PERRI KLASS   DAVID KLASS

SECOND IMPACT

SQUARE
FISH

FARRAR STRAUS GIROUX │ NEW YORK

We would like to thank Dr. Jenny Frances of the Department of Pediatric Orthopedic Surgery at the Hospital for Joint Diseases, New York University; Dr. Jaime Levine, Director of Brain Injury Rehabilitation at the Rusk Institute at NYU Langone Medical Center; and Dr. Michal Eisenberg of the Department of Neurology and Rehabilitation at New York University for their help with medical aspects of this manuscript. Any errors are the responsibility of the authors. We also thank Josephine Wolff for her help with blogging formats and the fun of Internet comments.

SQUARE FISH

An Imprint of Macmillan
175 Fifth Avenue
New York, NY 10010
macteenbooks.com

Square Fish books may be purchased for business or promotional use. For information on bulk purchases, please contact the Macmillan Corporate and Premium Sales Department at (800) 221-7945 x5442 or by e-mail at specialmarkets@macmillan.com.

Library of Congress Cataloging-in-Publication Data
Klass, David.
    Second impact / David Klass and Perri Klass.
        p. cm.
    Summary: When Jerry Downing, star quarterback in a small football town, gets a second chance after his drunk driving had serious consequences, Carla Jenson, ace reporter for the school newspaper, invites him to join her in writing a blog, mainly about sports.
    ISBN 978-1-250-04436-5 (paperback) / ISBN 978-0-374-36590-5 (e-book)
    [1. Football—Fiction. 2. Conduct of life—Fiction. 3. Sports injuries—Fiction. 4. Blogs—Fiction. 5. High schools—Fiction. 6. Schools—Fiction.]
    I. Klass, Perri, 1958– II. Title.
    PZ7.K67813Sec 2013   [Fic]—dc23   2012040873

Originally published in the United States by Farrar Straus Giroux
First Square Fish Edition: 2014
Book designed by Andrew Arnold
Square Fish logo designed by Filomena Tuosto

10 9 8 7 6 5 4 3 2 1

AR: 6.0 / LEXILE: 980L

For our mother, Sheila Solomon Klass, the best writing teacher in the world, and in memory of our father, Morton Klass

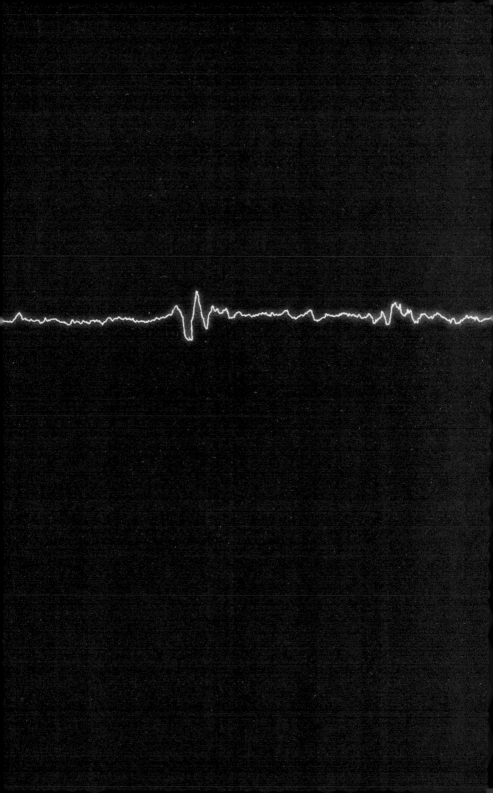

SECOND IMPACT

GAME DAY

Posted by user **JERRY** on November 2 at 9:00 p.m.

On game day, I usually wake very early and lie in bed thinking things over. I've got a small room with one window that faces east, so the first light filters through the curtains and hits my trophy shelves at about six a.m. Most of my trophies have miniature gold football players on top, and when the light strikes them, the figurines seem to come alive and play a little game. I lie in bed and watch them and think how dumb I was, and how lucky I am to get a second chance.

You all know what happened. Everybody knows what happened. Lots of people screw up and no one ever hears about it, but what I did was posted on the Internet and written about in newspapers, and it even made local TV. Some of the hardcore fans in town felt it was the worst thing to befall Kendall since the church burned down.

I'd like to say that what happened that night last October was a freak occurrence, that it was the first time I'd been to a keg party or the first time I drank too much and did something stupid. But that wouldn't be telling it straight.

Okay, here's some honesty. It's very hard to be the quarterback of the high school football team in a town like Kendall and not have it turn you into an arrogant jerk. You're anointed at age twelve. You are the star. Girls want to talk to you, even though deep down you know you're not that brilliant or charming. Guys want to be your friend. Gradually, you start to think you can do no wrong—or at least that's the idiotic conclusion I came to.

There are a lot of football towns like Kendall in Florida, Pennsylvania, and Texas, but not so many in New Jersey. When you push in through the doors of Kendall High, it's not a coincidence that the first thing you see is the enormous trophy case. There must be five hundred trophies inside, some of them dating back nearly a century. When I lie in bed watching the morning light hit my own much smaller trophy collection, I can feel the weight of that forest of school trophies and the tradition behind them.

"Pride," Coach Shea always says on the first day of a new season. "It's all about pride." I think he's right. For our town it was always about pride. Years ago, when we had our amazing run and won three state championships, I used to sneak into the games with my friends, wriggling under the fence because we couldn't afford the buck ticket. Those were hard times for a lot of people in our town, and it was thrilling to see the pride in people's faces as they stood up to cheer, as if our town was going to war against another town, winner take all, with no quarter asked for or given.

On game day, I remember those faces as I get out of bed and pull on some sweats. My parents are still asleep, and our house is dark and quiet. I walk downstairs in my socks, holding my sneakers so as not to wake my dad, who works the late shift as a security guard at a warehouse. I slip out the door and stretch on our front lawn, and then I head up Sylvan Avenue at a fast jog.

Here's the truth, the stinking truth, and nothing but the lousy truth. I had been to dozens of parties like that, and I had done worse things. I don't want to write them down because they involve other people who are still my friends, but I had bullied kids. I broke a kid's nose. I teased girls and sometimes it got out of hand. And I got away with it because when you're the quarterback of the Kendall football team, who's going to blow the whistle?

Two blocks away I stop at the house of my best buddy, Danny Rosewood, and rap gently on his back door. Danny is always dressed and ready, and he slips out the back and joins me. He puts on headphones and runs to music, but I like to hear the sounds of the world waking up. We don't need to talk. Danny feels the same weight that I do on game day. I have to throw the touchdowns, and he has to catch them.

Danny is the fastest kid in our school—and possibly in the entire county—but he's a sprinter, and when it comes to grinding out the miles, I can stay with him. We soon leave the town behind and run past the factory, with the chains on the gate and the busted windows. Then there are the fields—corn and alfalfa—and after that the first stubby trees and soon the pine forest takes hold.

Danny listens to Usher, but I listen to the wind in the pines and the birds and my own breathing. The run helps relax me, and even though we don't talk, it gets Danny and me in the same space. I bet a lot of people don't realize how close a quarterback and a wide receiver have to be to get it right. It's not enough that we practice the routes endlessly, both with the team and on our own. We have to be able to anticipate each other's actions and think almost with one brain.

Danny was there that night at the Sullivans' party, but he never drinks because his dad's a cop. He left early, but my other friends stayed late, standing around the keg in the backyard, cracking jokes and making small talk with a few girls.

I can't remember who suggested we head to the reservoir for a late-night swim. I do remember a little argument about whether I was sober enough to drive, and me getting into my car and switching on the ignition and grabbing the wheel and saying, "Get in or get left behind." And they got in, three buddies from my team and two girls I barely knew, one of them just a ninth grader.

Why did I get behind the wheel that night? Why didn't I let someone else drive, or just stay at the party? I was the quarterback, the go-to guy, the leader of the pack, and things like alcohol that derailed other, lesser people had no effect on me. I was invulnerable, immune, all-powerful, and so when I said get in or get left behind, they piled in.

The road to the reservoir is narrow and winding. I remember driving out there in the moonlight, feeling totally in control, while my buddies were passing a bottle back and forth and fooling around. I didn't drink on the way out, but I made up for it once we got there.

No doubt you've seen the photos that got posted and texted until they went platinum on local and even national news. I don't know who took them, and I don't care. Because yes, it happened. Yes, I was doing shots and, yes, I stripped and went for a swim and, yes, I was the one tilting the wine bottle while a fifteen-year-old girl in her underwear drank.

Danny veers off at his house, and I do a final sprint to my front door, and even on the coldest game days I'm sweating and loose. I jump in the shower and get dressed in jeans and my game shirt and go down to breakfast.

Dad is usually at the kitchen table when I get there, reading the paper and eating cereal. He always asks something silly on game day, like "Hey, beanhead, how's the old chicken wing?"

"Loose as the caboose on a goose," I tell him.

Mom ambles into the kitchen right about then and usually hands out some free diet advice. "Carbs," she'll urge. "Eat toast so you don't get toasted."

"No one's gonna toast me today," I assure her, and she gives me a look. I catch myself. "Yeah, carbs, thanks," I say quickly, and fix myself some toast with strawberry jam, and maybe a banana or a protein bar.

I walk the half mile to school and stow my stuff in a locker, and soon I'm walking the halls in my game shirt. Part of the reason I wear it is for luck, and part of it is for team unity, but I admit that I still like to show off and strut a little bit. Last year, as a junior, I felt proud to saunter down the hall in my jersey with its captain's stripe. They made Danny the captain when the school suspended me last season, so I no longer have the stripe, but I'm still the quarterback.

When it's game day and you're going to be running the

team, everyone watches you. They don't always ask the questions out loud 'cause they're afraid they're going to jinx you, but from class to class, from homeroom bell to dismissal, everyone's excited and keying on you. "How's the arm?" they're wondering. "Are you feeling good?" "Are we going to win today?" The tension builds inside of me from hour to hour, till I can barely stand it.

After school we go suit up, and it's like putting on your armor with the rest of your army. My locker's right next to Danny's, and we go over our routes one last time. I do some deep breathing and extra stretching that my mom taught me, and Coach Shea calls us in for a talk.

The Supreme Court has ruled that team prayers are illegal, but when Coach finishes, we stay down on one knee and have a silent minute. I can guarantee you that most of the guys are saying a prayer—not just for victory, but that they'll play well and come through the game okay. We're fired up and ready for action; at the same time, we all know the risks of going to war.

And it does feel like war when we stand up and enter the tunnel. You can hear the band playing our fight song and our fans screaming outside and stomping on the bleachers. We draw five thousand to home games, and let me tell you, they can be loud.

We run toward the field exit, and Coach Shea likes me to run out last. I wait and listen as the roar builds, and I take a second and remind myself of who I am and what I've been through and how lucky I am to get a second chance. Then I follow Danny out of the tunnel, into daylight, between the line of cheerleaders, and I raise my arms, and the crowd roars.

There's always some kid watching me who probably crawled under the fence, and if he gets close enough he'll ask for my autograph. I take the pen and I sign, and I know what he's thinking. I see that look of hero worship in his eyes, and I remember driving back from the reservoir at forty, fifty, sixty miles per hour and a scared girl's voice in the back begging me to slow down. But I didn't slow down, I sped up, because I owned those turns, I owned that midnight highway, I owned the whole moonlit world, and nothing could touch me. And then I remember the horrible shriek of the tires, and wrestling with the wheel, and the sickening, exciting, electric jolt of certainty that it was really happening and we were all going to die a second before we veered off the road and crashed down a slope into the trees.

What I remember next is all the police and ambulances, and my first thought—what a surprise—was for myself. Surely I had busted myself up big-time and football was gone forever. But the weird thing was that everything felt okay. While they fished me out of the accordion of a car, I took inventory—I moved my arms and my legs—and then they tried to load me on a stretcher but I stood up. An EMT tried to push me back down, but I actually shoved him away. Because I sensed the truth then. I could hear someone moaning. The ambulance crew was focusing on one of us. I glanced over and saw just enough to realize it was the fresh-man girl whose name I didn't even know.

I remember going to the hospital and getting checked out, and then the police started asking me questions.

I recall the expressions on my parents' faces when they came and heard it from my own lips.

A stern lady judge with white hair gave me a speech I will never forget if I live to be a hundred and fifty. "You are get-ting a second chance that you probably don't deserve," she said, staring right into my eyes. "Look around this court-room at all the family and friends who have come today to support you." I obeyed her command and looked at them, and they didn't know whether to meet my gaze or look away. "You have disappointed all of them," she said. "But even worse, you have hurt someone very badly. I've thought long and hard about this, and I'm going to give you a second chance, Jerry Downing. Find it in you to make them proud again. Don't make me regret this."

I remember my speech to the team, when I apologized to them and left them there in their armor and walked away from my army.

Then came a month of community service, picking up lit-ter on Main Street, and everybody in Kendall who drove by knew who I was and why I was doing it. Some people honked. A few slowed and shouted insults. Most drove by in silence.

It's game day. I'm the quarterback. We go into our pre-game huddle. The excitement that has been building all day reaches a crescendo. My senses come alive in a way that's almost freakish. I can see, hear, feel, taste this coming football game. It all revolves around me. If I want a towel to wipe my hands, a team assistant will bring it. If I want a drink of water, I have only to wave. It would be so very easy to get sucked in again. "Ready?" Coach Shea asks.

Am I ready? I take a second. Look around the football field at the fans in the bleachers and the goalposts and the American flag flapping high above.

And then I close my eyes and lower my head and say a prayer, very different from the ones my teammates whispered to themselves in our locker room. The crowd is roaring, and my heart is thumping, and I know how lucky I am to have this second chance.

I open my eyes and look at the coach and nod. "Ready."

"Then let's go," he says. And the game is on.

View 4 reader comments:

Posted by user **DanTheMAN** *at 10:13 p.m.*
To clarify, JerJer, you can keep up with me on the long runs cause I let you. Oh, and nice blog. You'll get the hang of it. Always a little slow on the uptake, if ya know what I mean . . .

Posted by user **TIGERS4EVA** *at 10:42 p.m.*
GOOOOOO KENDALL. WOLVERINES SUCK.
WOLVERINES SUCKKKKKKKKKKKKKKKKKKK!!!

Posted by user **CrustyAlum** *at 11:03 p.m.*
When I played football for Kendall, there was a sense of real pride and accomplishment fostered among the teammates

and young gentlemen who populated our once-great team. It is always distressing to hear about the further exploits and indiscretions of the near delinquents who now represent our fine institution on the playing field. Should the disgrace of this young man and his fellow ruffians really be receiving greater attention and publicity? It seems to me this was not the purpose to which an interactive media presence for the Kendall sports teams once aspired. I, for one, would like to see a return to the honor and purity that the young men of Kendall once exhibited on the playing fields and off.

Crusty McFirecracker, Class of 1975, New Jersey State Football Champions (cornerback)

Posted by user **WOLVERINESSUCK** *at 11:58 p.m.*
WOLVERINES SUCK WOLVERINES SUCK WOLVERINES SUCK. WOLVERINES GOIN DOWNNNNNNNNNNNNN.

I know what you're thinking. You're wondering why I would sign up Jerry Downing to write for the paper and expect you to read his stuff. You saw his space, all set up with a new blog, right in the middle of the *Kendall Kourier* Web site, so his photo was the first thing you saw when you opened us up this morning—and you're probably wondering if I've been bought. You're thinking, Why does the football team need more attention? Don't we get to see enough photos of Jerry Downing in the news? Or, depending on which photos you're remembering, maybe you're thinking, The guy's a bum, he may be a half-decent quarterback, but how proud can you be of someone when you're also ashamed of him? Or maybe you're just thinking, Shut up and play football.

Okay, but what did you think of his writing? It took me by surprise, and that's why it's up here. So don't yell at me about who you think I am or who you think Jerry Downing is, or was, or will be, just put all that aside and tell me what you thought of "Game Day." Post a comment, let us have it, Jerry and me.

As I say, this whole thing took me by surprise. There I was in honors creative writing, day one, and I tell you, I didn't have particularly high expectations for Jerry Downing, to put it mildly. I thought what anyone would think: they've stuck another dumb jock in here who is looking for an easy course, looking to read no books, download some dumb essay off the Internet, hand it in. Tough luck, Jerry, you were badly advised, I thought. Mr. Cooper is one of the toughest teachers in this school, the reading list is a killer, and you'll have to write your aerobically overdeveloped athletic heart out—and then watch Mr. Cooper and the rest of us tear it apart.

And then, like Mr. Cooper could read my mind, he asked Jerry to read first. And right there and then I decided I'm signing this guy up. He has things to say, and it's his voice that we should hear narrating this football season. So let's all put aside our prejudices, whatever they may be, and welcome our new columnist, Jerry Downing.

Oh, and you know perfectly well what I mean by prejudices. Some people think he would have to be dumb. Well, he's not. Some people think he's a degenerate who brought shame on our team and our school and he should either be kicked off the team (if you think Ryan Hurley did an okay job as qb finishing off the last season) or maybe (if you think Ryan Hurley is out of his depth) Jerry should be allowed to play quarterback but otherwise keep his head down and his mouth closed and his pants on (sorry, Jerry, but if you're gonna be out here, on the blog, you better learn to take a joke).

(And don't worry, Ms. Edison goes over everything before it goes up—that's what happens when the First Amendment meets high school journalism—and she'll probably take out that gag about the pants, and she'll certainly take out this whole parenthesis; she hates how I'm always sticking in long parentheses.) [*Edit by user Ms_Edison: Happy to have a conversation, either online or off, about the First Amendment, but don't think you can always rely on me to be saving you from your parentheses! I think you'll find that a really good writer finds the way to make her important points in the body of the text and does not have to resort to long parenthetical asides.*]

Actually, I want to say, here and now, that I kind of like Jerry Downing, kind of liked him even before he turned up in honors creative writing and knocked our collective socks off. I'll never forget Spirit Week last year, when he brought the guys from the football team to cheer at our girls' soccer game. Maybe you don't think that was a big deal, seven varsity football players showing up to cheer? Maybe you're one of the soccer boosters, like a certain would-be-French intellectual in honors creative writing (you know who you are, and I love you dearly, but the beret is really getting old), and you like to go on and on about how graceful soccer is (*balletic*, I believe, is the word I've heard you use, and I'm not sure it really is a word), and how European, compared to violent American football, and blah blah blah. Well, I just want to say this: you weren't at the Spirit Week game last year, or at any other game. None of you were. We'd have noticed you—we notice whenever students come because, frankly, students don't come. Not to girls' soccer, balletic though it may be. Now that I can't play anymore, and I go to the games to root for the team and, of course, to make sure the *Kourier* maintains the brilliant, incisive level of sports coverage (or should that be koverage?) you've come to expect— well, now I am more aware than ever of our tiny crowds. There are just a few loyal parents (and man, I have to tell you, I have come to appreciate my dad, who used to skip out on his office now and then to watch me play—hey, Dad, I want to apologize for having asked you to keep your voice down. I was a twerp to be embarrassed, you were great to keep coming). But you know what? Those of you who have loyally followed my writing for the last couple of years know that this is a familiar rant. So let me just say that seven varsity football players, stripped to the waist, each with a huge black letter drawn on his chest so that they could stand in a line and spell out *Kendall*—well, that was just about the biggest thing, in every sense, that ever happened at a girls' soccer game.

Jerry, I remember, was *K*. Of course. And I might comment (oh, c'mon, Ms. Edison, leave it in), his pecs and abs were reasonably impressive, though by no means the most stunning in the lineup. By unanimous girls' soccer team opinion, that prize went to Danny Rosewood. Clear favorite. But it's a good memory, overall, Spirit Week. A chilly October afternoon, fall in the air, warming up with my team, the bus from Riverwood arrives with the other team . . . and suddenly the air is full of cheers, and along comes the football team, jogging in formation, letters on their chests, stomping so as to shake the earth, and there's Jerry, Mr. K himself, leading the troops.

Well, of course, that was before he got in trouble. Back when he was, like he says himself, the big hero. But I'm not going to get into that story—that's for him to write about.

But what I was thinking was that for both of us, Jerry Downing and me, that was Before, with a capital *B*. I was in my soccer shorts and jersey and, of course, my cleats and shin guards. I used to think that was the real me, but I haven't been that person in a couple of months. She's gone. I lost her that day in summer soccer scrimmage when I decided to try a fancy crossover, and I came down just a little bit wrong and I felt it, I felt my knee just buckle under me, like there was nothing holding the two parts of my leg together—and suddenly, there wasn't. Or not enough.

Well, I've told this story before. I'll probably tell it again. I'll probably be telling it on my college applications. (My ACL tear and how I learned from it and grew and became a stronger, wiser person with better board scores. And ended my high school soccer career. So take me into your freshman class, even though I may not be playing soccer for you. Please!)

And so here I am, not having the senior year I had planned. (My dad still can't quite get used to it. He wanted to get another second opinion—well, I guess you'd have to call it a third opinion—even before I had the surgery. Now he keeps finding things on the Internet about athletes who made quicker than usual recoveries after ACL tears. But he's honest about it. When he read about Jerry Rice, who came back to pro football after only fourteen weeks, he told me the whole saga—how he made a touchdown catch and cracked his kneecap on the play. My mom had some choice comments to make about that one.) But you all know my sad story. No pity parties, please. I'm a big girl.

But I don't know—maybe confession is catching. I just read over "Game Day" one more time, and I have something I want to tell you, something I've never discussed in all those pieces I've written about soccer, or even about my ACL tear. Here's what "Game Day" makes me think: how sure he is. Oh, I know he thinks this is all about making up for what he did, and I know he prays, they all pray, but he never thinks, not for one minute, Oh, what the hey, if it's not me, it'll be Ryan Hurley quarterbacking, and that's fine, too, and sometimes you win and sometimes you lose, whoever's playing. That's not Jerry. He wants to be the one with the ball. He really wants it.

And the funny thing is—this is what I want to tell you—I don't know if I ever felt that. I love suiting up. I love playing. I love looking for my moment, and moving fast—let's face it, I love being a striker. But even as I'm writing this, I keep wondering if I should be putting it all in the past tense (I loved taking a pass from midfield, I loved scoping out the goalie and planning my shots). Because here it is: when I came back after my injury, they let me sit on the bench, of course, and they tried their best to include me, and so I sat there. And you know what? It was okay. I wasn't playing, so Jeannette Markowski got serious time as striker, and she did really well. And when she flubbed a penalty kick, I didn't think, Oh, I would have made that. I thought, Well sure, that happens. It's her turn.

And that confirmed something that I think I had already begun to suspect about myself—that I'm not an athlete the way some of the other girls on the team are athletes. I think I always knew there are limits to how far I was going to go with this. (My parents disagree—big-time—about whether I will ever play seriously again. My dad is a big believer in getting back on the horse, and my mom keeps pointing out that after one ACL surgery, you're at an increased risk of another injury and another surgery. And she reminds him how, after the injury, I was in such bad pain. And then he gets upset, too, because my dad can't stand to see his child in pain. And I just try to stay out of the conversation because what's clear is that I won't be playing soccer this year, so what I need to do is get into college, without soccer, and figure things out for myself.) And when I felt my knee fold under me, I think some part of me knew right then that there are limits to how far I am going to go.

On the other hand, when I sit down at my laptop, I don't think there's any limit whatsoever. When I start writing—when I think of all of you out there reading my writing—I feel I could do anything. I could go and go, I could write and write. Well, you know that about me. But I feel like I could do things, like I could make everyone listen to me. I could change lives. I could remake the world. (Oh, no, I think I'm writing a college essay again—I want to end world hunger and violence against women, that's why I want to be a writer. And sure, while I'm at it, I'd also like to fix the environment and maybe reopen the factory in Kendall so everyone could have their jobs back.) But that's not the real point.

The real point is how I feel when I sit down to write. And you know how Jerry says about the football game, that he can see it, hear it, feel it, taste it? That's exactly what it's like.

View 5 reader comments:

Posted by user **Photog_Sophie** *at 10:03 a.m.*
Click here for photos from the girls' soccer game last Saturday. Photos from last year's Spirit Week are available here. Take the online poll to vote for which player has the best six-pack! And, Carla, I'm not too worried about your college application essay.

Posted by user **Ms_Edison** *at 10:23 a.m.*
Thanks for posting photos, Sophie. The poll is no longer active, but the pictures are still up.

Posted by user **@Ms_Edison** *at 10:45 a.m.*
You never let us have any fun!

Posted by user **No_Poll_Needed** *at 11:07 a.m.*
Rosewood's the clear champion. AMIRITE?

Posted by user **GOTIGERS** *at 11:43 a.m.*
WOLVERINES SUCK!!!

DING DONG

Posted by user **JERRY** on November 10 at 6:00 p.m.

Last week, when Carla asked me to write a blog on the *Kourier*, I didn't know if I should do it. I was afraid it might seem like showing off. But the reaction to "Game Day" has been very positive, and it's important to me that people know the truth.

Mr. Cooper thinks it's a great idea and said that if Carla and I want to blog back and forth about the season—"narrative blogs," he called them—we can get credit for his class. "But the writing has to be polished," he said. He warned me that there's a lot of lousy prose out there on the Internet. He won't give me any credit if I just spew or post supershort blogs with sentence fragments and inside jokes that only my football teammates will get. "If you want to do this," he told me, "write it for a general audience, for people who don't know you unless you introduce yourself and won't understand your story unless you tell it well."

So I'm going to try to tell our team's story this football season in that kind of blog—as honestly and personally as I can—and what happened last Friday night in the Midland game is a great place to start.

Just for the record, Carla, I can't claim credit for our team turning out at your soccer game last year during Spirit Week. My buddy Danny had a thing for one of your teammates, and he suggested it. But I admit the letters on our bare chests was my idea, and I'm glad we didn't horrify you with all the hair and flab.

I wouldn't be too modest about your soccer ability. I admit I'd never seen a girls' soccer game before, but I remember you as being the best player on the field that day. Both goals that you kicked were bullets. That's really tough luck about your knee. It's easy for me to say this, but when it heals, I'm on your dad's side—I think you should give soccer another try. You gotta get back on the horse after it bucks you.

Which brings me to today's blog posting. I'm calling this one "Ding Dong" because I got my bell rung really good on Friday. I didn't get dinged because I was wearing my helmet and suit of armor, so there were only a few minor cuts and bruises. But I did get donged, and even now, three days later, the chimes are still ringing.

You may be wondering what it feels like to get donged, or why I didn't just go down on my own before the hit. As you probably know since you're reading a football blog, if a quarterback goes down voluntarily and slides feetfirst, opponents can't hit him. But in a tight game, with the whole season on the line, sometimes it's harder to go down than to stay up and take a massive hit.

I know a lot of you reading this were at the game on Friday, so I won't bother with a recap. You know it was a perfect fall day, a great crowd. I don't usually pick out faces from the crowd, but I couldn't help noticing that there was a coach from an in-state college I visited last spring sitting there taking notes on a pad. I wanted to give him a show. Our offense was clicking, and my arm felt strong—in three quarters I threw four touchdowns.

The only problem was that Brian Dumars, better known as the Midland Express, ran for five. I couldn't blame our defense—the guy's unstoppable. So when I trotted onto the field with three minutes left in the fourth quarter, we were trailing by seven points. The math was real simple. If we got a touchdown and a two-point conversion, we would win the game and stay undefeated. If we didn't, our season and all our championship hopes would go down the drain.

Three minutes sounds short, but it's actually plenty of time for a final drive. When we huddled up, I could see how nervous some of the underclassmen were. "Okay, guys," I said, "before we talk football, I've got a more important question." They looked at me, waiting. What could be more important than football at a moment like this? "Granger," I asked, "have you taken a shower yet this season?"

Granger is a giant lineman who has muscles the size of cantaloupes, but I don't think he'd mind me saying that he's not exactly known for his personal hygiene. He wears his sweat and grime the way soldiers wear their medals, and he considers it a point of pride not to take showers often. "I got caught in the rain two weeks ago," he said, playing along with the joke. "Does that count?"

I saw a couple of the sophomores crack smiles.

"Rain doesn't count," I told him. "There's gotta be soap involved. Change places in the huddle. Stand downwind, next to Peters."

"No way," Peters, another senior, said. "I got allergies, and he sets me off."

There were laughs and grins, and I could feel the mood lighten. I said, "Okay, guys, let's talk football. We're gonna march in for a touchdown and not make any stupid mistakes. Since they're guessing pass, we're gonna start it off with a run."

We mixed up short passes and runs and were soon over the fifty, steaming full speed ahead into enemy territory. Their defense was worried about getting beat with a long pass, so they were giving our receivers too much room at the line. I kept hitting Danny and Glenn Scott with crossing patterns, gobbling up seven or eight yards with each play.

Fifty yards turned into forty, then thirty. I threw a short square out to our super soph Mike Magee, and he was supposed to step out of bounds and stop the clock, but he tried to stretch it and got dropped inside the line, so we had to burn our last time-out.

Fifty seconds left. Fourth and three from the twenty-seven. I knew they'd think we were going for the first down, so I wasn't too surprised when Coach Shea sent in a play from the sideline. He decided to gamble everything on a stop-and-go to Danny. It's just what it sounds like—he runs out three steps, stops, and turns. I pump him a fake short pass. And then he *goes*—straight out to a corner of the end zone.

We got to the line, and I waited an extra beat, conscious that this was it—our whole season was on the line. Then I took the snap and Danny sprinted out three steps, stopped dead, and turned. I rolled to my left and sold the pump fake. Their defender bit hard, and at the moment he jumped in to try to break up the short pass, Danny started running again, switching gears and directions in an instant. We had them exactly where we wanted them. I was about to loft the ball into Danny's hands and start celebrating our victory when I saw that the unthinkable had happened.

Danny is normally as sure-footed as a mountain goat, but when he stopped and started, he lost his balance, his arms windmilled for a second, and he fell down right on his butt. Suddenly I had no target to pass to, and I could feel the pressure coming behind me. One of their pass rushers got his hands around my waist, but I spun free and looked for Glenn Scott, my secondary target. He was covered by two guys who were draped all over him.

There was only one thing to do. I'm not exactly the fastest runner in the world, but when I need to pick up yards the hard way I can usually do it. I started downfield, slanting for the sideline. I had to pick up three yards to get the first down, and then I needed to get out of bounds to stop the clock. A Midland tackle had a clear shot at me. I was about to try to juke him, when he dove at me for a leg tackle. I saw him coming low and vaulted over him, and somehow came down running again.

Time slowed. I could hear the roar of the crowd. I took a stride. I was pretty sure I had picked up the first down. The sideline was less than five feet away, but Gonzales, Midland's all-league humongous defensive end, was speeding right at me. Drop, I told myself. Slide, feetfirst. If I had picked up the first down, there was time to get to the line and spike the ball to stop the clock.

There was only one problem: I didn't know for absolute sure that I had made the first-down yardage. If I went down voluntarily and they marked me short—even by an inch— the game and our season would be over. So instead of going down, I stayed up and kept moving forward and tried to get out of bounds.

I saw Gonzales getting ready for the hit, and I knew I had made the wrong decision. He was as big as a mountain— at least four inches taller than me and fifty pounds heavier. He had been sprinting right at me at top speed and now launched himself at me like a guided missile. No doubt about it, he was going to rip my head off.

I wrapped up the ball in both hands, hugged it tight, and lunged for the sideline. The hit came so fast and hard that I felt no pain. There was a flash of light and a bone-jarring reverse thrust that I felt with my whole body—my spine, my ribs, my teeth—as Gonzales's mass and momentum smashed me backward to the turf, and all I could think was, Hold on to the ball. Don't let it go.

That single thought became a rope, a lifeline, tying me to daylight and consciousness with a sense of purpose, even as it frayed to a cord and finally a single gray thread stretching over a chasm. But the thread never broke, and I never completely blacked out. I felt the ball in my hands the whole time and never let go of it—not even when Coach Shea was standing above me asking me questions and trying very gently to take the football from my grasp.

I was lying on my back, watching the sun filter around his face, which seemed to mushroom larger and shrink down again like a character in a cartoon. "Jelly?" his voice said. "Jelly?"

But it wasn't *jelly*, it was Jerry—my name. "Jerry, are you okay? Can you hear me? Can you talk?"

I could hear him and see him, but there was some kind of a disconnect. He was speaking into a tube, whispering into a windy echo chamber, and someone had stuck a vacuum down my throat into my chest and sucked the air out of my lungs, so I couldn't make a sound in reply.

Another shadow blocked out the sunlight, and then I saw the concerned face of Dr. Anderson, who comes to all our games. He had joined Coach Shea and was kneeling over me and asking me questions: "Jerry, can you move your hands? Can you blink your eyes? Can you move your feet?"

And suddenly, of course I could! I blinked my eyes on command and moved my feet and my arms, and I even let Coach Shea take the football out of my hands.

Dr. Anderson started asking questions: "What day is it? Come on, Jerry, answer, what day of the week is it?"

I looked back up at him. "Down?" I whispered.

"What?"

I took a breath and spoke louder. "First down?"

"I'm asking the questions," Dr. Anderson said with a little smile. "What day of the week is it today?"

"Just tell me if I made the freaking first down."

He gave up on the day of the week. "Who's the president? Come on."

"Lincoln," I said.

He stared at me. "Don't mess with me, Jerry."

"I got stopped short? We lost."

"No, you made it with plenty to spare and you also got out of bounds," he told me. "Now, don't try to get up. We're going to take you to the hospital for some tests."

They lifted me onto a stretcher and carried me away. I gave the crowd a thumbs-up, and they stood and cheered. I was feeling better, and I wanted to stay and watch the end of the game, but they loaded me into an ambulance with my dad sitting next to me and sped off to Pinewood Hospital.

During the ride, the EMTs were shining lights into my eyes and firing off questions, but I kept asking: "Did we win the game?" Dad finally got on his cell phone and called another team dad. He bent over me and whispered: "Ryan Hurley threw a touchdown to Danny and they ran it in for two points, so you guys are still undefeated. Now, why don't you cooperate a little bit."

The medics looked surprised at my reaction. I guess they're not used to seeing someone let out a cheer in an ambulance. "Ryan Hurley, huh? How about that!"

We reached the hospital, and the docs ran every possible test on me, including a CT scan, but all they could come up with was that I had a possible minor concussion. Except for a headache, I felt fine. I've been donged before. Never that hard, but it's part of the game.

Now they tell me they want me to sit this week out, just to be on the safe side. No practices. No playing time this Friday. They even want me to stay home from school for a few days. I don't mind missing school, but I'm sure I could play on Friday.

On the other hand, since it's the Mumsford game, why not let Ryan have the start? He earned it. No disrespect to Mumsford, but we could beat them with a chicken as our quarterback.

So you might be wondering whether it was worth my taking the risk and getting my bell donged. They tell me that I had the first down by two steps, and I should have just slid. Coach Shea was apparently standing on the sideline yelling, *"Down, go down!"* But I didn't hear him over the roar of the crowd, and I had to make absolute sure of it.

I did what I thought I had to do to win the game, and I'd do it again in a heartbeat. Football is not for the timid. It can be a brutal contact sport, and I took a big hit for the team. I'd do it again any old time, but hopefully not from Gonzales, the human missile.

| View 4 reader comments: |

Posted by user **GOINGSTRONG** *at 7:23 p.m.*
Still no shower, folks! Kisses, Granger.

Posted by user **Photog_Sophie** *at 7:53 p.m.*
Pictures from the game are posted <u>here</u>!

Posted by user **MidlandSUX** *at 8:02 p.m.*
VICTORY IS OURS!

Posted by user **Friedman_HealthTeacher** *at 8:15 p.m.*
Just a quick note, kids, to remind you that daily showers,
particularly following vigorous athletic activity, are an
important part of a personal hygiene & health regimen.

Posted by user **@Friedman_HealthTeacher** *at 8:47 p.m.*
~~Just don't drop the soap . . .~~

Comment deleted by user Ms_Edison *at 9:03 p.m.*

Good morning, Kendall High!

How about that Jerry Downing, guys? How about that Ryan Hurley? How about that undefeated football team? But honestly, Jerry, now that I know what I know—now that I read what you know—I have a couple of things I need to tell you. First of all, kid, think about an out-of-state school. I'm not saying you're going to play Big Ten ball, but for right now, football is your ticket out to see the world. Go someplace a little bigger, a little stranger. Sometimes a person needs to get the heck out of the place he thinks he belongs.

The more I read your stuff, the more I think that you should find someplace for your next act which will be harder in every way—harder academically, harder socially, harder athletically. You ought to ride that passing arm of yours to someplace where it will get goosed a little bit.

Sorry, that's patronizing. I sound pretty obnoxious, and I'm probably just jealous—in my own petty girls' soccer way, I'm probably more than a little jealous. Jealous of the crowds you draw, you warriors in your armor, jealous that you got to be a hero, but most of all, jealous that you can be out there playing and running on a perfect fall day, and that you can fall down but still get up again.

And while I'm examining my own motives, let me add that I might even be jealous of your firepower as a blogger—jealous and proud, all at the same time. Let it be known: since Jerry Downing started blogging the football season on the *Kourier* Web site, traffic has tripled. We're getting hits like never before, and a lot of people are sticking around to read the other stuff as well. Comments are up, and I'm getting lots of credit for recruiting Jerry. And yes, it makes me a little bit jealous, but I tell myself that in journalism, like in sports, some serious competition can only improve your game. So get set, guys, this is going to be a long and (attention, Mr. Cooper!) superbly well-written post.

So let's start over. Jerry Downing's game this week was a lot more than getting his head banged. Those four touchdown passes he threw were pretty slick, and even when we were losing, you couldn't help being proud that we had a team capable of that kind of grace and style—the running game that Midland was playing was fierce and tough, but it was like watching our side take to the air. Like we were the soaring birds, and they were the dinosaurs clomping down below. And of course, you could hope that in the end, evolution would hold and the birds would triumph, but you knew that might not happen this time around.

And that last drive—till Jerry got hurt—that was the kind of drive that makes you think the team can do no wrong. "We mixed up short passes and runs," he says, describing it like it was kind of random, but it wasn't like that at all. It was choreographed, everything clicking, every player following the script. Until Danny fell and Jerry had to move the ball himself.

It's funny, though. I've been to plenty of Kendall football games. I've even covered them for the paper sometimes. But knowing Jerry a little better changed my feelings about watching our players take those hits. (Or maybe it's that now I know, in the most personal way, that high school bodies really can get broken in serious ways. Maybe it's sitting there and every now and then testing out my knee to see, does this hurt, does that hurt. Maybe that's part of it, too.)

Those hits are hard. Everyone is screaming—I'm screaming, too, of course—and the noise is building as the play begins and the ball gets hiked and the day is chilly but the bleachers feel warm because everyone wants the same thing, everyone is screaming for the same thing. And then, over that crowd noise, or maybe under that crowd noise, comes the different dangerous noise of big body hitting big body, of boys hitting the earth—and when you know one of those boys, one of the ones getting hit, something in you just can't believe that anyone anywhere is built to take this, that they'll all stand up and walk again. (Or, again, maybe I've just been spooked because I've learned the hard way that sometimes people actually don't.)

Watching Jerry go down was scary. Just plain scary. That guy Gonzales is a giant; you can practically feel the earth shake when he moves. He makes ordinary pumped-up jocks—like Jerry Downing, for example—look like little scurrying rabbits. Or if we're going back to prehistoric times again, to my other metaphor, maybe Jerry could be the early mammal, trying to survive by his wits, and then, Stomp! Don't count the dinosaurs out yet, they're still dangerous.

Anyway, I was close enough to see that the coach was signaling Jerry to go down, close enough that I thought, even at the time, that Jerry was making some kind of crazy decision to run it out. So I'm taking the liberty of telling him that taking one for the team is all very well, but if he makes choices that get him badly hurt, everyone loses, especially the team. Agreed, football is not for the timid. But while I would never say football is not for the dumb, on the whole, quarterbacking is not for the extremely foolish. Your team needs you and your school needs your team and even those of us who don't think we're going to war against Midland or Mumsford think that your town needs your team. And if redemption is really what you have in mind, you'll want to stay in one piece and win some games. So next time, Jerry, no making eye contact with college scouts who are maybe a little over the line already in terms of their level of contact, if you know what I mean. Pay attention to your coach instead. For all of us.

Okay, you all know the score. I mean, literally, you know that thanks to Jerry's first down and then Ryan's touchdown pass and conversion we beat Midland 36–35, leaving us still undefeated, ready for the Friday game against Mumsford, who has only won two so far this season. Catch tomorrow's issue of the *Kourier* for an interview with Ryan Hurley about strategy.

I'm thinking I might follow up on Jerry's "Ding Dong" theme with an interview with someone who does sports medicine, partly because of what happened at the Midland game. I went with my dad—he isn't actually from here, as you may know, and for the first couple of years we lived here, he was actually kind of snooty about the high school football scene. I mean, kind of snooty about that whole tradition that Jerry talks about, the century of football, the glass case full of trophies. My dad loves football, but what he thought he meant was that he was pretty happy to have his turn at the corporate box at MetLife Stadium. You know, big-ticket professional stuff. In college, he never missed a game, but of course, that was the Ivy League, boola boola.

It took a couple of years living in Kendall before he made it to a Kendall home game, and I think he was pretty knocked out by the intensity of it all—the intensity of the playing, the intensity of the cheering. And then for a while (sorry, Dad, but this is just the kind of lame thing you do) he pretended to think it was some kind of good public relations for him to go to high school football games—like he was mixing with the people and they would be thrilled. Except, of course, nobody was thrilled, nobody ever even noticed. And after a couple of years, Dad was just plain hooked. He was entering every game on his expensive little electronic calendar and offering to drive me to away games. He was a fan—that old Kendall magic had him in its spell.

So sometimes I go with him to football games. Other times, of course, I go with friends from the soccer team, or with kids from the paper. Sometimes my mom goes along, but she works a lot of evenings and weekends these days.

I don't think my dad would mind me telling you this (and, anyway, we have a standing joke in our house that nothing is ever off the record when your daughter is an aspiring journalist), but after we moved here, he went through a phase of wanting me to go to private school somewhere. It's kind of typical of my father that we would live in a town at least partly because it was supposed to have a good public high school and then he would start to worry that maybe it wasn't really good enough for his own daughter. My dad is the guy who asks the hotel clerk whether there's a category of deluxe rooms. He believes the more expensive wine always tastes better than the cheaper wine (Ms. Edison, I don't know if I'm allowed to admit this in public, but when my parents open a bottle of wine at dinner, my dad always gives me a taste and asks me to describe it—and it is therefore my somewhat educated opinion that most wine tastes pretty much like most other wine, and someday I am going to challenge my dad to a blind taste test, and there will be a ten-dollar wine, a twenty-five-dollar wine, a fifty-dollar wine, and a hundred-dollar wine. I guess it will have to wait till I have $185 or so to waste, and maybe till I'm old enough to do my own buying. And if this is going to get my father arrested, you can just cut it out). [*Edit by user Ms_Edison: I don't think your father is actually breaking the law, as long as he only offers the wine to you, at home, under strict parental supervision, so I think you're safe.*]

So my dad went through this phase of thinking I should go to Something Academy or Somewhere Country Day, and I said no. We moved around an awful lot during my first years of elementary school, and I learned to make friends pretty fast, and I had already made friends at Kendall back in middle school. My whole fantasy at that point, you might say, was about living in a place and belonging there and going to school with my neighbors. Most important, I had met Sophie West, and we were clearly going to be best friends forever, and no way was I changing schools one more time, let alone getting on a school bus every morning in a stupid little plaid skirt (Something Academy) or even worse, a blazer (Country Day, you know who you are). So here I am, and was I right about Sophie or what? I mean, here we are in our senior year, still so tight that, as you probably know, she's the photo and technical editor of the *Kourier*. She took that photo of Ryan Hurley lofting the winning pass that you're looking at right now on your screen. Anyway, what I am probably getting at here is that I chose to be at this school because I wanted to be at this school. And maybe my dad did go through some phase of thinking I was the princess deliberately choosing to be educated democratically with the common people, but he got over it. By this time, by this year, by last weekend when we went to the football game together, I think we were just father and daughter being true to our school. My mom was working, and I thought about her as we climbed to that place in the bleachers not so far behind our bench. I wondered, Does she give this a thought, does she think about the beautiful fall day and the bite in the air that tells you to enjoy the football season, because after football comes winter? Or is she thinking about law and legal papers and things that have to be filed?

Right after my dad and I sat down, somebody waved to me and started heading in my direction, walking along the bleachers. And for a minute I wasn't sure who it was—a short, dark-haired woman, younger than my dad, with her curly hair gathered back into a big bushy ponytail, wearing jeans and a bulky white cabled sweater and expensive running shoes.

My dad recognized her before I did—of course, he's seen her a lot more than I have. "Dr. Abbot!" he said. "I didn't know you lived in Kendall!"

"Now I do," she said, and stuck out her right hand, almost aggressively. My dad shook her hand. "I just bought a place," she said. "Over on the west side of town, right near the park. Moved in last week."

Now that I knew who she was, I couldn't believe I hadn't recognized her. I mean, I've only seen her a couple of times, but they were what you might call "key encounters," deeply fraught for me with pain and tension. The kinds of encounters that you would think you would remember. It's as if I had walled them off in my mind, pretending they happened in another world or something.

Anyway, that's next week's piece—the final surgery is happening on Monday and, as promised, I will blog it, so whether you like it or not, you're going to get all the gory details. For now, let me just say that I first met Dr. Abbot in the emergency room right after the ER doctor had looked me over and done an X-ray and probably wasn't so very glad to realize that my dad had already been on his cell phone and demanded to have me seen by an orthopedic surgeon. Dr. Abbot was pretty cool about it. She was wearing blue scrubs and a long white coat, and you couldn't really see all her curly hair; it was pinned up behind her head. She spent about ten minutes or so with us, and there was something about the way she talked to my dad that really impressed me—and really impressed him, too. It was like she was saying, "You are the head of the hospital, and I'm sorry your daughter is hurt, but I have a patient waiting to go to the operating room, so right now my time is more valuable than yours, and don't pull anything." And he didn't. He said "Yes, Doctor," and "No, Doctor," and "Thank you, Doctor," and she did her stuff with me and went off to operate.

So I saw Dr. Abbot that first day in the emergency room, when I was so dizzy and scared and confused, and then again in her office a few days later, and then two weeks after that, and now we're scheduled to go back later this week for the pre-op visit. But instead, we ran into her at the football game, and she sat with us and cheered like a maniac.

I said something to her about how hard the hits were looking to me, and she explained some technical stuff about protective equipment and showed me how the tackles were actually angling themselves in specific ways—I mean, football tackles always look a little basic and brutal, but she showed me how the tackles were trying to keep their heads up. You tackle what you can see, she said, you never tuck your head down, and she explained some things about the shape of the skull and the way it fits on the spine. There's more science and skill to this than most of us realize, and she got kind of excited, yelling out when someone did a perfectly positioned tackle, like she'd just watched an Olympic dive. Once she even yelled out for a Midland tackle, then apologized to me. "I'm kind of a sports physiology geek," she said. "I guess you can tell."

At the end of the first quarter, Dr. Abbot got up to go look for some of the other hospital people she thought might be at the game.

My hands were full with my reporter's notebook and my pen and my tape recorder, but I reached out anyway and grabbed her wrist. "Could I interview you about this?" I said. "Could I talk to you about preventing injuries—all the stuff you've been pointing out?"

"I'm not really the person to talk to," she said. "There are sports medicine specialists who spend their whole lives researching this."

"You're enough of an expert for the *Kendall Kourier*," I said. "Plus, you're local—and there's a personal angle for me. You're the one who's fixing my knee."

"Sure," she said. "But we won't have much time to talk at the visit—my patients are scheduled pretty tightly."

"I'm glad to hear it," said my dad, trying to make a joke, but also trying to let her know that patient productivity matters.

"Don't worry about our group," Dr. Abbot told him. "We could take care of twice as many people if you guys would get that new operating suite built."

You could tell my dad was a little taken aback, but he just nodded and pumped his fist, like he was saying, "Go team!"

Anyway, I'm going to get to interview Dr. Abbot during what she calls her "paperwork time" the day after my pre-op visit, and we're going to talk about sports injury prevention. So watch this space—I can already see the title: Injury Prevention and the Sports Physiology Geek.

View 2 reader comments:

Posted by user **Photog_Sophie** *at 9:23 p.m.*
Thanks for the shout-out! And for the sake of the friendship I'll even photograph the rest of the season, even though as far as I'm concerned we could just pull pictures of guys and footballs off the Internet and no one would ever know the difference. Just saying. Click here if you'd rather see pictures from Thursday's performance of *Fiddler on the Roof*! No naked abs in those, Ms. Edison, don't worry.

Posted by user **CrustyAlum** *at 9:23 p.m.*
In my day, men were men, and we didn't spend so much time whining about our injuries. If you were tackled, you got back up and shrugged it off and kept right on playing. It reflects poorly on the state of today's high school students that they are unable to shake off some of the tough knocks in the game of life; how will these young men fare should they,

heaven forbid, one day be asked to defend our fine country if they cannot even protect a piece of pigskin? It surprises me less to hear that a young woman (I understand we are no longer supposed to call them girls!) is fretting about such minor scrapes and scuffles. I should certainly hope that her male classmates, however, are more able to rise above such incidents.

BLOGGING THE PARTY

Posted by user **JERRY** on November 16 at 8:00 a.m.

We sliced and diced Mumsford on Friday night, 30–3, and it felt very strange for me to be all suited up but not playing. Of course, Ryan Hurley was more than up to the task. His accuracy and the way he ran the team were impressive—he's come a long way since last year. I was pulling for him, but I confess I was also a little jealous.

Carla says that after she got injured she could go to a soccer game and cheer on her replacement at striker and not feel that she should be the one out there. I admire her for that attitude, but I guess I'm hardwired differently. Each time our offense ran onto the field, I was eating my heart out. I wanted Ryan to succeed, but at the same time I also wanted to be the one setting up the play in the huddle, the one taking the snap, the guy cocking his arm and dropping back to pass.

Instead, I stayed glued to the bench, watching along with five thousand other cheering spectators. All through the game, I was conscious of our fans roaring their approval, and I kept turning around to scan for familiar faces. I picked out dozens of people I knew—students, parents, and townspeople who come to all our games and cheer me on. But they weren't watching me—they didn't even know I was there.

They were focused on Ryan Hurley. Only one fan seemed aware of me sitting on the bench, and when I looked at him he met my eyes.

My mom was at her clinic on Friday; she's a physical therapist and stays late two evenings a week so that patients can come in after work for their rehab. But my dad hasn't missed a home game in years.

He always sits on the same high bleacher, wearing the same blue coat, in the same tense pose. Back straight. Arms on knees. Hands clenched nervously. Thinning brown hair blowing in the wind. And then—when we make a good play—he's on his feet in an instant, clapping and shaking a fist. My father's a peaceful man, but when he cheers for Kendall it's as if he's punching the air, trying to score a knockout. On Friday night he was cheering for our team and Ryan Hurley, but whenever I glanced at him he seemed to sense it and looked back at me.

I don't think my dad ever played tackle football in his life, but he hasn't missed a game of mine since I starred in Pee Wee. When he watches our team play, his black eyes come alive and gleam like tropical fish flashing around a tank. He sometimes stands and cups his hands and calls out surprisingly violent things: "Yeah, way to rip into them! Bust it up the middle! Take no prisoners!"

My dad is very different from Carla's dad. He never would have sent me to private school, not that he had the money anyway. He drinks beer rather than wine, and we've never sat in box seats in our lives. Dad was a pretty good miler back in the day, and there are three track trophies in our school's case that have his name on them. He once ran a mile in four minutes and forty-seven seconds, just two seconds off the Kendall record.

When my father lost his job at the factory, he couldn't sleep. He'd spend all day looking for work and take any kind of job there was. He washed dishes. He pumped gas. He packed and hauled for a moving company. But sometimes there were simply no jobs out there, and it absolutely killed him. He would knock on doors all day and then pace at night.

I could hear him downstairs, walking circles around the living room, and then the back door would shut as he slipped outside. He would be back home when I woke up, his eyes red and his face haggard from sleeplessness. I'd sometimes mention that he looked tired and ask where he'd gone. "Just out for a late stroll," he'd say with a brave grin. "Don't worry, Jerry, I'm doing fine. Never better."

A buddy of mine told me he was up at 3 a.m. one night and spotted my dad all alone, walking the track of our high school in a cold drizzle. The track is a quarter mile around. Dad ran around it four times in four minutes and forty-seven seconds when he was eighteen. I wonder how fast he circled it at forty-two, in the darkness and the rain, worrying about providing for his family. But I never once heard him complain, and he wasn't trying to walk away from his troubles. He just needed some kind of movement.

After the Mumsford game, there was a party to celebrate the blowout. I wasn't planning on going, but my teammates gave me the hard sell. "Come," Danny urged me. "You don't have to stay late, but hang with us. I'm heading over with Deb. Show up and have a little fun, Jer. It'll do you good." So I went to the party—the first one I've gone to all season. Nice house up on a hill. Parents gone.

Heads turned when I walked in, but five minutes later the music and the dim lighting had swallowed me up. It felt wrong to me that it felt so right, that I could slip so easily back into this scene. I talked to Danny and Deb for a while— they're a great couple. Teammates walked by and gave me high fives. "Welcome back, bro." Girls who I used to party with smiled at me. Someone tried to hand me a beer and I poured myself a ginger ale instead.

I spotted my fellow blogger, Carla, swaying with a tall dude from the lacrosse team. Is he your boyfriend, Carla? Not that it's any of my business, but bloggers are supposed to paint the full picture, aren't they? I've never heard you mention him, or lacrosse. And if you don't mind a word of advice, I don't pretend to know too much about ACL tears, but I'm not sure you should be dancing—even if it's slow dancing—just before your operation.

Two bloggers in one corner of the room seemed like too much press, so I started to walk away. And then I froze. Because right there—*directly in front of me*—was the girl who had been in my car the night of the accident and gotten badly hurt. I hadn't spoken to her since then, and now we were less than five feet apart.

She was dancing with some guy I recognized from the JV

football team, her eyes half closed. She must have felt my gaze because she opened her eyes and looked at me. I stared awkwardly back at her for a few seconds till she turned away from me and put her head back on her guy's shoulder. I didn't have the nerve to say what I should have said, so in case she's reading this blog, I'll say it now: it's not enough, but I'm sorry.

When the song ended, we left the floor in separate directions, and I decided I had had enough of that party. I said goodbye to Danny and Deb and left on my own.

I didn't feel much like going home, so I just walked. I headed down the main street of Kendall, past the bank and the grocery where I work summers as a bagger and the funeral home where I said goodbye to my grandpa two years ago. The shops were all closed, and the lights were off, and not a soul saw me.

I veered down Christie Lane without even thinking about where I was going, and soon our high school swam into sight. I circled the grounds—the baseball field, the track that I always think of as my father's track, and the football field that is my own patch of Kendall dirt.

I'm not sure how long I walked, but at some point it started raining, and by the time I got home, I was wet and shivering. My mom was making herself a cup of tea when I walked through the door. She was still dressed in her clinic uniform—she wears white, like a nurse, with a blue patch near the heart that says, "Amy Downing: Kendall Wellness Physical Therapy, Licensed PT." She took one look at me and got me a towel, and poured me some hot tea. "Where were you?"

"Just out for a late stroll," I told her.

She studied my face. "Jerry, is everything okay?"

"Fine," I told her, with the bravest grin I could muster. "Don't worry about me, Mom. Never better."

View 3 reader comments:

Posted by user **ProudTigerMom** *at 10:13 a.m.*
Go Ryan Hurley! We in the stands always knew you had it in you! Ryan Ryan Ryan rah rah rah!

Posted by user **DanTheMAN** *at 11:27 a.m.*
Hey Jer, glad to see your head's stopped spinning enough to hit up the party, even if only for a second, and post some moderately coherent bloggy thoughts. Too bad you'll never know what happened after you left that night!

Posted by user **Tigers4EVA** *at 1:11 p.m.*
Mumsford suxxxxxxxxxxxxxxxxxxxxxx

TAKE CARLA'S MIND OFF HER OPERATION!

Posted by user **CARLA** on November 16 at 12:00 p.m.

Slow dancing with a lacrosse player? Is that what you call it? Jerry, I think you may have the makings of a sportswriter, or even a non-sportswriter, or let's say, a writer about other things even beyond sports. In other words, you're making up stories. No, he's not my boyfriend. And you must be kind of out of things over the last six months if you don't know who his girlfriend is—or was, up to last August—but I've taken sort of a pledge not to cover high school dating relationships on this blog. I get into enough trouble as it is. Let's just say, ask your friend Danny to ask his girlfriend for the story behind "Love and the Lacrosse Team." And we'll leave it at that.

But the guy you're talking about is a pretty good friend, and he and my best friend, Sophie, had kind of formed themselves into an unofficial Committee for Helping Take Carla's Mind Off Her Operation. First, Sophie started in on how I can't sit home all weekend worrying, and there's going to be this party, and she'll drive me there, and everyone will be there after the game, and what's the fun of being a senior if you never go to parties, and who the hell cares if you have something wrong with your knee and you can't move around too easily. And I was saying no, I really don't want to go, it'll just be the same old people and the same old stuff, and Sophie, who knows me better than anyone else in the world, was correctly interpreting this as me being much more scared of the operation than I was willing to admit and planning to spend the weekend at home obsessing. And she wasn't going to let that happen. (And so, among other things, you have Sophie to thank for the fact that you are not reading several thousand words of angst-filled stream of consciousness that I wrote while spending the weekend alone in my room, Googling the complications of knee surgery and generally driving myself crazy. So next time you see Sophie, you might thank her—I already have, several times.)

Anyway, while I was putting up my I-don't-feel-like-a-party defense, I did say, and honestly, that what I like best about parties is dancing, and I really can't dance. And Sophie, like the true friend she is, recruited a couple of friends—two lacrosse players and a runner, Jerry, if you want their varsity jacket IDs—who promised to take me out on the dance floor and hold me up for a couple of go-rounds, if I so desired. So what you called slow dancing, with its romantic overtones, was actually me draping myself over a tolerant and well-muscled young man in such a way as to put no weight at all on my knee. It didn't quite feel like dancing. From my side, it felt kind of like learning to walk with crutches all over again, and I would guess that from the guy's side it felt like some slightly bizarre conditioning exercise in which a weight of more than a hundred pounds (there are limits even to what I am willing to reveal on this blog!) is fastened around your neck and you have to make it through a mixtape.

Sophie was right, of course. She pretty much always is. She came to pick me up, looking like she always looks, totally great, with the wild curls and the bright red lipstick, and she made me get a little bit dressed up. Nicer, tighter jeans, a silk blouse she made me buy last month on what I suspect was another therapeutic endeavor, a take-poor-Carla-to-the-mall-to-get-her-mind-off-her-knee shopping trip. But Sophie being Sophie, it might also have been designed as a take-poor-Carla-to-the-mall-because-her-clothes-are-boring shopping trip. She got me to buy a turquoise silk spaghetti-strap blouse, even though I said I wasn't going to wear it. And then she got me to wear it. She, naturally, was wearing something that you can't buy at the mall, which was either crocheted by tribespeople somewhere who had been dipping into their opium crop or else assembled by Sophie herself from a bunch of doilies that she found in her great-grandmother's hope chest, the great-grandmother who spent time as a Fauvist painter, I mean. She looked like Sophie. She looked great, and I was glad to be at the party. I did a little "dancing," but not that much, out of kindness to my partners; if you hadn't been driven away by whatever odd mix of motives, Jerry, you would have seen me hobble over to the side and sit down very soon.

Mostly, though, I hung out and looked at who was dancing with whom, with maybe a little more expert decoding than certain quarterbacks are capable of, and I talked to friends, and I felt good, I felt like a high school kid doing what high school kids do on a weekend and not someone about to have doctors cut holes in her leg and insert high-tech instruments—although, of course, I was both. A high school kid and a person about to have the holes cut in her leg, I mean.

I even ended up, later that night, talking about Jerry Downing. I was watching some videos with a gang of kids, mostly footage of the Kendall football team over the past couple of years that the kid whose house it was had collected. We were being kind of silly, screaming and cheering over plays that happened a year ago, two years ago, and talking about the ways that the players have grown and changed, and a play came on from last year, from before Jerry had to quit the team. It was a game against Forest Park, the one where the whole thing turned on Granger catching an interception and then Jerry Downing driving the ball down the field in something like seven completions, one after another. And we were all just howling, like it was a game going on right in front of us on live TV and we didn't know how it was going to end. By the last play, first and goal, everyone was standing up—well, not me, but everyone else—and cheering for that long-ago touchdown and a quarterback showing his stuff in a season that was about to go sour. Kind of impressive, I have to say.

So yes, it was a party. Jerry should have stuck around; sounds like he let himself get driven away more by his own demons than by anything anyone else was actually feeling. The usual people did the usual things, most of which cannot be mentioned on this blog, and I hung out with the people who don't do so much of those usual things, but it felt noisy and friendly and like the place to be, and I was glad to be there, even though on some level I knew I was also the person about to have holes cut in her leg.

And even though I was saying up above that thanks to Sophie, you are all being spared the gory details about surgical complications, I need to warn you that you are about to get the other gory details.

View 3 reader comments:

Posted by user **Photog_Sophie** *at 6:13 p.m.*
Here's a link to a photo Carla doesn't know I took of an outfit she refused to buy . . . comment if you think she should have worn that!

Posted by user **@Photog_Sophie** *at 6:17 p.m.*
HAWT! Who says New Jersey girls don't know how to shop?

Posted by user **CrustyAlum** *at 8:22 p.m.*
In my day, girls wore appropriate clothing to school and social activities. We weren't Puritans, of course, but it was expected that young women would cover their shoulders and not flaunt their various body parts all over as if they were working in clubs of dubious intent. It is always

upsetting to see today's youth attempting to imitate the seedier versions of nightlife that have come to encroach upon our otherwise wholesome town. What such young ladies see in these characters as role models is frankly beyond me, but it suggests a severe lack of parenting!

UNDER THE KNIFE

Posted by user **CARLA** on November 18 at 4:00 p.m.

Well, the painkillers are making me a little groggy, but I'm going out of my mind with boredom, so let me tell you about my special day. So first of all, you have to stop eating and drinking at midnight the night before. My mom had taken the day off from work, and she was kind of fixated on that rule, like she thought I was going to forget and next thing she knew, she would look around and I would be drinking my glass of orange juice or spooning up my morning yogurt and granola. I guess she was just anxious about the whole thing; it made her hover kind of close—we aren't usually a particularly clingy mother-daughter pair—and it made me act all let-me-alone and hey-I-get-it.

The truth is, if you think about it, it *should* make you nervous, this whole thing about not eating. They tell you not to eat right before surgery because they're afraid that if there's anything in your stomach, you'll puke it up under anesthesia, and the vomit will get into your airway, and you'll suffocate. So that's a pretty thought from every point of view and should remind us that surgery really is full of dangers.

Both my parents drove with me to the hospital. We took Dad's car, since it has the Head of Hospital parking sticker on it, and they wanted me to sit in front next to him. But I made my mom go in front, because somehow it seemed more normal that way, the two parents in the front seat, the child in the back. And to be honest, we don't go that many places that way anymore, because I'm grown up and I can drive myself (except for this little knee issue, of course) and because my parents are as busy as they are with their jobs, and for whatever other reasons come into play in our family dynamic. But it felt to me like the right way to get driven to surgery, with Mommy and Daddy both in place. Sorry, but I really wasn't feeling very tough that morning.

So we got to the hospital, and Dad parked in his super-high-powered parking space, which is ridiculously close to the entrance and has a little sign with his name and the CEO title. It's part of a row of VIP spaces, the chief of surgery, the chief of internal medicine, and so on. My dad is kind of proud of this, and I was glad when my mom made a fuss when she said, "Wow, this is real status, Joe." He waved his hand like it was nothing, but I could tell he was pleased.

We walked slowly up to the entrance, me in the middle, like the little girl, Mommy on one side, Daddy on the other. He was carrying my soccer gym bag, which for some reason had felt like the right thing to pack, with a couple of books and a ratty stuffed animal for luck and some protein bars of the particular brand that I like for when they would let me eat again.

So we went to Admitting, and with Dad there, of course, it's totally streamlined. We were hustled right past all the other people waiting to check in, and the clerks couldn't do enough to fill in the forms for us and hustle us off to Day Surgery. It's the only way to travel, and I said so to my dad, as the people at Day Surgery, with similar alacrity, hustled me right into a changing room. But in the changing room, I started to feel weird. I had thought about bringing my own pajamas to wear, but at the pre-op visit they gave us a pile of papers, which I actually read pretty carefully—which I bet that not that many people do. That's how I got started on the idea of not eating being about not puking and suffocating to death, though that's not quite how the hospital puts it. Anyway, the papers said don't wear your own clothes, there could be a problem with germs, though I'm not so sure why clothes that come out of the hospital laundry should be that much cleaner than the ones that come out of our perfectly good machine at home. But I felt weird, taking off my own clothes, as instructed, and putting on the yellow hospital johnny. I snapped it up the back, and then I put on another one, with the opening in the front, and used it as a bathrobe. I had to take off my necklace, which was a present from my parents on my last birthday, a garnet on a chain, and my bracelet, which was a present from Sophie, and I put them in my pants pocket. I didn't have any barrettes in my hair, or I would have had to take them out, and I wasn't wearing my watch, and I don't wear glasses. But just putting on the johnnies makes you feel so weird, like you aren't you anymore, you're just patient number whatever.

I don't really like hospitals, which I know is kind of a

funny thing for someone whose family fortunes, so to speak, are made on hospitals, but I've never really liked being around them. I'm happy to admire my dad's parking space, but then, if it's all the same to you, I'd just as soon go home. That's why it's so strange that since moving here to Kendall, I've become so aware of the hospital as the place that keeps this town going—the place where so many of my classmates' parents work, the major employer for miles around now that the factory is closed. I've started to feel differently about it than the other hospitals where my dad has worked, but I still didn't want to be a patient there.

They moved me into a little cubicle with a hospital bed and all that weird stuff on the wall—dials and machines and tubes. I tried not to look at any of it. I sat on the bed, and my parents came in. There was one hard plastic chair, and my mom took that. Then the anesthesiologist came in and said to me, "So you're the one who wants to be awake for her operation," and all hell broke loose.

Well, not *all* hell. That's an exaggeration. But certainly some hell.

The anesthesiologist was a wiry little guy in scrubs, with bushy white eyebrows and blue eyes that kind of matched the scrubs. He talked to me, not to my dad, which I appreciated, and clearly he did know about me, I mean, given what he said.

"So you're the one who wants to be awake for her operation."

"What?" said my father. "What did you say?" He kind of

barked it at the anesthesiologist, and since he was maybe six inches taller and standing up and wearing a fancy charcoal-gray business suit—and most of all since he was the CEO of the hospital—you would have to say that his aspect was intimidating. But the little anesthesiologist with the bushy eyebrows seemed kind of unimpressed.

"Hi," he said up into my dad's face, "I'm Dr. Dickinson. And my understanding is that the patient has expressed a strong preference for being awake during her procedure, and that Dr. Abbot has agreed, subject to my approval." He turned and looked at me again. "Is that right?"

"Yes," I said, trying to sound very mature and very definite, though it wasn't exactly how I was feeling right then.

"Your approval?" My dad exploded. "She doesn't need your approval, she would have to have *my* approval! What kind of nonsense is this?"

"Dad," I said, "I talked about this with Dr. Abbot. She said that normally she doesn't give people the option of staying awake if they're under eighteen, but I told her about my blog. I told her I want to see this so I can write about it. I told her I'll be eighteen in a couple of months—"

"And she agreed," my mom said. "And so did I."

"You what?" Now my dad was turning on my mom. It's what he does whenever he's scared about anything: he gets mad at people, he barks, he announces that he's in charge. It used to scare me a lot in return, but now it usually just makes me feel bad and sad, like people must be thinking he's full of it. Which he really isn't, or at least not usually. He's a pretty cool guy, really, my dad. I could tell you some stories that would surprise you.

But we shouldn't have surprised him about the anesthesia. The thing is, after I discussed it with Dr. Abbot and she and my mom agreed it was okay, it never occurred to me that my mom wouldn't have passed it on to my dad. I always think there's this major-league top secret parental back-and-forth going on. Parents ought to be talking behind your back, that's part of what makes them a team.

"And neither of you thought to mention this to me?" my dad went on, still that accusing bark. "Neither of you thought I might have an opinion about violating hospital policy and allowing a teenager to be awake during a major operation?"

I told him I was sorry that I hadn't warned him about this, and I was. I pointed out that I had been pretty freaked out about the whole operation and that when I found out I could be awake, and I had this idea of blogging about it, that made the whole thing easier to face. I never stopped to think about whether that was kind of weird, I guess.

Here's the thing about my dad. He's a hospital CEO who is kind of queasy about the sight of blood, and medical procedures, and all that kind of thing. When he's not all mad and blustery, he can admit it about himself. He even uses it sometimes as a joke. Take him to a movie, and I happen to know he closes his eyes during shoot-outs—he also closes them if someone's getting a shot. He's always been like that, and as I said, I've seen him make a joke about it and get people laughing. But I know perfectly well that if he were having any kind of surgery and they said, "Do you want to be awake?" "Do you want to see what's happening?" he would be horrified. So I don't think he can really understand why I might be more scared of the idea of going to sleep and missing it.

"Dad," I said, "I've been really scared about this. The idea of being awake made me feel better. Please. Please, Dad."

He didn't look at my mom. He didn't look at the anesthesiologist. He just looked at me. I thought about saying it again, "Please, Dad," or even, "I'm sorry." But I didn't say anything, I just looked at him, and I shrugged a little, like, what can you do, I'm your weird blogging daughter.

"Any other little surprises you two have in store?" Dad asked, and it was okay, just like that.

"No surprises," said Dr. Dickinson. "Just a pile of consent forms."

So that was how I ended up in the operating room, more or less awake. They had given me something to relax me, as he called it, but I told him really specifically, "Don't relax me too much, I want to see what's happening." Whatever he did give me, though, changed my sense of time. After they put the IV in my hand (they let my parents stay in the room for that, and of course my dad couldn't watch), I could just feel the time slow down, like there was some kind of syrup in the air. I guess it really did relax me—but by relax me I think they mean undoing some of the links that hold me into my life. I was watching everything go by, and it was all just fine with me. But I was not asleep.

So I can tell you what they did to me. I can't tell it exactly in my own voice, because the person in that room wasn't exactly me, but I concentrated, and I checked it over again with Dr. Abbot when she came to see me after I was in the recovery room, and she laughed and said, "Pretty good, you got it pretty much absolutely right."

Here's what she did:

She put my knee in a legholder that propped it right exactly where they wanted it.

She put a tourniquet around my leg.

They put up a blue paper curtain so I couldn't see what they were doing to my knee, but I could hear them talking and I know what they did.

Dr. Abbot cut two little holes, one on either side of my kneecap. She called them portals. Then she put little tubes in through those holes, up inside my knee. And one of those tubes had a tiny camera in it, and all of a sudden, everyone could see the inside of my knee, up there on a video screen.

So I was lying there in this really cold room, breathing that very relaxed syrup air, and I could feel that my leg was weird, weird, weird, but I was looking up on the video screen, like the other people in the room.

Except not like Dr. Abbot, because she had on this science fiction headset, and I guessed that's how she could guide the tools that were—I still feel weird saying it—actually inside my body, inside my knee. And there she was, under her mask and her headset, saying what she was doing: here's the meniscus, here's the torn ligament, I'm removing some fragments of this or that, I'm repairing, I'm preparing the bed for the ACL, I'm drilling a hole for the ACL.

I might actually have fallen asleep once, because I kind of jerked myself awake, and Dr. Dickinson, who was standing near my head, said to me, "Hey there, you're doing great. Stay calm now, almost done." And I almost started laughing, probably again because of the relaxing drug, lying there and thinking, Here I am, people are digging inside my knee, and I'm falling asleep, and isn't that just the funniest thing!

Dr. Abbot took a piece—a long strip—from my patellar tendon, which is the tendon that connects my patella, the little roundish bone of my kneecap, to my tibia, the big bone in my leg. She just sliced out a rectangular strip of that tendon, and she used it as a graft, a kind of strap to hold my knee back together, instead of my old, torn ACL. I know this more from the diagram she drew me in her office, though, than I do from what I watched on the screen, and when I try to picture the graft, I see the neat little rectangle she drew on her pad. But I watched them, I really did.

To attach the graft, they have to drill tunnels in your legbone and in your thighbone and pass the graft through. And then there it is, a new connector, and the knee has meaning again. My thigh and my leg were no longer separated.

What did it look like on the video screen? The funny thing is, I thought a lot of it was beautiful, a kind of undersea world with these seaweed shapes waving—I think that might have been meniscus. Or maybe it was the pieces of my torn ACL. But it was really clear, watching on the screen, what were the pieces of my body, even the torn pieces, because they somehow looked so alive, especially in comparison to the metal instruments you could see moving in there like in a construction zone, trimming and prodding and constructing.

Or, at least, that's how I remember it. I did fall asleep, once and for all, after they had taken out the camera and the video screen went blank. Dr. Dickinson leaned over and asked me if I was okay one more time, and I said, "Yes, yes, I'm fine," and he said, "Good job, Carla." Then I have to wonder if maybe he dialed up the relax juice, because I think I passed out, right then and there, while they were cleaning up on the other side of the drape. I woke up in the recovery room, and my parents were sitting right there at my bedside. I was glad to see them and glad to see that they were holding hands, but the first thing I thought, when my vision focused and my head began to clear, was not actually about my parents, or even about me and my knee and my operation. What I thought was, Now I understand about bodies. What's inside the knee is real, if you know what I mean, real pieces of bone and tissue, ligament and meniscus (and I still don't really get what a meniscus is, even though everyone keeps explaining it to me). If something gets torn in there, then you can't rest your weight on your leg, bend your knee, kick a ball into a goal.

I don't know, am I totally dumb not to have realized this long ago? I mean, I dissected my earthworm and my frog and my rat in ninth grade honors biology. Drew my diagrams, too. But somehow this was like stop the presses news, this idea that kept coming over me again and again, this understanding that everything we are and everything we do is made up of pieces of material, hooked together in complicated ways. That's why we can do what we do—and it's why we can get broken.

View 3 reader comments:

Posted by user **ACLSurvivor** *at 7:13 p.m.*
Thanks for posting this. I actually had the same procedure about a year ago but all I remember was just being knocked out cold and waking up in the hospital with no idea what had happened except it felt like an elephant sat on my leg. Now I finally know what they were doing, thanks to you!

Posted by user **Ms_Edison** *at 9:11 p.m.*
You deserve a Pulitzer for combat reporting, Carla. Leave it to you to stay on the job even as you're going into the operating room. We're all wishing you a quick recovery here at the *Kourier*!

Posted by user **SoccerGirl#17** *at 10:17 p.m.*
We smashed Mumsford in girls' soccer in your honor, Carla! Get well soon!!!!

DINNER WITH FRIENDS

Posted by user **JERRY** on November 20 at 10:00 p.m.

My mom pulled into the driveway early this evening and saw me walking Smitty and shouted, "Jerry, we're having company for dinner. Put Smitty away."

Smitty is our golden retriever, and he's very friendly, so I couldn't imagine why I had to put him away. He likes children—he even likes the mailman. I walked closer to the car to see who our mysterious guest was. I saw dark blond hair, and then the person sitting next to Mom turned and I recognized my fearless fellow blogger.

I was surprised to see Carla, but it made perfect sense. She must have been referred to the Wellness Clinic after her knee operation. Mom doesn't usually bring her new patients home for dinner, but I knew she had been reading Carla's blogs and was a fan.

"Hi, Carla," I called. "Glad you survived the operation. I hope my mom isn't killing you with rehab."

"She tried her best today," Carla told me. "She made me scream so loud I had to bite a pillow."

"The first few weeks are the hardest," Mom assured her. "I have to bend the knee to get the full range of motion back. Then it gets easier. Do you need help getting out?"

"Might as well learn to do things myself," Carla said, and hoisted herself out of the car. I saw her wince—her knee was wrapped in a protective bandage and clearly very tender. She tugged some crutches out after her, and in a second was balancing precariously on the sidewalk, studying our house and then glancing warily at Smitty, who wanted to make friends by leaping all over her. "No offense, but get that humongous mutt away from me."

"He's no mutt and he's friendly," I assured her, keeping a tight leash on Smitty.

"Too friendly and too big. I'm a cat girl, anyway."

Smitty bounded at her, and I pulled him back. "You shouldn't have said that. I think you hurt his feelings."

"Jer, get him into the house before he knocks her over," Mom commanded.

I tugged Smitty inside, and the smart dog knew what was coming, so that I had to practically drag him down the stairs into the basement. "Sorry, old fellow," I told him. "You're dining alone tonight." I gave him some food and water and left the light on for him, but he followed me back up the stairs whining and pleading. I told him to chill out, locked him in, and turned to see Carla hobbling through our front door on her crutches.

"You're pretty handy on those," I told her.

"Sarcasm is the last thing I need right now," she said, looking around at the inside of our house. "Why don't you just call me Tripod or Long John Silver and get it over with."

I admit I felt a little self-conscious. Our house is nice and reasonably clean, but I've seen Carla's family's mansion from the outside, and it makes my home sweet home look like a shack. "Be it ever so humble," I muttered.

"Get off it," she said. "This place is great. And so are your parents. I'm a big fan of your mom, except when she's twisting my leg into knots. And your dad sounds great, too, the way you describe him on your blog." Carla paused, and looked a little embarrassed. "Hey, Jerry, I hope it's okay that I kind of invited myself over. Your mom and I were talking during the session, and I happened to mention that my parents are out of town, and she said that your dad was barbecuing chicken tonight . . ."

"It's fine," I told her. "As long as you don't blog about it."

"No promises," she warned with a smile. "Everything you say and do may end up posted for the world to read."

My father walked in from the kitchen, holding a heaping tray of chicken and some of his home-brewed barbecue sauce. He mixes the stuff up himself, and I can't tell you exactly what he puts in but it's smoky and delicious. "Dad, this is Carla Jenson. She's the one who got me started writing the blogs."

"I know who you are," Dad told her. "I'm a Kendall sports junkie, and I've been reading your stuff for years. I've seen you at two thousand Kendall sports events." He extended two fingers from the tray of chicken. "Welcome."

Carla poked out her pinky from her right crutch and they shook fingers. "Thanks for reading my stuff."

"You write about sports really well," he told her. "But you

need to cover a few track meets. Now I'd better get this chicken on."

Dad walked off with his chicken, and we were alone. "Your dad's a sweet man," Carla told me.

"You're just saying that because he likes your blogs."

"No," she said, "I'm brutally honest about people. Now, would you mind showing me your room?"

I looked back at her. "My bedroom? Why?"

"I'm a snoop," she admitted. "It's the reporter in me. You can tell everything about a person by their bedroom."

I shrugged. "It's upstairs. There's no elevator. And, anyway, there's really not much to see."

"Lead on," Carla said. She followed me up the stairs without complaining, but every step up looked like a painful struggle. She clumped down the hall after me, and I felt self-conscious again. The second floor of our house is small and low-ceilinged—there's my parents' room, my room, the bathroom we share, and a tiny study.

I hesitated at the door. I don't usually give girls tours of my bedroom. When I led Carla in, my room looked smaller and more cluttered than usual. My bed takes up almost half the space, and then there's my desk by the one window, with shelves on either side that hold books and trophies. "Wow," Carla said, "have you won every trophy they've given out in our town since kindergarten?"

"No, I missed a couple of archery and swimming ones," I told her.

"These must be your favorite football players?"

"Quarterbacks," I explained. "The Gods." My finger moved down the row of photos. "Joe Namath. Joe Montana. Dan Marino. Peyton Manning. Tom Brady. Eli Manning . . ."

But Carla had already moved on to my floor-to-ceiling bookshelf and was scanning titles. "So this is where the unexpected verbal facility comes from?"

"I have an uncle who collects books. He got me hooked on reading when I was six. Don't blow my cover."

"Too late, jock bookworm. I'm posting it on the Web. Have you actually read *Bleak House*?"

"No, I just looked at the pictures," I teased her back. Then my mom came in and told us she had appetizers and lemonade ready, and we headed downstairs.

It was one of those cool and beautiful fall nights. My dad's chicken tasted even better than usual, and the four of us ate enough for ten people. Carla seemed to like my parents and was especially interested in what had led my mom to become a physical therapist. Mom explained how she was the first one in her family to go to college, and that she paid her way through by working long hours at the field house. At first she did grunt work like mop the floors and fill the water bottles, but she soon got to know lots of athletes from different sports.

"You were probably flirting with them," Dad suggested.

"A few of them," Mom admitted. "I had never been around talented athletes before, and I was fascinated." She watched them hobble back from practices, sore and injured, to get iced and bandaged. There were two physical therapists on staff, and she watched them and learned from them, and pretty soon she was assisting them.

"What was it about the college jocks that fascinated you?" Carla asked. "Besides their muscles."

"Their competitiveness," Mom told her. "I liked their swagger. And when they got hurt, I saw how their whole sense of self changed."

Carla nodded. "Yeah, I know how that works." She looked down at the drumstick on her plate and muttered: "One day you think of yourself as a soccer star and your whole world revolves around practices and games, and the next . . . you're on crutches, reading about ligament autografts and allografts and thinking that you may never score another goal in your life."

There were a few seconds of awkward silence. I should have just changed the subject, but instead I said: "Come on, Carla. Of course you feel that way now. You just had an operation. But I've seen you play and I know how good you are. You'll score lots of goals in college."

She looked across the table at me. "No, I won't," she said, and there was a warning in her voice that I should have heeded. "I'm not going to play in college."

"You can't possibly decide that now," I told her. I was trying to make her feel better, but I should have kept my big mouth shut. "Just wait a few months and see how you feel when my mom gets through with you."

And just so you don't think I'm the only clueless one in

the family, my mother—who's a professional—chimed in: "He's right, Carla. Your surgery went well, and you're young and strong. All the research shows that after rehab you can return to contact sports and play as hard as ever. It's true that sports where you need to make fast pivots—like soccer— offer the greatest chance of reinjury, but I've worked with fifty-year-old men who return to the soccer field after ACL reconstructions and play another ten or fifteen years."

"Some of them," Carla said.

"Mom's point is . . ." I began, but Dad cut me off.

I was a little surprised that he took her side, because he's usually the most gung ho about staying the course and climbing back on the horse after it bucks you off. "I think Carla has the right to decide for herself," he said. "None of us has walked in her shoes and felt what she's felt. And I think we all need to respect that." He spoke softly but with enough quiet authority so that my mom and I got the message.

"Sure," I said. "Sorry, Carla, I didn't mean to push. I just think you're a great soccer player, and if you enjoy it, you shouldn't give up and quit too soon."

She stood up from the table, and her eyes flashed. "I'm not a quitter, and it's not about giving up," she told me in a low but furious voice. "Excuse me. I'll be back in a minute."

She headed off to the bathroom, and we looked at each other.

"Let it alone, Jerry," my father counseled.

"Believe me, I will," I told him. "I really didn't mean to push."

"Of course not," my mother said, "but your father's right. This is a very personal decision, especially for young athletes."

When Carla returned, we ate some pie and shared some laughs, and gradually the awkwardness went away. Carla stayed till ten, and my mom said she would drive her home.

I walked next to Carla as she crutched herself to our car. "Hey, Long John Silver, thanks for coming."

"Any time you're having chicken and pie, invite me back," she said.

"Standing invitation," I told her, and held the door. There was a moment when she was looking at me and I wanted to apologize for calling her a quitter, but I didn't and the moment passed, and Mom climbed into the driver's seat.

So, since I've been told that all that happens is fair game for blogs, and everything everybody says can and probably will be posted for the world to read, let me apologize now, Carla, for what I said the other night. I think I was really talking about myself—about how important football is to me and how I could never think of giving it up. Every minute I'm not playing is torture for me, and somehow I put myself in your shoes—your soccer shoes—which wasn't fair at all.

I've never gone under the knife and I've never had my knee bent to restore motion, and I won't soon forget the sight of you climbing the stairs on crutches, wincing at each step but making it to the top.

I'm still just getting to know you, but I definitely don't

think you're a quitter, and I hope you come back soon for some more chicken.

View 3 reader comments:

Posted by user **ACLSurvivor** *at 10:25 p.m.*
Jerry, if you haven't been through this procedure you have no idea what your friend is actually going through. Let her be, and she'll recover at her own pace. The worst thing for her right now would be to push her body before it's ready.

Posted by user **DanTheMAN** *at 10:33 p.m.*
What the hell is *Bleak House*? Carla, don't fall for this; I know what this guy reads in his spare time and it mostly involves publications with glossy centerfolds . . . His dad's BBQ is pretty damn good, though, I'll give him that.

Posted by user **PhysicalTherapyAdvocacy** *at 11:13 p.m.*
Physical therapy is often underappreciated compared to the surgical interventions. Check out my blog <u>Feel Good Get Physical Therapy</u> for more on how this underpaid and often unrecognized profession plays a major role in the recuperation of surgical patients. As always, the surgeons get all the glory but the real heroes here are the PTs. Feel good. Get physical therapy.

From: Cjenson@kendallhs.edu
To: JerryQB@kendallhs.edu
Subject: What your dinner guest was thinking

Jerry, I am sorry I wasn't the world's easiest dinner guest last
night. But I have a confession to make: it's all your mom's fault.
She is one fierce physical therapist, as I gather you've guessed,
but I would bet that professional ethics or whatever probably
prevent her from really working on you, even if you get yourself
banged up and twisted around on the football field. Here's the
piece I didn't have the sense to say—after that session with your
mom, and then after I made myself climb up and down the
stairs in your house so I could scope the place, I was sitting at
the table and however much my mouth was saying, "Oh, what
good barbecued chicken," my knee was saying, "Cry, baby, cry,"
or sometimes, "Die, baby, die." It just wasn't a good moment for
me to do the get-right-back-on-the-horse conversation. Sorry, I
know I was touchy, but the truth is, when I got up and clopped
clumsily off to your bathroom, what I needed to do was break
down for a couple of minutes, and it didn't have too much to do
with anything you or your mother had been saying. I mean, I
know you're a jock and you know from pain, but I thought I was
a jock and I knew from pain too, and this was something
different. Something was *wrong* inside my knee, right then, and
after the physical therapy and the stairs, to be honest, I didn't
really know if I could go on tolerating it and eating my chicken.
I held on to the sink in the bathroom and I looked at my face in

the mirror and there were tears sliding down my cheeks, and I did this weird silent howl, where I just shrieked at myself but without any sound coming out. I just mouthed the shriek, and then I mouthed the words, over and over, *I cannot stand this I cannot stand this I cannot stand this.* And after about ten times, I started to relax a little. I swallowed one of my painkillers, and I washed my face with cold water, and I clomped back to the table and ate a little more chicken.

So I'm usually better company. Sorry, enough about me. Let's talk about someone else.

It was nice of your mom to invite me home, and your parents are great, and you can tell they're proud of you, but I also felt like they were just a little on guard, just a little like they're watching out over you. Maybe it's because they didn't quite know what to make of me. Hey, Jerry, have you ever brought home a girl who clearly wasn't a girlfriend? Or even one who was? Or maybe it's what happened last year, when you got into trouble? If I were writing this as some kind of story, that would be a possible structure. You have this kid and he's the quarterback and he's a star and it's all good, and then one night the phone rings and you wonder, Do we really know our kid at all? And then you wonder, Is his whole life wrecked? And you stand by him, but maybe you don't actually feel safe again.

Or maybe that's total nonsense; maybe anyone hanging around with any one of us seniors and our parents would pick up the same vibes. Maybe it's just about what it's like to live with one of us right when we're on the point of leaving and going out into the world. That's one of the reasons I made you show me your room; I think about how we're all still living in our childhood rooms. Right now, you can look at them and see something related to the shells which shaped us as we grew. But someone who meets Jerry Downing next year and looks at your college room isn't necessarily going to see any of that. I mean, you're obviously unbelievably sentimental in a sort of sweet way, but I would guess that even you are unlikely to cart your elementary school trophies off to college with you.

I was sorry that I was so out of it with the pain. Just trying to behave like a mildly good guest and paying polite attention to other people was hard for me right then.

Anyway, thank you for the dinner, Jerry, and please thank your parents.

Carla

KNEES OF THE LIVING DEAD

Posted by user **CARLA** on November 21 at 10:35 p.m.

My knee felt a whole lot calmer and better this morning. I took one of the most powerful painkillers at bedtime, the one they had told me would knock me out totally, and it did, although I will swear on anything you say that my knee was throbbing while I was falling asleep, and that if I could remember my druggie dreams from that night, they would be knee-pain dreams. But in the morning, I could manage okay, though I wasn't looking forward to another physical therapy session. Today was my appointment to interview Dr. Abbot about sports injuries, and I showed up on time, crutches and all, with a slick new tiny digital tape recorder that I got by trading in the present my aunt sent me on my last birthday. (Don't get me wrong, it was totally sweet of her to send me something so beautiful, more like a piece of jewelry than a watch. My father promised to smooth it over with his sister, and I took the watch back to the fancy watch store at the mall. They gave me cash, not just a store credit, and that's how I came to have this nifty digital recorder and a pretty good little video camera as well. The complete investigative journalist, that's me.)

I knocked on Dr. Abbot's office door. It was her afternoon

for administrative work, she had said, so I was surprised that she was dressed for the operating room, wearing scrubs.

"I was down in the OR longer than I expected this morning," she said, "and I was afraid that I wouldn't get up here in time to meet you."

I couldn't help looking to see if there was any blood or anything gross on her scrubs, but they looked clean and blue, like they were just out of that special hospital laundry, which kills all germs.

"Besides, why not be comfortable while you're doing paperwork, right?"

I sat down in the chair in front of her desk, the same one that I sat in when we were discussing my own surgery, and I thought about how glad I was that this time I was here to discuss something else. I mean, even if we did start with ACL tears, it still wasn't about me.

And we did start with ACL tears. She diagrammed the tear for me, just as she had done when she was showing me how the surgery would work, but this time I could really pay attention. Then she took out her 3-D plastic model of the knee and went over it again with me, the ligaments, the bones, the way that the ACL stabilizes the whole knee. She talked about why girls are at especially high risk for ACL tears.

"The truth is, no one knows for sure," she said. "A lot of people think it's because after puberty boys add muscle and strength more rapidly than girls do. It takes less conditioning to get them strong. It may have something to do with having the strength to stabilize your joints, but also your whole upper body when you're running, so you don't find your body swinging to one side or the other, twisting your knee."

"So it's because I'm not strong enough?" I asked. I've never loved the weight training we do; I do it, but I do the minimum. Maybe it was my own fault that this happened to me.

"Maybe it's strength, maybe it's hormonal. Some people think that the estrogen in girls' bodies makes the ligaments a little more lax and that sets you up for these injuries. The bottom line is, no one has proven it's definitely any one thing, but there's a lot of belief that a good general conditioning program can reduce the risk."

She showed me a study in one of her journals from a couple of years ago. They took more than eight hundred girls who played soccer and gave them a special training program where instead of their usual warm-up, they did agility drills and strength training and something called plyometrics, which involves very fast intense movements. And you know what? When they compared those girls to the ones who didn't get the special warm-ups, their ACL injuries went down 88 percent over the first year.

I actually felt a little mad when she explained this. I mean, I never heard of plyometrics, and maybe if I had had a special warm-up, I wouldn't be in this situation. Still, there was something very cool about the way she talked about surgery, but also something really gross about some of it.

"Oh, here's a study you'll like," she said, clicking through some links on her computer. "This guy took knees from ca-davers and studied them."

"Just the knees?" I asked, feeling a little queasy at the thought.

"Yes, just the knees. And he looked for cadavers with ACL damage. And then he attached the knees to this ma-chine he built that simulated the forces of various athletic activities."

I was thinking maybe Dr. Abbot had gotten a little car-ried away. I mean, just because I was willing to watch my own surgery from a happy-juice haze didn't mean I wanted to think about zombie knees, cut from corpses, hooked up to torture machines. Why would she be going on about this and looking so enthusiastic? Any minute, I was afraid, she would click a picture onto her screen and there they would be, Knees of the Living Dead.

"And so what he found—and this is really interesting, Carla—is that it's pretty individual. Some of the male ca-daver knees tore right away, some of the female knees with the same forces, no damage at all."

"Wow," I said, trying not to picture it. "Interesting."

"But anyway," Dr. Abbot went on, "it's pretty clear that even if we can't specifically identify all the reasons, female athletes are at higher risk here. Maybe it's the physiology and the hormones, maybe it's the conditioning, maybe it's even the style of play. But there are way too many girls—and good athletes, too—getting ACL reconstructions these days."

So anyway, I took a lot of notes, and I recorded everything

she said. She was so eager to talk about this stuff that she had actually put aside a big pile of X-rays and MRI scans to show me some of her favorite injuries. I mean, it sounds silly to say it that way, because of course she doesn't want to see people get injured, but it was pretty clear that she just loves talking and thinking about things that can go wrong with the knee and the elbow.

I spent the whole week working on this, and I've done my big story on "Injuries and Athletes: The Sports Doctor's Perspective." Sophie is working on some great photos— Dr. Abbot let her photograph a couple of the MRI scan images. The story will run in the *Kourier* on Monday next week, so I just want to hype it here—but it won't just be about ACL tears. We also talked a lot about Tommy John surgery, which is something that baseball pitchers get on their throwing-arm elbows. The surgery is related because it's about replacing another important ligament, the ulnar collateral ligament, with a tendon that you take from somewhere else in the body. We cover why younger pitchers are getting operated on and whether the rules about pitch count really make a difference. The thing is, pitchers don't suddenly blow out their elbows by landing wrong, Dr. Abbot said, it's more the wear and tear of throwing hundreds and thousands of pitches. So there's this belief that if you restrict pitch counts, especially in younger pitchers, that might protect them.

Anyway, I'm not going to give away the whole article here, but I think it's pretty interesting. Dr. Abbot gave me some great quotes about what it feels like to repair these things and send kids out again so they can play. I also interviewed Mr. Feldman, the honors biology teacher, about how joints work, and Dr. Abbot connected me with one of the guys she did Tommy John surgery on back when she was doing her fellowship, and he told me about what it felt like to pitch before and after. I also called up Jerry's mother, and she talked to me some more about doing rehab with athletes. It's a pretty solid story, if I do say so myself, with a nice Kendall Hospital spin on it. All of which is to say, check out Monday's *Kendall Kourier* for "Athletes and Injuries, Part I." Yup, I've decided this is a pretty interesting subject, and I'm going to keep working on it. I mean, what else is my life all about right now?

So now I'll stop scooping myself—you'll have to read the paper to find out what the pitcher told me, and whether his arm really did come back to where it was before, and all the cool statistics I dug up.

But here's what I wanted to write about, because it comes back to that story that Jerry told about me at his house. After I did this long interview with Dr. Abbot, and we looked at some of the films, and I was getting ready to close my notebook and turn off my tape recorder and head on home, we got to the question of reinjury and athletes going back out there on the field.

"No question," she said, "some of the repairs and reconstructions we do leave girls at higher risk to hurt their knees again. It's not supposed to be like that. The reconstruction is supposed to solve the problem, but you have to work with the materials you have."

"What about emotionally?" I asked.

"What do you mean?"

"Do you ever find that people play differently after they've been hurt? That they're more cautious, or more self-conscious?"

Dr. Abbot isn't a fool, and I could see that she knew I was talking about myself. She leaned forward across her desk, and I could see a thin gold chain around her neck, hanging down into her scrubs, but I couldn't see what was on the chain.

"Sure," she said. "For some people, maybe especially some athletes, maybe especially some young athletes, it's kind of surprising news that they can really be hurt, they can really be stopped by an injury. Just like that, one minute you're fine and your body is doing what you tell it to, your athlete's muscles are working, and your athlete's heart is pumping away, and then something slips or something breaks or something sprains and you just can't tell your body what to do. And that's kind of a shock to the system in two ways, first because of the pain and the medical effects of whatever you've done to yourself, and second because you just can't will yourself over this particular hump."

I flipped my notebook closed, but I left the tape recorder running.

"When my knee heals," I said, "when it's finally all better—"

"Which it will do," she said, and smiled at me. "It will heal and it will finally be all better."

"Well, when it does," I said, "the thing is, I don't know if I want to get back out there and play. You know, if I want to get back on the horse."

There, I had said it. I had even captured it on tape.

"Ah, yes," Dr. Abbot said. "The proverbial horse."

"You know what," I said, and I realized I was talking kind of fast, because I was so relieved to have finally said this, on my own terms, "I don't think I would enjoy trying to make myself play really, really hard, like you have to if you play serious soccer, when all the time I'd be thinking about what I went through with my knee. And I'd just be waiting for that random twist, or that bad landing, or that kick that gets a little out of my control, and there it is, I've undone the whole thing. I've broken it again, all the healing was for nothing, and all your work was for nothing, and the pain comes back . . . I don't mean that this would happen, I just mean how would I ever play without thinking about it a little, and won't it get in my way?"

"It might," she said. "There are people who are so relieved to be playing again that nothing gets in the way. There are people who have to psych themselves up in a whole different way. But as I've just been showing you, there are probably some training regimens that can change the odds for you, so if you decide you do want to play—"

I interrupted her. "I'm not sure I want to play," I said, a little too loudly.

Dr. Abbot looked at me with a kind of considering look, like she was adjusting whatever she had planned to say.

"For years I've figured that my senior year would be all about convincing colleges that I was their future girls' soccer varsity player. But now it turns out that my senior year is going to be about arthroscopic surgery, pain, and rehab—"

"And so that's making you rethink?"

"I don't know," I said. "It's complicated. Part of it is that I'm thinking, well, I'm not selling myself to colleges as this big soccer player, so does that mean I don't have to be a big soccer player once I get there? That maybe I can do other things for the next four years, and know some different people, and just kind of keep my options open?"

I had meant to sound confident, but when I listen to that part of the tape, I can hear that my voice gets kind of squeaky.

"That's how I felt," Dr. Abbot said. "I had a knee injury back when I was in college. I didn't need a graft like you did, but I had to have a repair done, and I had lots of physical therapy. And I just realized that, well, I was actually more of a weekend warrior."

"What do you mean?" You know, my dad always says that surgeons are weird—can you imagine that she's been checking my knee and taking care of my knee and operating on my knee and up till right then she never mentioned that she had had knee surgery, too?

"I thought about it, after I spent most of a semester on

crutches—we weren't rehabbing people as quickly back then—and I realized that if it were really up to me, I would play pickup games with friends every now and then, but I wasn't cut out for serious college sports, especially combined with premed. And that's what I told my coach and my team-mates. I told them I needed to buckle down and get the pre-med grades, and that was my priority. And it sort of was. But it was also this realization that I was, well, like I said, a weekend warrior."

"Maybe that's what I am, too," I said.

All of a sudden, and I'm not sure why, I wanted to know all kinds of things about Dr. Abbot. I wanted to know whether she always knew she would be a doctor, and whether she always knew she would be this kind of a doctor, and whether it ever grossed her out to think about cutting the knees out of corpses, but I also wanted to know what her house looked like, what she actually did on her weekends (besides attend the occasional Kendall football game), and whether she was married, or had a boyfriend, and what she really thought of my father and the way he was running the hospital. I had been in her office interviewing her for almost an hour, and I suddenly wanted to start all over again with a whole new list of questions.

But she was already answering the question I hadn't quite asked.

"You can't decide that right now, Carla," she said. "Or at least, you shouldn't. You're in pain, you're too close to the surgery. Concentrate on the physical therapy, concentrate on getting better. This is a bad moment for life decisions. Your body's still traumatized, and so is your head. When you feel better, when your knee is working, when you aren't spending every day playing games with yourself about when is the pain so bad I need a painkiller—"

"How did you know that?" I asked.

"I know athletes," she said. "I would bet anything you don't like the fuzziness that comes with the painkillers. I bet you're toughing it out through the school day—"

"And then," I said, "when I get home, I don't want to cloud up my brain because that's the time I write. That's when I blog, that's when I do my articles."

"But you're in a lot of pain by the time you get home, too, I bet."

"Sometimes," I said.

"So wait till this all gets better. I promise you, I'm not just saying to get back on that damn horse. I'm telling you this is the wrong moment to make decisions. Get better, get your body back, and then think it over."

So that was the interview, with Carla's little therapy session thrown in for good measure. I packed up my tape recorder and my notepad and the research articles she had printed out for me.

I thanked her for her time and told her what a great subject it was, the athletes and injuries. She said I should think about some of the other categories of injuries and even about the whole history of protective equipment, especially for football. You could write about spinal injuries, she said, and about head injuries. You wouldn't want an orthopedist for that. You'd want to go after a neurosurgeon.

So I'm working on it. I haven't tracked down a neurosurgeon yet, but I've learned a lot about the brain and about the ways that you can protect it, even when huge, strong guys are trying their best to tackle one another. I'm planning to talk to a couple of athletes who've had these injuries and hear about their version of rehab, and so on. So read part one and watch for part two!

View 3 reader comments:

Posted by user **StrongerThanEver** *at 11:13 p.m.*

I had my ACL repaired two years ago, and the first time I set foot on the soccer field after that I was running on egg shells, but pretty soon you forget everything that happened because it's true what they say: it heals stronger than it was to begin with. I'm running just as fast and cutting just as hard now as I ever did; I even run stairs! Your body will let you know when it's ready and then, if you love soccer, go for it!

Posted by user **SoccerMom** *at 11:13 p.m.*

In my opinion there needs to be more emphasis on conditioning in girls' soccer from the youngest ages. There's not enough stretching and not enough drills that strengthen the important muscles. Science has shown that girls' bodies are demonstrably different from boys', and the only way to protect the feminine physique from overexertion

and irreparable damage is to engage in regular stretching
and conditioning.

*Posted by user **@SoccerMom** at 11:14 p.m.*
~~Also, they look hot in Lycra when they're stretching . . .~~

Comment deleted by user Ms_Edison at 11:15 p.m.

SAND RIVER

Posted by user **JERRY** on November 22 at 8:47 p.m.

It started snowing during the night, an early season dusting, so that when I woke up and looked out my window, the dawn light that filtered through my curtains and glistened off my trophies seemed to sparkle with magic dust. A name came to me right away. Sam Taggart.

I lay in bed and watched my trophy shelf come alive, and thought about the matchup to come. We hadn't faced each other last year, because of my suspension, but now it would happen. I was the best at my position, and he was the best at his. I wanted to throw in his direction, at him, over him, and through him. Taggart was being heavily scouted by major college teams, and I wanted those scouts to see us going at each other full on, mano a mano.

I pulled on an extra layer for my morning run and headed over to Danny's house. I rapped on his back door, and when he opened it he was zipping a fleece jacket over a thick sweatshirt that I believe covered a long-sleeved cotton team practice jersey. His dad spotted me from the kitchen, where he was making coffee. Mr. Rosewood is the deputy captain of our town's police force.

Danny's mom died of cancer when he was four. His dad

nursed her through the long illness and then raised Danny on his own. They're as close as a father and son can be. I remember riding with them in a police car when Danny and I were six, and Mr. Rosewood let us turn on the siren and flasher, and even speak through the loudspeaker. At the time, I thought it was the coolest thing a dad could do.

He turned to me and waved with his coffee mug. "Hey, Jerry. Kick some butt today."

"Gonna try, Mr. Rosewood. You coming to the game?"

"Yup. Freed myself up for it. I've been reading the sports pages. Taggart sounds like a beast."

"The Monster of Sand River." I nodded.

"You'll slay him," Mr. Rosewood said.

Danny came out the door pulling on what looked like ski mittens and banging his hands together as if they were already feeling frostbitten. "Let's get this over with."

"Sure you've got enough layers on?" I asked him.

"Unlike some people, I'm not part Eskimo," he grunted.

Actually, my ancestors are mostly Irish, and I doubt I have any Eskimo blood kayaking around in my veins. But I do like the cold. There was a sharp bite in the air. "Football weather," I told Danny. "You gotta love it."

"I hate it," he said, and took off down the block.

The fresh powder was still soft enough not to be too slippery. Wind gusts stirred up snow devils that hovered and swirled before disappearing back onto the roadway. We ran three miles side by side, our breaths fogging the winter air, and I knew the same name was hammering away at both of us with every footstep.

"You ready for Taggart?" I asked Danny as we circled the old factory. "Or should I throw away from him?"

He gave me a look back that said he welcomed the challenge of being covered by the best pass defender in the county. "Just make sure you lead me."

"Danny, I gotta say, I think he can run step for step with you," I told him.

"We'll find out soon enough," he responded with his usual mix of modesty and quiet confidence, and picked up the pace.

I stayed with him for half a block more and then started to fall back. I could only watch as he set sail for home through the silent white streets of Kendall, his elbows swinging rather than pumping and his track shoes rising and falling in that loping stride that should have been a jog but ate up ground like a full-on sprint.

During my darkest days, when I was picking up trash for community service, keeping my distance from the team, and wondering who my friends still were, Danny made it a point to jog by every day. I'd spot him far off, motoring toward me with that easy stride, and he'd stop to chat and tell me some news from the team or a bad joke. Then he'd flash me that goofy grin of his and say, "Don't get too down on yourself, Jer. You'll be back soon."

Now it was game day at Sand River, and Sam Taggart was waiting for both of us. I knew Coach Shea was thinking about sitting me out for one more game, to be supersafe, but I was determined to play. Of course, when you get your bell rung as hard as I had against Midland, it's always in your mind that you could get hit again, even harder, but I pushed the fear as far away as I could.

I had looked up concussions online and was sure that mine had been mild. I hadn't completely blacked out or had any memory loss. I had no repeat vomiting, no dizziness or ringing in my ears, and no drowsiness. Except for a head-ache that soon went away for good, none of my symptoms had come back. I had taken a pop, let it heal, and now I was good to go. I've played whole seasons without taking a hard shot to the head. What were the odds I'd take another one in my very next game?

Coach Shea brought it up when I saw him third period. "I don't care if Sam Taggart is the best safety in all of New Jersey—"

"Which he may be," I interrupted.

"He can't beat us on his own," Coach Shea growled. "The rest of the Sand River team is mediocre. Take one more game off. If we need you, I can always put you in."

"The docs have cleared me," I reminded him. "If I don't play, I'll be rusty for the States."

"You've been practicing hard," he pointed out.

"It's not the same," I replied.

Coach Shea reluctantly nodded. He had been a high school star at Kendall, and then had played in college for Fairleigh Dickinson and nearly turned pro. He knew the difference between practicing and game time. "True," he admitted. "Listen, Jerry, you know how much I want to win it all. But I really don't think we'll need you today."

I looked back at him, at his craggy face, as if a sandstorm had blasted away at his cheeks and forehead, at his white hair, which he cuts so close to the scalp that it makes him look like an old army sergeant who has seen his share of combat, and at his coal-black eyes that during tight games seem to ignite with intensity and inner fury. Yeah, he wanted to win it all, and he wanted it badly.

Coach Shea led Kendall through its glory years when state titles came to our town in bunches. The last few seasons, we haven't won it all. I hate to even write this, but lately there's been talk that he's too old, which is ridiculous. Coach hasn't lost a step, and he's still razor sharp. But people here expect state titles, and when that doesn't happen, somebody's got to take the fall.

We would have won it all last year, if I hadn't gotten suspended. This season could be a last chance for both of us. It's my senior year. And for Coach Shea, if we don't win they may try to replace him with someone younger. That would be a damn shame.

"You're the coach," I told him. "But I feel great. No headaches. No dizziness. And if you want me to come into the state tournament sharp, I need this."

He studied me carefully for a few seconds, looking down at me with those intense black eyes. I'm not a small guy, but Coach is five inches taller, and his shoulders are a lot wider, and at sixty-three he can still do more push-ups. He finally put a beefy hand on my shoulder. "Okay, Downing. You want it, you got it. Just take it easy."

"You know a way to play football and take it easy?" I asked him.

He shrugged. "Just try not to lead with your head."

Our bus rolled through pitch pines, and soon Sand River's brick high school swam into view, and behind it their football field with its cobalt-blue metal bleachers. I could hear the music from their marching band, especially the rhythmic pounding of the bass drums. The Sand River Blue Devils were ready for us.

It may have been enemy turf, but when I ran onto their field, I heard the roar from a thousand of our loyal fans who had made the half-hour drive. There must have also been two thousand Sand River faithful sitting there, cheeks painted blue, wrapped in winter coats with scarves around their necks, sipping hot chocolate, and waiting for their hero.

SAM TAGGART—THE MONSTER LIVES! a sign read, and another proclaimed TAGGART—SAND RIVER—RUTGERS—NFL—HALL OF FAME. I could see him warming up, running short sprints forwards and backwards—not the biggest guy on their team, but perfectly put together. Call it extra muscle-twitch fiber or genetics or superstar charisma, but whatever it was, Sam Taggart had it in spades.

When the game started, it looked like maybe Coach Shea was wrong—Sam Taggart *could* beat us all by himself. I threw my third pass up the middle to Glenn Scott, and Taggart—who should have been taken far out of the play—read my eyes and somehow got a hand on it.

The deflected ball bounced off Glenn's shoulder, high up

into the air, and Taggart leaped up and snatched it back to earth. In an instant, he was running the interception back the other way, and it looked like he was moving twice as fast as our players.

Three Kendall Tigers took off after him. I tried to cut him off, but a lineman blocked me onto my butt, and I watched the race from the grass. Taggart pulled away from two of our players like they had concrete in their shoes, but one stayed right on his heels, and I saw that it was Danny.

The two of them seemed to cover the forty yards to the end zone in a couple of heartbeats. It was a blue streak followed by an orange lightning bolt as Danny matched him stride for stride and even gained half a step. At the twenty, Danny launched himself in a desperate dive. His flailing right hand brushed Taggart's right ankle, but Taggart ran it into the end zone, where he spiked the ball and raised his fists to the roaring Sand River crowd.

It's a dangerous thing to let a home team get a lead. Suddenly they started to believe that they could beat us, and we were in a world of trouble. Their defense stopped us cold, so that we had to kick. Our punter was told to kick it away from Taggart, but he squibbed it.

The Monster of Sand River stepped up and fielded the pooch punt on his thirty, juked back and forth twice, superlight on his feet like a dancer, and then found a seam and ran the ball all the way back for his second touchdown in four minutes.

I tried to lead Kendall back, but Danny is my go-to guy in

these situations, and every time I made him my primary receiver, Taggart was practically inside Danny's shirt. I had to find a secondary receiver, or even a third option, or run the ball myself.

I was surprised to find that I was a little gun-shy. When I had to search the field for open receivers and buy us a little time, I couldn't shake the premonition that I would be hit in the head again, from behind, and slammed to the ground. I kept flashing to that moment when Gonzales had launched himself at me like a guided missile and I ended up flat on my back listening to Coach Shea ask: "Jelly? Jelly?" I wasn't rushing my passes, but I also wasn't giving my receivers the extra seconds they needed to free up.

I brought us close enough to hit one field goal, but we went into halftime down fourteen to three. As we ran off the field, someone from our cheering section shouted, *"Put in Ryan Hurley!"*

Coach brought us back into the team bus for our halftime meeting. He started off quietly, but his black eyes were flashing, and I knew it was the calm before the storm. "You guys must have been reading the papers," he told us. "You thought these guys were going to roll over, and you were already in the States. Well, bad news, guys, they're not rolling over, and we may never make it to the States. Our season could end here at Sand River, with their marching band tooting their horns and their fans cheering as we walk off the field. I've seen plenty of games like this, where great teams choke away a whole season's hard work. Do you want that to happen today?"

There was silence on the bus, a gut-wrenching silence as the picture he had conjured up sank in. I thought about what I had been through during my suspension, and the vow I had taken to redeem myself and lead us to a championship. "No, Coach," I answered first. "That's not gonna happen."

Other voices immediately took up my answer with different words, the tone swelling louder and growing more confident and angry, like a rising tide: "No way, Coach." "We'll step up." "We know what we need to do."

Coach Shea let it build for thirty seconds or so and then cut us off by punching the steel wall of the bus with his bare fist, so hard he put in a dent. BAM!

"All right, listen to me!" he shouted, and believe me we were listening. *"It's not up to them. Do you understand that?* It's not up to their quarterback or their receivers or Sam Taggart. *It's up to you.* You played a stinking half, you can play a great half. *You can make the decision to take back what's yours.* Where are my seniors?"

We raised our hands.

His eyes fell on Danny and me. "You can go out with your heads held high, or you can remember this game of shame for the rest of your lives. Now, I'm not gonna diagram any plays for you or change up personnel—*to hell with that.* But I am going to tell you that I've been coaching for thirty-three years and this is one of the best teams I've ever had, and if you want it *you'd better take it from them. Fight for it! Claw it out! Win the one-on-one battles. Kick some ass. Let's go!"*

We got off the bus and headed back to the field, and I

was thinking, to hell with the fear of another hit. I would hold the ball and buy time and take whatever shots came my way. Coach was right—this was something we would have to live with for the rest of our lives. And that's when Danny took my arm and tugged me away from the rest of the team and said, "Jer, you gotta throw it to me."

"I'm trying, but he's all over you," I told him.

"I've got half a step on him," he said.

"I'll keep looking," I promised.

Danny didn't let go of my arm. His usual relaxed expression and goofy grin were gone. He hadn't caught one pass the whole first half, and he looked angry. "Four years of work, Jer," he reminded me softly. "We got here together. You threw them, I caught them. Don't you dare throw away from me now." Then he stalked off.

Two quarters. Twenty-four minutes. We ran back onto the field, and I took a deep breath and looked at our cheering section, drawing strength from the faces I knew—my dad and Mr. Rosewood looking tense, Carla typing away on her iPad, and on a high bleacher I spotted Leo Keller. Leo was the only Kendall grad to ever make it big in the NFL. He played outside linebacker for ten seasons and has two Pro Bowl rings. He's a handsome African American with a rugged face and salt-and-pepper hair. He doesn't come to many of our games, but there he was in an orange Kendall Tigers jacket, massive arms folded across his chest. I felt him staring down at me and me alone as if to say, "It's money time. This is on you, baby."

In the huddle, during our first possession, I wasted no time. "It's a post to Rosewood. I'm gonna fake it short to Glenn and let it fly. *Let's get one back!*"

I grabbed the snap and took a five-step drop to give Danny a few precious extra seconds. Glenn slanted across the middle, and I pump-faked it to him so realistically that one of their tackles jumped high to bat down the pass that never came. I felt the pressure of their rush coming from my right, and I slid left. A panicked voice inside me warned, "Throw it now. Get rid of it or you'll get creamed." But I held on to the ball, dodged a rusher, and looked desperately for Danny.

He was already twenty yards deep, slanting toward the goalpost at full sprint. My fake to Glenn hadn't fooled Taggart—he had a good inside position on Danny and was running right with him. People think quarterbacks gauge distances and aim long passes based on calculations, but that's not true—there's no time for that kind of thinking. I just heaved it high and hard, trying to put it in a place where only Danny could possibly catch it.

As soon as I let the ball go, I knew I had overthrown him. No one could catch this one. POW! I got hit a good shot in the small of my back and fell to my knees. I knelt there as if praying and watched the ball spiral through the cold air. There was no way Danny could possibly catch it, except that no one had told him that. My old friend from Pee Wee turned on the afterburners.

He pulled a half step in front of Taggart, and then a full step, and it was like watching a graceful antelope dart away from a hungry lion. Somehow Danny ran under my prayer of a long pass. At full sprint he reached out his long arms and caught the ball in his fingertips, and then it was Taggart's turn to dive at Danny's ankles and miss.

I don't remember getting up off my knees, but I suddenly found myself sprinting to the end zone and giving Danny a flying high five that turned into a tight embrace. "WAY TO GO! Damn, I didn't know you could run that fast."

"I didn't know it, either," he admitted, still gasping.

Fourteen to ten. As quickly as that, the game turned. Sand River fought hard, but their confidence had been shaken. We scored again on our very next possession, this time on a run right up the middle by Brian Hart, our sophomore running back, who had started the season on the bench and played himself into the starting lineup.

We took that three-point lead into the fourth quarter and held it as the clock ticked down. "I'm going to take you out," Coach Shea informed me with four minutes left. "No reason to risk a late hit. Ryan can close this out."

"I'm sure he can," I told the coach, "but we're only up by three. If they score a late touchdown, they win. Leave me in for one more possession to seal the deal."

He thought it over and nodded. "One more set of downs, Downing. Just keep it simple."

Our defense held them, and we ran onto the field with three and a half minutes left. *Hold on to the ball,* I implored our guys in the huddle. "We're gonna eat up time and win this thing as long as we don't fumble it away." Sure enough, we picked up a first down on three straight runs, and now there were only two minutes left.

The Sand River players looked desperate. Time was running out for them. If we got another first down it was all over. Twice we tried to run it, and both times they stopped us behind the line. On our second run, Sam Taggart came off Danny, blitzed, and stuffed the run behind the line himself. Suddenly we were looking at third and twelve. There were still ninety seconds left. If they got the ball back, they'd have a chance to drive it in. We have a solid defense, but I didn't want to leave the game and our whole season in their hands.

Coach Shea called a time-out. He looked worried. "They're expecting another run," he said. "Taggart is cheating up. Let's fake a handoff to Magee to draw Taggart in and then hit Rosewood on a slant up the middle. One more first down, guys, and this game is history. Come on, seniors. Execute this play and we're in the States!"

We ran back onto the field, and for a long second I locked eyes with the Monster of Sand River. He was studying my face, trying to read what we had planned. I'm sure I didn't give him any clues, but monsters have sharp instincts, and I saw him back up half a step.

I took the snap and dropped and wheeled to my right. Magee came roaring up, and I stuck the ball in his belly. He put his arms up as if cradling it, and I pivoted with him and rode the fake a full step before I popped the ball out. Magee slammed into the line, his arms now cradling thin air, while I bootlegged right and looked for Danny.

Sam Taggart hadn't bought the fake. He was a quarter step behind Danny, the two of them slicing up the middle. Danny needed just a little more time to open up daylight. I sensed the pressure coming from my blind side and knew I might be crushed at any second. "Go down," that panicked voice called out inside my head. "Take the loss. Kick it away. Trust your defense. *Go down now!*"

I stayed up, sliding to my right, trying to buy a few more seconds. When you play quarterback as long as I have, you can feel a pass rush closing in, and I knew my blocking had collapsed. I steeled myself for a hard hit, drew back my right arm, and threw a dart to Danny, seven feet off the ground and two steps in front of him.

Just as I released the ball my knees got chopped out from under me, and I spun to the turf. I hit the ground hard but never lost sight of my pass.

Taggart put on a burst of speed and reached out to tip the ball, but I had placed it too well. Danny leaped high and to the side and unfolded his lanky body like a bird spreading its wings. He caught my pass with both hands, and that was when the blue freight train ran him over.

It was a big lug of a kid named Schultz who should've been too chunky to play cornerback, but he had unexpected speed. Glenn Scott was supposed to take Schultz deep on this play, but he had come steaming back in. He found himself in a perfect position to make the hit of a lifetime with five steps of sprinting momentum and an unsuspecting target. Receivers are never as vulnerable as when they're led up the middle and fully extended. Danny was wide open, and the collision of bodies sounded like a thunderclap.

The ball bounced free, and there was a wild scramble before one of their players fell on it and one of our players fell on him.

Meanwhile Danny lay there, flat on his back, not moving or even twitching. The Sand River lineman who had tackled me still had me wrapped up, and it took me a few seconds to disentangle myself and hurry over.

By the time I got there, Coach Shea and Dr. Anderson were on the field, and I had the déjà vu experience of watching them stand over him just the way I had seen them standing over me two weeks before. "Danny," Dr. Anderson repeated, clapping his hands. "Danny, can you hear me?"

I got up off one knee and walked close, so that I was staring down at my oldest and best friend. Danny's eyes were open, but for the longest time he didn't respond. There was complete silence on the field and in the stands. I noticed a tall figure standing stock-still on the edge of our sideline, as if tempted to move forward but frozen in place. It was Mr. Rosewood, standing alone. My father walked next to him and gently took his arm.

Everyone on both teams got quiet, and I'm sure prayers were said on both sides. I know I whispered one. The only sound to be heard out loud was Dr. Anderson repeating, "Danny? Daniel Rosewood?" And clapping his hands loudly. In the distance came the shrill wail of an approaching ambulance. "Can you hear me, Danny?" Dr. Anderson demanded.

Then Danny blinked, and said, "Yeah?" in a surprisingly loud and steady voice, as if he was suddenly ready for a conversation.

I let out a breath and walked even closer.

"Do you know what day it is?" Dr. Anderson asked.

"Today," Danny answered. "Game day. Friday. Sand River. Did I hold on to the ball?"

You could feel the waves of relief from both teams and from the sidelines as more questions and answers and physical responses followed.

"Can you move your arms, Danny? Good. And your legs? Excellent. No, don't try to sit up. We're gonna carry you off the field as a precaution. Just lie back and keep your head and neck still. That's good."

They strapped him to a board and carried him off the field, and by then Danny was totally alert and talking to us. He gave a thumbs-up to the fans who stood and cheered for him.

"Did I hold on to the ball, Jer?" he asked as they reached the doors of the ambulance.

"Don't worry about it," I told him. "Just chill. We'll win this one for you." And we did.

When I got to the hospital, Danny was sitting up, totally alert, and all he wanted to talk about was the game. "How did it end?"

"They got two first downs, but then we stopped them

cold. We're in the States!" I saw him wince and blink his eyes quickly. "What's the matter, Danny. Are you in pain? Should I get a doctor?"

"Nah, I'm fine," he said, lying back on the examining table. "It's just a headache. The docs said it's normal when you get your bell rung. You should know."

"I do know," I told him.

He smiled up at me. "The States! Son of a bitch. How about that Jerry? We did it!"

He held up his hand, and I slapped him five, but very gently. "Yup, we did, old buddy. Now chill, and rest easy."

View 6 reader comments:

Posted by user **MONSTERofSandRiverMyAss** *at 9:13 p.m.*
GOOOO Tigers! Eat dirt Blue Devils! You think you've got a monster but we're going to STATEEEE

Posted by user **KENDALLLL** *at 9:15 p.m.*
WE ARE THE CHAMPIONS.

Posted by user **DanTheMAN** *at 10:02 p.m.*
Totally worth it!! You better believe I'm back on my feet and ready to play, Jerry.

Posted by user **TigerMom** *at 10:13 p.m.*
I was terrified for you, Dan, glad to hear you're doing better. I was one of the people praying for you when you went down,

and I hope you'll take it a little easy at least for the next few days until you're completely back to normal.

Posted by user **CrustyAlum** *at 10:28 p.m.*
Coach Shea is the finest football mind our town has ever seen. To all who say he needs to be replaced, I would direct you to the trophy case in the lobby of Kendall High.

Posted by user **MONSTERMASHofSandRiver** *at 11:57 p.m.*
King Kong got his. Godzilla got his. And now the so-called "Monster" of Sand River lives no more!! GO TIGERS!

FOLLOWING MY STORY

Posted by user **CARLA** on November 22 at 9:23 p.m.

I drove to the hospital behind the ambulance carrying Danny Rosewood. Well, actually, my father drove. And actually, we weren't right behind the ambulance, because of course he had to wait and see Kendall win. We were right down near the sideline—me with my special press privileges—and there I was, pulling on his sleeve. I was practically begging, so we got up and started moving toward the exit, but I could feel he was hanging back, wanting to see the final plays, so I just turned toward the field myself, once we were close to the exit, and we watched Kendall block Sand River's final attempts, and the big clock count down, and then, as our side started to celebrate, I dragged my dad out into the parking lot and we took off. It could only have been a ninety-second or so delay, because that was all the time remaining, and what surprised me was how impatient I was. I didn't even care that our team was winning, that we were getting into the tournament—I just wanted to follow my story.

So that's what this blog is going to be about, following my story. And I warn you, it's going to take some unexpected twists and turns, and something in me wants to write it in a kind of angry and bitter voice. But I'm trying not to do that. I'm trying to tell it the way it happened and show you the way I was feeling and thinking while it was happening. Following my story.

Because all of a sudden, Danny Rosewood was my story. I guess I should explain that since I turned in the athletes and injury story that I hope you all read in the school paper, I've been working on football injuries, reading about them, thinking about them. I mean, it's been practically all head trauma, all the time, so when I saw Danny knocked unconscious on the field like that, all I could think about was how will he be assessed, what kind of care will he get—it was like my story coming to life. Talk about a Kendall spin!

When we got to the hospital, I did something just a little bit sleazy, I guess. I let my dad walk with me into the emergency room, walk me right past the desk and into the back. It would never occur to him to stop and identify himself, everyone knows who he is, and it would never occur to him that there's any part of the hospital he can't just walk into. So I walked back there with him, and it looked pretty quiet in the back. You could see a bunch of empty hospital beds, each in its own little yellow-curtained alcove. There was a family over on the side with a little blond girl who was breathing in medicine from one of those machines they use on kids with asthma, and all the way over on the other side, a white-haired old lady asleep in one of the beds. And that was it—nurses checking on the little girl, a guy in scrubs listening to the old lady's heart without her waking up. And Danny Rosewood strapped to a board on the bed in the middle.

I walked up to Danny's father, who was standing right next to the head of the bed. "Hi, Mr. Rosewood," I said. "I'm Carla. We've met at some of the games."

He looked worried, but not crazed, and I guess it helps to be a cop sometimes. I bet he's seen bad and worse and worst, and this was clearly only in the bad category. I mean, Danny had woken up and talked right there on the field. But on the other hand, he had taken a pretty powerful hit, and there had been this moment, like Jerry said on his blog, when a lot of people had been praying. Including me. (Though I was also already packing up my stuff and thinking about how I would get to the hospital to follow the story—does that make me a terrible person?)

My dad stuck out his hand and introduced himself. "I work here," he said to Mr. Rosewood. "I think my daughter wants to interview the fallen hero, but I just came along to be sure that you're treated right."

He said it nice and loud, to be sure the nurses and the ER docs heard him, and I guess it was well-intentioned, and for all I know it meant a lot to Danny's dad, but I can't say I really liked it. On the other hand, I didn't have a leg to stand on (pun intended), given how I had used him to get me in there.

"Appreciate it," Mr. Rosewood said.

"Hi, Danny," I said. I went and stood right next to his head, on the other side from his dad and mine, because his neck was in one of those big orange braces, and he clearly wasn't supposed to move his head around to look at me. "It's

Carla," I said. "I don't want to bother you if you aren't up to talking. But I'm going to write up this game for the *Kourier*, and I bet people would like to know what you have to say."

Danny's eyes slid over to look at me. He's a good-looking guy, and his face wasn't messed up or anything. He actually managed something that looked a little like a smile.

"Who hit me?" he said softly.

"The cornerback—big guy named Schultz," I told him. "You had everybody pretty scared."

"Just tell me we won," Danny said.

Just at that minute, a young doctor in scrubs appeared at the side of the bed.

"Hi, folks," he said. "I'm going to need to do an assessment on Daniel here, so I'd appreciate it if everyone could back off a little and give him some space."

"I'm his father," Mr. Rosewood said.

"Pleased to meet you," said the doctor. "I'm Dr. Ahwadi, and I'm one of the emergency medicine fellows. You're welcome to stay here while I'm talking with your son, but I need you to stand back a little ways for right now."

"How is he?" Mr. Rosewood asked.

"That's what I need to try and figure out," said Dr. Ahwadi. He had a round face and big dark eyes, and he didn't look all that much older than Danny to me, except that he had a very small, very neat black beard, and I was sure he had grown it to make himself look more mature.

Mr. Rosewood stepped back to the next bed over, and my father and I went with him. I could see that my father was considering making some statement, "Hi, I'm the big boss, don't take any notice of me," that kind of thing, so I tapped him on the shoulder and said, "Hey, Dad, thanks so much for driving me here. I'll be fine if you need to get going."

"Well, actually," my father said, "I was thinking of stopping by my office."

Which was no surprise. My dad is always thinking about his office on the weekend. Any time you drive past the hospital with him, there's a risk he'll want to go in and check something or find something or just sit down and do some work. It used to make my mom crazy that he would go out to play tennis or do some shopping at the electronics store and then, somehow, mysteriously, he would end up in his office for the whole day. They used to fight about it, but lately she's just as likely to be out working herself, which could be either a good thing or a bad thing, I suppose.

Anyway, I was relieved to see my dad head off to his office. I stayed there, standing next to Mr. Rosewood, and took out my notebook and started taking notes.

"Tell me what you remember," Dr. Ahwadi was saying to Danny. "Tell me what happened."

"The Monster," Danny said. "There's this guy they call the Monster. He was almost beating us, and we had to win this one. And I got hit. In the game."

"And what happened after you were hit?"

There was a short silence. Then Danny said, "Can you take this thing off my neck? Can't I sit up?"

"Not right now," the doctor said. "We're probably going to

need to take an X-ray of your spine before we let you up off that board. But that's part of what I'm trying to figure out right now. Look, Danny, can you tell me what day it is today?"

"It's Friday," Danny said, though I didn't think he sounded too sure.

"And where were you playing?"

"What?"

"Which field were you at?" the doctor asked.

"We were at Sand River," Danny said, sounding kind of confused. "I told you, the Monster of Sand River!"

"Okay," the doctor said. He looked over at us, at Danny's father and me, like he needed us to confirm that, and we both nodded.

"And do you know where you are right now?" he went on.

"I'm at the hospital," Danny said. But again, he didn't quite say it like he meant it, more like he was trying it on for size.

"Danny, do you know who the president is?" the doctor asked.

"The president of what?" Danny asked. "What does that have to do with anything?"

"I'm trying to get a sense of whether you're feeling a little confused," Dr. Ahwadi told him. He took a little light and started shining it in Danny's eyes, first the left side, then the right. "That's one way we can figure out how badly you got hit in the head, so we know how to take care of you." He paused. "Keep moving your eyes so you follow my light, please."

We all waited while he moved the light, left, right, up down. Then he turned it off, and Danny closed his eyes for a few seconds. With his eyes still closed, he said, "I'm going to be okay to keep playing, aren't I?"

The doctor tried to make a joke out of it. "Well, not today," he said. "But I gather the game is over, anyway."

"No, really," Danny said, and his voice, I thought, was just a little thicker than it should have been. "You aren't thinking that I'm going to have to miss any games, are you?"

"Daniel, if you could just answer my questions," said Dr. Ahwadi. At the same moment, his father called out, "Hey, Danny boy, let's just make sure you're okay! First things first!"

"They'll be taking your son to X-ray in just a few minutes," the doctor said. "And as far as we can tell, there's no evidence of anything that would make us worry about his neck—his sensory and motor exams seem okay—but that was a major impact, and we just need to clear his spine."

"Yes, sure, thank you," said Mr. Rosewood, and I thought again about him being a cop and probably knowing all the things that can happen to boys in car crashes and other accidents.

"I'd just like to ask again about what he remembers from the actual impact," Dr. Ahwadi went on. "The report I got was that he lost consciousness for a period of perhaps two to three minutes."

"I didn't!" Danny said loudly. "I never lost consciousness!"

I thought about that time when we were all watching Danny lying cold as stone on the football field. About how there was time to think about what it would mean if he didn't start moving again, and time to look around the crowd, like maybe someone else knew what to do, and time to pray. You could have told me it was one minute or ten minutes, and I don't know that I could disprove it, but there had definitely been some time there when it seemed like Danny Rosewood had left the stadium.

"Hey, Danny," his dad said, "don't get excited. We're just trying to get you taken care of."

"Do you remember the impact?" the doctor asked. "Do you remember exactly what happened?"

"Yes, of course I do," Danny said. "I caught the pass. Game was almost over. And then I got hit."

"How did you get hit?"

"Their cornerback. Big guy named Schultz," Danny said, and I had the weirdest feeling.

"And then?"

"I guess I had everybody scared," Danny said. "I mean, I went down. I had all the air knocked out of me, you know how that is? I just lay there for a couple of minutes, I guess, before I felt like I could really talk."

"Did everything go dark?"

"Hell, no," Danny said. "I could hear everyone talking, and the coach—and I guess Dr. Anderson. I mean, I wasn't out of it or anything."

"Did you see any flashing lights? Any stars?"

"I just kept my eyes closed and tried to get my breath back, like I said."

"And when you opened your eyes?"

"Everything looked normal," Danny said. "Everything was fine, except now I'm strapped down here with this collar thing around my neck."

A nurse came hurrying up to the bed. "Radiology is ready," she said.

"Let's get your spine cleared," the doctor said. "Then we'll be able to let you sit up, and we can go over it all in a little more detail."

He unlocked the brake on the wheels, and the two of them, the doctor and the nurse, began to roll the bed away. Mr. Rosewood took a step like he was going to follow, and the doctor told him to wait, they would be right back.

After they had gone, I thought of asking Mr. Rosewood, "Did that make sense to you? Do you believe that Danny never lost consciousness? Do you believe he remembers everything?" I had a strong feeling that it was the question he really didn't want me to ask, though. Sometimes, you know, having that feeling when I'm interviewing someone makes me really eager to ask that question—whatever it is—that I think the other person doesn't want to talk about. Like I can tell that here's where I'm going to find my most important information. But I didn't feel like doing that with Mr. Rosewood. Instead, I felt like he had had about all that he could take. I couldn't even imagine what he had been feeling during that time that Danny wasn't moving or talking or opening his eyes, and I couldn't imagine what he was feeling right now.

Dr. Ahwadi came back. "It'll be about fifteen minutes for the spine films," he said. "And when he comes back, I'm going to get him set up in that room over there. I'm going to need to examine him, once he's off the backboard, and I'll need to take him through what happened one more time. So maybe you guys want to have a seat in the waiting room?"

"Can't I stay in the room?" Mr. Rosewood asked.

"Well, maybe one family member," said the doctor, "but I think that's it."

"I'm going to get going, anyway," I said. I had already closed my notebook. I mean, I hadn't lied to anyone or anything. I had told Danny straight up that I wanted a quote for the *Kourier*, but still, I didn't feel comfortable. I told myself that it was because I didn't really belong there. It was a private thing, getting examined, and of course that's true. But it's also true that I didn't want to hear what Danny was going to say next time around.

So instead, I went and found my dad's office. The executive suite was dark because it was after hours, but he was busy on his computer, and I had to wait almost twenty minutes till he was ready to go.

"So how's Rosewood?" he asked me as we were walking out to his parking space.

"Okay, I guess," I said.

We drove home, and I got on my laptop and pulled up some of my research notes for the second installment of my athletes and injuries series. I just couldn't stop feeling weird about what had happened in the emergency room. About how I had fed Danny some information about the game, and he had used it to convince the doctor that he remembered everything. Amnesia around the actual accident is a key sign of concussion. So is losing consciousness, of course. And Danny didn't want to admit any of that, and I knew why.

I sat on my bed, looking at research studies about the brain on my computer screen, thinking about Danny, thinking about my story. Thinking about how much it meant to the whole team that they made it to the state championships. To the whole town.

The next afternoon, after my last class, I headed for the *Kourier* office. I was supposed to meet Sophie there; we had an appointment to look at brain story graphics. But instead, when I got to the office, Ms. Edison told me that the principal wanted to see me. And she gave me this look, which I interpreted as "What have you done now, Carla?" But I didn't know the answer.

So I went to Mr. Bamburger's office. And Mr. Bamburger cut pretty much right to the chase: "Nice article on knee problems and elbow problems," he said. "But I think you should hold off on part two."

"What do you mean?" I asked.

"My spies tell me," said Mr. Bamburger, "that you're working on a story about head trauma and football."

Amazing what a spy network that man has. Why, one of his agents must have read the line at the end of part one in the school paper that said that part two was coming up soon.

"I am," I said. "It's a hot topic right now."

"But I am letting you know that right now is not the best moment for that story, here at Kendall High School," Mr. Bamburger said.

I was kind of shaken. This hasn't exactly ever happened to me before, not in three-plus years here at the high school. I mean, don't get me wrong, there have been some disagreements with the high school administration, there had been some delicate negotiation about how we cover certain subjects, but I have never found myself face-to-face with the principal, being told to kill a story. And he's a pretty impressive guy, Mr. Bamburger. He's used to having people do what he says.

So I sat up straight in my chair, which I suspected was carefully made to be an inch or two lower than his (they probably teach you that in principal school).

"You mean because of what happened to Danny Rosewood at the Sand River game?"

"Young lady," said Mr. Bamburger, and I wondered if they teach that one at principal school as well. "You cover our athletic teams for the *Kendall Kourier*."

"Yes, sir, I certainly do," I said. "I love doing it."

"And you do it very well," he said. "And I think that's because you care about our school and our students and our athletes."

"Yes, of course," I said.

"Well, surely you can appreciate that right when we make it into the State Tournament and our football team has a shot at a championship is hardly the moment for a big piece on football injuries," he said.

"But it's part of the story," I said. "Part of our team getting to the tournament—that good players get injured, that the coach has to make these calls about who can play and who sits out."

"This is not the right moment for that particular part of the story," Mr. Bamburger said. "That would be a good article, potentially, which you could write after the season is over. Looking back, thinking it over, from a distance. I'd be glad to look it over and see what you can do with it. But after the season. Not now."

I made myself look him in the eye. "Mr. Bamburger, you're asking me to hold the football head injury article back for now, not run it at the height of the football season when a key Kendall player has just suffered a head injury. Do I have that right?" I wanted to add, "And are we on the record here?" but I didn't have the nerve.

"I'm not asking you, Carla," he said. "I'm telling you. You, and Ms. Edison, and the rest of the staff. Wrong story, wrong moment. Not good for the team, not good for the school. And I know you care about what's good for the team and what's good for the school."

Period, end of discussion. I bet they teach them that in principal school.

So I went back to the *Kourier* office. I told Sophie what had happened, and she said, perfectly sensibly, that a few more weeks of working on the story would probably make it a better piece.

"Gives me more time on the graphics as well," she said. "Here, look at this."

She touched a button, and her screen filled with an image of a brain floating in space. Touched another key, and some boldface labels appeared: frontal lobe, parietal lobe, cerebellum.

"I'm thinking maybe drawings, not photos, when the story actually does run," she said, and I could see she was trying to get me over my snit. She knew I was still fuming. She wanted me to focus on the article that would one day run, not on the article that I had hoped would make such a splash next week.

"And then I could put up a lot more images online," she went on. "MRIs and even some photos—the kind of gross stuff you like—and there could be a link on the site for anyone who wanted more pictures."

"You think he's right, don't you?" I said. "You think that my story is bad for the team."

"Carla, I think you should leave this alone and let the season finish," Sophie said. "Guys get hurt in football, always have and always will. But they don't always get to play in championship tournaments. Let them have their moment. Then later you can come along and reveal the dark underbelly of the sport."

"That's not what I'm trying to do," I said.

"Yes it is," Sophie said cheerfully. "That's what makes a big story."

She got called over to look at the layout for the next issue, and I sat there, staring at that picture of the brain, thinking about the stuff I'd been reading about sideline assessment after head trauma. That is, the way the coach is supposed to ask a player a list of questions right after the player takes a hit, to help figure out if he knows the score. I mean that literally. There's one set of questions that are actually based on the game—what period it is, what the score is, what happened earlier in the game—to assess whether the guy who got hit is confused or has had any memory loss.

But no one got to do a sideline assessment on Danny Rosewood. Because Danny Rosewood, whatever he says now, was not with us for a couple of minutes there.

I thought about the articles I'd read on how doctors and coaches should make the decision about when football players can return to play. That's the technical term, the return to play decision. I wondered who was making that decision about Danny.

So I made a decision. And maybe it's a dumb one. I'm going to go ahead and post this blog, and I haven't run it by Ms. Edison. It's my blog, my story, my responsibility. And everything I have said here is as true as I can make it.

Here's the thing, guys. My knee. It's healing, I guess. It may eventually do all the things it used to do, or it may not. It may stop giving me pain, or it may go on hurting. But it's not the same knee that it was. It's been repaired, healed over, patched back together. It's not just a concept, it's a physical change. It's not the knee I started out with. It's something more damaged, more difficult. That's what I've been learning this year; that's what all of this has been teaching me. We're made out of meat and bone and other kinds of tissue, and those pieces of meat and bone and tendon and ligament and nerve and meniscus (whatever that is) add up to us and what we can do. Everything that we think and do is thought and done by the pieces of us, if you get my meaning. When we damage the pieces, we damage ourselves, and you don't always come back the same. So what does that mean about your brain?

TAKE IT DOWN

Posted by user **JERRY** on November 23 at 9:47 p.m.

Okay, Carla, so I just sat down to do my math homework, but instead I read your blog, and now I can't concentrate on trig at all.

I have three simple words for you: *take it down*. I know you believe you have the right to write anything you want and that freedom of the press and the need to know trump all other considerations, but I have a scoop for you. In this case you're flat-out wrong.

Danny had a right to privacy. He was being examined in a hospital by a doctor when you snuck in to follow your story. I'm sorry, but that's the only way to put it. At least you're honest enough to admit that you felt a little uncomfortable being there. You should have acted on that impulse and left right away. Your dad may be the CEO of the hospital, so he can waltz past security, but that doesn't give you the right to listen to a private conversation between a doctor and a patient. And it certainly didn't give you the right to post it on your blog so everyone in the world could read it.

Take it down. Sophie West was right. We're trying to bring a state championship back to Kendall and we don't need distractions. Let us have our moment.

Two games. That's all that lies ahead of us now in our division of the States. Granted all four teams in our championship bracket are undefeated and tough as hell, but we have a great shot. Listen to Sophie. Let our team alone. Let us finish what we started.

Mr. Bamburger was right, too. Your reporting serves the Kendall School community, which includes students, parents, and all our fans. We've had a sweet season, and now let them enjoy the icing on the cake. Don't try to freak everyone out, even if it generates a record number of blog hits for you.

Danny Rosewood is my best friend in the world, and if he's not ready to play next Friday against Jamesville then he won't play. Simple as that. But that's a decision for Danny to make, with his doctor and his father. So stay out of his private business.

And by the way, Carla—a word to the wise—I don't think you're going to do yourself any favors by posting private conversations you had with our principal.

I've gotten to know you a bit in the past month and I respect you a lot. I'm sure your blog entry came from a good place and you put it up with the best of intentions. Now, do us all a favor and take it down.

TAKES ONE TO KNOW ONE

Posted by user **CARLA** on November 23 at 9:53 p.m.

Oh, come on, Jerry Downing. You've turned into quite a blogger, haven't you? You know as well as I do, you don't make something more private and less "out there on the Internet" by writing about it on your blog, now do you? You just double the chance that people will come across the story—because now they can read your reaction and go looking for my original post. And then, gee whiz, you can be all hot and bothered because all you were trying to do, really truly, was make it go away, that's why you wrote about it . . . so you get to have your cake, with self-righteousness for icing, and eat it, too.

Well, no dice. You want to talk it out here in the blogosphere, I'm up for it. But let's not play games about how we're really keeping secrets.

Okay, then, your call. Here goes. First of all, you're right, I felt funny in Danny's room, and I got out of there pretty quick. But there was no sneaking in. I identified myself to his father, and I told Danny I was writing about him. And the story I was following was Danny—Danny playing like he did, Danny getting hurt—and yes, I knew a whole lot more about that than I would have known if I hadn't just spent some time looking into head injuries in football players. And I can sure see why it would upset you, and some of the other players, to have someone who knows even a little bit about that particular subject covering a story like this. Next time we'll have to send our fashion reporter.

But you know me pretty well by now, Jerry. I'm not really very pushy. I may manage to get pushier as I go on working, but you know as well as I do that if Danny, or Danny's dad, had had any problem with me being there, if they'd said, "Wait outside," if they'd even said, "Maybe later," I would have been out of there. Funny thing, they didn't.

So that leaves you in sort of a sticky little dilemma, doesn't it? I mean, in your fine high-minded blast of analysis, you left out two kinds of important points, didn't you?

The first one is this: I was actually reporting on a conversation that Danny Rosewood had with *me*, wasn't I? I mean, the new piece of information in my story was the conversation between Danny and Carla, two people who knew one another, one having said clearly she was writing a story. You can hardly be worried about my reporting what he told his doctor. That's the public information part, the party line, no loss of consciousness. That wouldn't bother you one little bit, despite all your fulminations about his right to medical privacy, if I hadn't happened to report the conversation between Danny and me. And that one, I think you'll have to agree, I have a right to report.

Unless, of course—and this is what I mean by sticky little dilemmas—you think that Danny Rosewood wasn't really in shape right then to know what he was doing. Maybe you're about to tell me that I took advantage of someone who was really woozy, really not with it, really didn't know what he was doing, because, after all, he had just suffered a big-time head injury? Was that your point? Think about it. Looking forward to your response!

But as far as taking down the blog, that's not going to happen. And to be honest, I don't really think you want it to; all you've done is expand the blog, made it more complete and more interesting.

And I'm afraid you're wrong about who my reporting serves. I mean, I do believe that it serves the school and the community to have good and thorough reporting, but it's not about writing the stories they want to read. It may just be a little high school paper, but it serves the school best when it at least tries to tell the truth, even when the truth isn't easy.

So this time, the truth isn't easy. I don't want this to be true, because, believe it or not, I love the team and I want them to win, and I want the people I like on the team— which includes you and your best friend in the world, Danny Rosewood—to be there and win that victory together. That's the right, heartwarming ending, both in your worldview, where principals are "stand-up guys" and football players are "warriors," but also in mine, where I see a team that's learned to play together so well that they almost transcend their level, playing for a coach they care about and a town that needs a win.

And, Jerry, I don't want this to be true because I don't want to see anyone I know get hit as hard as Danny got hit that day. I don't want to hear those noises, or watch someone lying there like that. I don't want to think about it. But I did see it and hear it and watch it, and I have to think about it.

You got hit hard in the Midland game. But what happened to Danny was a different order of magnitude. I saw both hits, and I saw Danny afterwards. And Danny's health and the inside of Danny's head matter a lot more than all the rest of this. You can try to convince yourself that he's not at risk, but you know what the truth is, I think. I really think you do. You wouldn't be half so concerned about what I posted, and privacy, and all the rest of it, if you thought it wasn't true. Deal with it.

HOW I DEALT WITH IT

Posted by user **JERRY** on November 24 at 1:16 a.m.

You may be wondering why I went storming out of my house at ten in the evening, heading for the golf course. If I can remain calm and focused on a football field with the seconds of a big game ticking down, why did a stupid school sports blog set me off?

First, understand, there was no chance of my doing any trig homework. Hell, I couldn't even stay seated in my chair. Carla twisted everything and made it sound like I was ready to endanger my best friend. That pissed me off, and the next thing I knew I was outside, jogging through the cold evening darkness in search of my partner in blogging for a real face-to-face.

You know one advantage of meeting face-to-face, Carla? Two real people stand in the same room and look each other in the eye. It's very different from sitting alone and typing something on your computer about somebody else.

I admit I've enjoyed telling the story of our season week to week. But I'm not sure I believe in blogs. What are they, really? They're not responsible journalism. No one's checking your facts or telling you to be impartial. They're an open invitation to spew and vent and name names and make accusations without any rules.

I can see the attraction of that to an aspiring journalist who doesn't pull her punches. But I can also see the dangers of it, and I hope you can, too, Carla.

I reached Overlook Lane and took the hill at a half sprint, fingers folded into fists, arms pumping like pistons. I sped up as the grade steepened—even Danny would have had trouble matching my pace. Anger was driving me forward, and I felt no pain.

Beneath me, the fairways and greens unfolded in the starlight in a quilt of gray and black shadow patches knitted together by darkness. Beyond the last fringe of that quilt, the lights of my hometown glinted. I felt like I wasn't even in Kendall anymore—at least not the Kendall I knew. These two dozen or so estates were spaced so far apart that some blocks had only three houses. The gargantuan homes were set so far back from the curb that you couldn't even see their walls or rooftops from the street. Winding driveways disappeared behind gates, and signs warned about security patrols and alarm systems.

I crested the hill and turned onto Overlook Terrace, the roof of our town. I had been up here before on training runs, but never in the evening and never planning to go inside one of these behemoths. I was getting so nervous that I was tempted to turn around and go back home.

Then I reached Carla's house, or at least the security gate outside her house, and before I could chicken out I jabbed the "Call" button on the keypad with my thumb.

I heard ringing and then a crackle of static. "Yes?" a woman's voice asked.

"It's Jerry Downing. I need to speak with Carla. I'm sorry it's so late. Can I come in just for a minute?"

There were a few seconds of silence. "Jerry Downing the football quarterback?" she asked.

Apparently they even know me this high up on Overlook Terrace. "Yes, that's right."

The gate slowly slid open.

I walked up a long driveway that twisted between grand old trees and trimmed shrubbery. The walls of greenery suddenly spilled open to a giant lawn, and I saw Carla's McMansion all lit up like a four-story wedding cake.

Lawn lights blinked on as I walked past, as if some sort of high-tech security system was tracking me. I climbed the front steps, but before I could knock or ring, the door was opened by Carla's dad. He's a distinguished-looking man who I've seen sitting next to her at games. "Jerry," he said. "Joe Jenson. An unexpected pleasure."

I shook his hand, and he had a pretty strong grip. "Sorry to bother you so late, sir," I said. "Is Carla around?"

"She's coming down," he told me. "She was taking a shower. Come this way. Have you met my wife, Vickie? She's in the kitchen. Don't ask me why, but that's where we all hang out. So how does it look for Friday's game?"

I followed him, muttering answers to his football questions, and tried not to stare too hard at the rugs and the leather furniture and the original art on the walls. Their kitchen was bigger than our living room and had a center island that a couple of people could be marooned on.

Carla's mom waved at me. She's a petite, dark-haired

woman, and she was sitting at a computer. That's right, they have a computer desk in their kitchen! They also have a flat-screen TV there, and it was tuned in to a basketball game. The kitchen smelled sweet; somebody was baking something. Mr. Jenson clicked off the basketball game.

Mrs. Jenson took off her reading glasses and smiled at me. I recalled from Carla's blogs that her mom's a lawyer. "Hi, Jerry Downing," she said. "I've heard a lot about you. If you stick around, you might even get a hot chocolate chip cookie. Would you like some tea?"

"No thanks," I told her. "Please don't go to any trouble. I'm sorry to come barging in like this."

"Barge away," she told me. "In this family, we don't stop for yellow lights." She saw me thinking that over and gave me a little smile. "I've read your pieces. They're as polite as you are. And very well written."

"Thank you," I repeated, hands in pockets, feeling awkward. "I don't really know much about journalism. I just try to write what's interesting to me."

"It's strange. Carla never says anything nice about anyone's writing, especially mine," her mom told me. "But she's a big fan of yours. I'm quite jealous."

Something on her screen caught her eye. "Excuse me," she muttered, and began banging the keyboard.

"So I saw in the paper that you guys are favored against Jamesville by ten," Mr. Jenson noted.

"I saw that, too," I told him. "But I try not to believe those predictions. They're a great team and they won their league. We have to go out expecting a fight."

"Yes, it's always good to expect a fight," a voice agreed from the doorway, and then Carla walked into the room in a yellow terrycloth bathrobe. Her hair was in a towel, and as she walked in, she took the towel away and let her wet hair fall down around her shoulders. She looked a little tense for someone who had just stepped out of a hot shower, and her eyes were red. She didn't even glance at her parents. I wondered what was going on.

Carla walked closer to me and gave me a tight smile. She smelled of lavender—either perfume or shampoo. Something was definitely on full boil. I could feel the tension in the room. Some battle had just been fought, some game was being played, and I didn't have a clue.

Mrs. Jenson watched us through her reading glasses.

"Dad, Mom, Jerry and I need to have a serious talk, so I'm going to take him up to my room," Carla said.

"Why don't you just talk in the study?" Mrs. Jenson suggested. "I'll bring in some cookies."

"No thanks. I'd rather talk in my room," Carla said, looking right at her. "Don't try to create a situation out of one of your parenting books. You don't need to make *all* the rules, do you? I mean, my room is still mine, right?"

"Carla," her father commanded, "take it down a notch. We have a guest."

"*I* have a guest," she said. "So let me entertain him in the place I choose. And I don't think he wants cookies any more than I do."

They all looked at me, but I kept my mouth shut.

"I think you'll be more comfortable talking in the study,"

Mr. Jenson said softly, but in his CEO voice that was meant to be obeyed.

"No, Carla and Jerry can talk in her room," her mother relented. "But keep the door open, Carla."

"Sure, and I'll open a window, too," Carla said.

She headed out, and I couldn't think of anything to do except follow her. We started climbing the curved, winding staircase to the second floor. She climbed slowly, limping noticeably. "The study might be easier," I told her.

"I got to see your room, you might as well see mine," she said.

We reached the second floor, and she pointed down a hallway. "The master bedroom is thataway. I'll give you the grand tour some other time. The kids' wing is over here."

"Kids?" I asked.

"That's my sister's room," she said, pointing to a closed door.

"Since when do you have a sister?"

"Since I was born," Carla informed me. "She's seven years older and lives in San Francisco. Doesn't come home very often, but they keep the room ready for her." She limped on down the hallway. "And this is my room. Come on in and leave the door open so my mom won't think I'm molesting you."

I followed Carla into her bedroom. It was large and beautiful, with three windows that faced downhill. Somewhere far down the slope I knew the lights of my family's small home were shining up at us as my dad read his newspaper and my mom went over her cases. My room in that house hasn't changed much since I was twelve. It's still in many ways the room of a boy, with posters of football heroes on the walls and rec league trophies on the shelves.

Carla's room, on the other hand, was like the room of a college student. There were no beloved old dolls or stuffed animals perched on her bed, and I didn't see any soccer trophies either, although I'm sure she's won her share. Instead, there were tons of books, computer stuff, and an impressive sound system with an electric guitar. I saw a vintage Rolling Stones poster on the wall, but there were also photos I couldn't identify.

"Who's that?" I asked, pointing to a black-and-white picture of a tall, serious-looking dark-haired woman in pants and a sweater standing next to an old prop plane. "I'm guessing she doesn't sing hip-hop."

"Martha Gellhorn."

"Right," I said.

"America's first and greatest woman war correspondent," Carla told me. "She was also a terrific travel writer. And she was Ernest Hemingway's third wife, but I don't hold that against her." Carla motioned me toward a swivel chair near the desk and sat down herself on a window seat nearby. There was a charged silence between us. "Go ahead," she said, "take your swing."

"What are you talking about?" I asked.

"Isn't that what you came over here for? Take your best shot," she said. "Join the club."

"Look," I told her, "I'm not sure what I stumbled into, but I didn't come over here to take a swing at you, and I'm going to leave in a second. But before I do . . ."

Carla shivered and put her arms around herself. It was hard for me to stay angry at her. She looked miserable and vulnerable. But she also looked tough and ready to bite my head off in an argument, and I remembered what had brought me over so late on a cold evening. "I think you should take your blog down right away," I told her. "For your own good."

"I can take care of myself, thanks very much," she said. "And you already gave me that advice on your blog, so you didn't need to come over here and repeat yourself."

"Well, I'm giving you the advice again in person," I told her.

"Face-to-face," she mocked softly. "Eye to eye."

She was repeating my own words, making fun of me. "That's right," I told her. "I can tell you're really angry about something. Well, I'm pissed off, too. You talk about Sophie West and how close friends you are. Danny and I have been like family since third grade. Do you really think I would put him in any danger just to win a football game? Do you think my teammates would go along with that? Do you think Coach Shea would?"

"I'm sure you're a loyal friend," Carla told me. "But there's a very old and powerful football culture at this school, and in this town, if you hadn't noticed. It's roaring along now, at full momentum and—"

"So the answer is yes," I cut her off. "Do you know how insulting that is? And unfair? You make a lot of jokes about how I call my uniform my armor and my teammates my army. But what you don't comprehend, soccer girl—"

"No need to stoop to sexist slurs," she cut in.

What you don't get, I pressed on a little louder, "is just how close the bond is on a football team. We care about each other like . . . brothers."

"You're not brothers," Carla pointed out, exasperated. "You're not in the army together, fighting a war. You just play on a football team together. And that's an important connection for a bunch of high school boys, but it's still just football."

"But sometimes that's a lot," I told her. "And it's not sexist to say that football is different from all other sports." I was speaking fast, looking into her flashing brown eyes. "From ballbusting two-a-days in the summer mud to blood on the winter snow and guys spitting up teeth and laughing and staying in the game, it's nuts and it's a rush and there's nothing like it. We *are* an army. We *are* brothers. We look after each other and care about each other and guard each other's backs. So stop insulting us—"

Her voice got louder. "So if I say I'm worried about one of your brothers, one of your warriors, if I say that I'm really afraid that something bad might happen to one of these guys you have this great beautiful bond with, that makes me a villain somehow?"

"You're the one who called it *your story,*" I pointed out.

"You said you were willing to do anything to follow your story. Even barge into Danny's hospital room . . ."

"He gave me permission," she fired back.

"He didn't give you permission to post stuff you heard there on the Internet. Even if Danny said you could stay, he was woozy and in no condition to give his permission!"

"You're damn right he was woozy," Carla half yelled at me, standing up from the window seat. "He was woozy because he had been knocked unconscious."

"And how do you know that?" I demanded, also standing. "Tell me how you can be so damn positive of that. Is it because Danny couldn't talk or sit up after he was hit? Well, I couldn't either for a few seconds, but I never blacked out. Have you ever been hit like that, Carla, by a big lug wearing a helmet? No, you haven't. I have. It rings your bell for a while but that doesn't mean—"

"It doesn't mean that it necessarily scrambles your brains?" she shouted. "Great! Terrific!" She gulped down a few breaths. "By any chance do the words *chronic traumatic encephalopathy* mean anything to you?"

"Carla, is everything okay in there?" her mother's voice asked from the hallway.

"Fine, Mom," she shouted back. "We're just having a *private* conversation. Leave us alone."

I stood up. "I should go," I said. And then, "Look, Carla, I may be a jock, but I'm not a fool. Sure, I've read about that stuff. But that's something NFL players who've been knocked around by giant linemen for ten or fifteen years have to worry about. Not high school players."

"How about multiple concussions?" she asked. "Or the dangers of second impact syndrome?" She stepped closer, getting right in my face. "Since you've read up on it, I assume you know that high school players who get concussions are more at risk than college or pro players because their brain tissue is still developing?"

"Danny didn't have a concussion," I told her. "End of story."

"Why don't you ask him?" she said. "I mean *really* ask him. Friend to friend. Brother to brother."

"I don't have to," I told her. "He already said what happened. He never lies."

"Maybe he wants to get back out on that battlefield with his comrades more than anything else in the world," she said. "If you care about him that much, *ask him*."

"I'm out of here," I told her. "Take the blog down, Carla. Do it before it takes you down."

She looked back at me, and her jaw muscles tightened. "It is down," she said. "As of half an hour ago. Bamburger called. He talked to my parents. And they made me take it down. Bamburger wants to see me at school tomorrow, to set some ground rules for my blogging." Her voice quivered. "So they've muzzled me. You won."

"You did the right thing."

"Thanks for stopping by," she said, turning away to look out the window. "I think you should go now."

I left her bedroom and found my way out of the kids' wing and walked down the stairs by myself. Mr. Jenson met me at the landing and apologized that Carla hadn't shown me out. "We've had a rocky night," he confided.

"No problem," I told him. "Sorry I intruded."

"Good luck Friday," he said. "I'll be there pulling for you. I know you guys are gonna go all the way."

I left the McMansion and headed back down the twisting driveway, and soon I was jogging down the hill. I sucked in breaths of cold night air. Now I understood why Carla had been so tense and angry at her parents and furious at me for showing up and piling on. If I had known she had already taken the blog down, I never would have come over.

From: JerryQB@kendallhs.edu
To: Cjenson@kendallhs.edu
Subject: Last thoughts

Carla, I hope this doesn't end our friendship. I really respect your passion for writing, and I understand how painful it must have been to have somebody force you to take your blog down. You looked so sad and frustrated and quietly furious sitting there in your yellow terrycloth robe with your pretty brown eyes flashing. I wanted to take your arm and tell you that you're gonna be a great journalist and there will be lots of chances to write about serious issues in the years ahead, and no one will be able to stifle your voice.

But on some level you probably know that.

Jerry

From: Cjenson@kendallhs.edu
To: JerryQB@kendallhs.edu
Subject: Muzzled

That last "blog entry" of yours was kind of sweet, though I keep wanting to tell you that when you get to college, you have to take a real writing course, with a tough-minded professor, and shake some of those cliches out of your system. Like, oh my god, the McMansion and the leather furniture and the original art on the walls? I mean, give me a break, kid. It's a big house for a family of four, I'll give you that, especially with only three of them living there, and there is indeed a brown leather couch in the living room, though it's been clawed by several generations of cats, and let's not get into a conversation about the quality of the paintings. The problem is that you have this need to make everything fit the dichotomies you set up in your head. Sorry, but you do, and you shouldn't, and you're potentially a better writer than that.

But not only did you feel the need to open up at me, and dissect my family, but you did so on a blog for the whole school and the whole world to read. I, on the other hand, am muzzled and can't blog back. But here's what I would have said to the school and the whole world:

So yes, there was Jerry Downing, the poor woodchopper (well, the high school celebrity with the history of bad behavior) in the castle of the Princess Yellow Robe, shuffling hesitantly through the marble corridors and worrying that his muddy workman's boots would stain the priceless Persian carpets. And as he sat in the princess's boudoir, hung with precious tapestries, he noticed that the princess had pretty eyes. (Never make eyes flash, Jerry. Promise me you'll never again make eyes flash.) Well, since this is really just between us, since it's not going up there for the public to see, I might as well go ahead and admit that there have been a couple of moments when you've looked kind of cute to me as well, though I was too furious right through that whole scene up in my room to have any tender thoughts.

But you know what, Jerry? I don't think this is going to turn into a romance. I just don't. Up till when you ganged up on me, I would probably have said that we were going to stay friends for years, go off to college and stay in touch, that I would cheer you on and you would cheer me on. But you know what? Gang up on me or not, I'm never gonna be the girl who dates the quarterback. Not ever. Not in college, and certainly not in high school. Sorry, but being who you are in a town like this opens up certain options and closes off certain others.

Okay, enough of that. Let's talk about what really matters here. Let's talk about freedom of the press. Bamburger called my parents. I was up in my room doing homework, so I didn't even know they were on the phone, but then came the fateful knock. You know that feeling when your parents appear together at your door, watches synchronized, all differences put aside, ready to steamroller you. I bet you've had the experience yourself—that feeling that you're being ganged up on. Of course, if you were imagining my parents, given the way you think, you'd probably still be stuck describing them synchronizing their watches; my dad would have a Rolex, and my mom would have something with diamonds. Which would probably flash.

I don't know all of what Bamburger said to them, but I do know what he said to me the next day, and you got some of it right. Pompous little speech about how the paper belongs to the school and the blog belongs to the paper. I did point out to him that there have been several state supreme court rulings supporting the idea that short of printing pornography or libel, a school newspaper does have certain First Amendment rights.

Well, not where Mr. Bamburger comes from. And anyway, he cut pretty directly to the chase. I was sitting in that scientifically lowered chair in his scientifically dreary office. I had dressed up to come to school, after the fight with my parents. I didn't want to blend in. I was wearing a white silk shirt and a black-and-white-checked bow tie, almost like I was making fun of Mr. Bamburger's outfit. At least, I hope he thought so, on some level or other. And a gray cashmere pencil skirt I borrowed from my mother's closet.

So there I was, sitting in Mr. Bamburger's office. And the hard thing about this for me to admit is that I was really hating him. I guess I haven't been in trouble enough. I guess I'm kind of used to being the good girl. I mean, I know there are sometimes fights between people who work on the school paper and faculty over articles and censorship, but to tell the truth, it hasn't come up in writing about sports. It just hasn't come up.

But I was sitting there and I was feeling on the one hand like I was in trouble, like I was being scolded, like it was my parents mad at me only louder, and then at the same time, of course, I was feeling angry, because I didn't say anything on my blog that wasn't true, I didn't cross any of the lines that we all know are out there in high school journalism. I didn't talk about kids drinking, or kids having sex, I didn't use any profanity—I just reported a story that started in front of hundreds and hundreds of people, and I followed it and I told the truth. And the whole truth and nothing but the truth.

But there was Mr. Bamburger, and he was leaning over me a little too much, and he wasn't being friendly. Well, he was being fake-friendly, you know what I mean? A smile that was really meant to be menacing, and a lot of slimy comments that were intended to mean exactly the opposite of what he said. "You've done such a good job writing about our teams," he said. "You've made such a place for yourself here since coming to town. I know you have the best interests of the high school at heart." Meaning, of course, you're an outsider, you don't belong, you don't care about this place.

"I do have the best interests of the high school at heart, Mr. Bamburger," I said. "And I think that those interests are always best served by transparency and honesty."

And that was it. That was my whole measure of standing up for myself. I got that far, and then I folded.

And I am ashamed to admit it, but I folded because he threatened me. He didn't even try to answer what I said about honesty, and you know why.

"Carla," he said, same cruel meaning, same kind words, "you're one of our most promising seniors, I don't mind telling you. Just like I told your parents the other night, I just hate to see someone who ordinarily represents our school so well, someone I've been thinking of as a top candidate for the most selective colleges, make a bad mistake in judgment. Especially a very public bad mistake in judgment. I don't want to believe that all this time I've been mistaken in my sense of who you are and how much you care about our school and our team. But you leave me no choice if you go on posting destructive stories just at the moment when we should all be sharing in what our team has accomplished. If you continue in any way to attack our players, or to suggest that our coaching staff does not have their best interests at heart, I am going to have to change my mind about you. And I would hate to do that."

Or words to that effect. I think I have them pretty close to what he said, but I wasn't taking notes or taping, so I wouldn't claim it's exact. Some phrases—"a very public bad mistake in judg-ment . . . you leave me no choice"—I know I have verbatim.

It was clear enough what he was saying, and what he was threatening: shut up, behave, stop arguing, or we will screw you over when it comes to college admissions. What could be more natural?

We sat there, looking at each other. I think that he knew he had won. Certainly, I knew he had won. But I didn't want to let him off without making him say it.

"My blog is down," I said. "My parents made me take it down. And I assume you're telling me that I'm not allowed to write anything at all in the paper now." I couldn't resist adding, "You should look over the other sports reporters and see who you think is good enough to cover the championship games. Those are going to be the issues that everyone reads, you want to be sure the writing is okay. So that we can all share in what our team has accomplished."

And we sat there looking at each other.

"How about this, Carla," he said. "Take a voluntary break for a week, or maybe two. No writing at all. No articles, no blogs. And then, when you've cooled down and you're willing to make the commitment that you won't write anything that violates people's privacy or that hurts the team, we'll give you another chance. But even then I want to see everything you write before it goes up."

I could have said no, of course. I could have walked proudly out of the room and risked my college future and taken him on. But I didn't. I caved. I said okay. I said, "I'll keep quiet this week, and if you let me next week, maybe I can write about the championship game."

"We'll see," he said. "As long as you restrict yourself to football, that's a possibility."

So that's the deal. I'm not writing anything this week for the paper, and I'm not posting anything on the blog. Just this private little diatribe for you.

But here's the thing, Jerry, since there's no one here but us—think about what it is that makes people afraid of words and stories.

Now, I'm not talking about secrets. Believe it or not, I can keep a secret. And I know that the truth can hurt. There are some truths I wouldn't tell out loud—on the Web, I mean, where anyone might see them—some truths I might only tell in a private place, like this private e-mail. Here's one: my dad is worried that the hospital might close, with all the budget cuts and the shifts in the health care rules. He worries a lot about reimbursement, and he worries a lot about what will happen to Kendall if the hospital closes or downsizes, especially now without the factory jobs. That's what keeps him at work for hours and hours and hours, I think.

And here's another, which might not surprise you since you picked up on some of the tensions in my family and broadcast them for the whole school to read: I think my parents will split up when I go away to college. It's just a theory, based on a conversation fragment I overheard a year ago and then on the vibe I pick up from the two of them. Things got really, really tense about two years ago, and they were fighting a lot, and I know they saw a marriage counselor. (I wasn't supposed to know that, but I'm a pretty good investigative reporter.) Then things got better, but it sort of felt different to me, not like they were really living together and being a couple, but like they had come to some kind of agreement so they could live together in the same house. And then I overheard them talking, and it was about me and how I was doing better. It was in their stupid language, my dad saying this is sustainable, my mom saying something about ROI—which means return on investment, in case you didn't know—and which is business-talk nonsense, as far as I can tell.

Damn it. Now I'm starting to cry. This is why I like to write for a larger audience. Write for just one person and you turn inward and you get sentimental and your writing starts to suck. Sorry, Jerry.

Maybe I was just trying to prove to you that we all have our issues to deal with. And that we all have to ask ourselves whether our private issues are getting in the way of seeing things straight and telling the truth. Because I think maybe your own private issues—about having messed up and about this story you're telling yourself about one more chance to make it right—I think all those things are getting in the way when you think about Danny and what happened to him and what might happen to him if he gets hurt again.

So like I said, what makes people afraid of words and stories? Why do newspapers get silenced, why do people get in trouble for what they say? Why would someone as powerful in his own little world as a high school principal need to take any notice at all of a smart-ass eighteen-year-old sports reporter? Because she was making up wild stories? Or because she was telling the truth? Which would be scarier, do you think, Jerry?

Very truly yours,
Carla

From: JerryQB@kendallhs.edu
To: Cjenson@kendallhs.edu
Subject: Sorry

Hey Carla,

That's really tough about Bamburger. You did the right thing.
There's no way you should let this endanger your college future.
He's trying to protect our football team and our season, but he
shouldn't have threatened you that way. I never thought of him
as a bully.

I'm sorry if I wrote anything in my blog about your family that
embarrassed you or upset them. You've been so open about
them in your own blogs that I didn't hold back. Maybe I should
have. Also, the way you justified barging into Danny's hospital
room really pissed me off—you seemed to be saying that when
it comes to writing the truth and posting it, anything goes. I
guess I felt like if that was true for Danny's medical condition, it
should also be true for you and your family. I've learned a
lesson—never blog when you're furious.

The secrets you told me really blew me away. I'm very sorry to
hear that about your parents. I hope you're wrong. I thought
they were both really smart and nice. I also hope you're wrong
about the hospital being in danger of closing. I'm not sure our
town could recover from that one.

As for you and Bamburger, I'm sure if you wait a week, he will cool down and let you cover the championship game. He must know you're our ace sports reporter and have a large and loyal following. Till you get back, I'll help out with the coverage and blog about this week and what the buildup to the Jamesville game is like for me. And I'll try to put in a plug for you, whenever I can. Bamburger reads my blogs, so I'll let him know that I think your voice is an important part of our season.

I also promise I'll never write about anyone's pretty flashing eyes again. Look, I wasn't exactly asking you out, but I also completely get it if you have a thing about not dating quarterbacks. We're an arrogant, controlling, headstrong bunch—even the ones who are trying desperately to be humble. But I'm hoping you and I can still be friends. It sounds like it may be a tough couple of weeks for you. Let me know if there's anything I can do to help.

From: Cjenson@kendallhs.edu
To: JerryQB@kendallhs.edu
Subject: What you can do to help

Hi Jerry,

Thanks for the message. You're a nicer person than I am, which for right now might not be setting a very high bar. And you're absolutely right that if anyone deserves to have her home and family described on a high school blog, that someone is me. I can protest, but that doesn't make you wrong, just like you can protest, but that doesn't make me wrong. See what a nice person I am, right back on my old soapbox.

Anyway, what you can do to help. Well, you can do what you said, cover the week, cover the game, and do it well, because I've invested a lot of my energy in the *Kendall Kourier* and its sports koverage, and I really do care, and it's making me pretty crazy to sit out the climactic weeks of the season. And you can watch Danny really closely and make sure he's okay, and be honest if you think he isn't. And, of course, you can win the damn football game, okay?

GETTING READY FOR A CATFIGHT

Posted by user **JERRY** on November 27 at 9:54 p.m.

The banner went up over Main Street on Sunday night. I saw it first thing Monday morning—white letters on an orange background stretching from the Co-op to the bank and spelling out: GOOD LUCK, KENDALL TIGERS!

Walking to school, I noticed hand-lettered signs in a dozen shop windows: KENDALL PRIDE!, NOBODY BEATS OUR BOYS!, FRANK'S HARDWARE SALUTES NEXT STATE CHAMPS, KENDALL TIGERS EAT JAMESVILLE JAGUARS FOR BREAKFAST!

An epic catfight was coming, and our whole town was getting ready for it. I tried to ignore the hype and the hoopla and just go about my business, but it's hard to ignore people hurrying out of stores to thump you on the back and wish you luck. A car screeched over to a stop near me on Broad Avenue, and a man I had never seen before ran out and pumped my hand. "Kick some butt, Friday. You're way better than Ricks."

Our home phone seemed to ring every few minutes. Sportswriters from papers I had never heard of wanted my opinion of Jamesville's dual-threat quarterback, Joshua Ricks. "I've never seen him in action," I told them. "I hear he's terrific, and I'm looking forward to playing against him. Now I gotta do my homework."

College coaches called to congratulate me on making the States. I hadn't heard from some of them in a year—since the car crash—but now they wanted to chat again like old friends. Kendall fans who I barely knew called us up late in the evening to suggest passing plays. Dad finally turned off the ringer on our phone.

But I can't turn the ringer off on my own central nervous system or unplug the current of electric excitement that I now carry around with me from when I first open my eyes in the morning till I fall asleep at night. It's real. It's here! Crunch time!

When I was booted off our team last year and at my lowest point, I fantasized about this moment. Once when I was doing community service, picking up trash, a blue van stopped near me and the window rolled down. "Downing, you scumbag!" a voice shouted. "You should be locked up!" As it drove away, I told myself not to shout back, but to wait and work hard and I would get my chance.

Most of all, I remember the judge delivering my sentence to a hushed courtroom. "Look around at the family and friends who have come today to support you," she commanded. I did, and many of them looked away. "You have disappointed all of them," she told me. "Find it in you to make them proud again."

The moment is here now, in the palm of my right hand. I can feel it when I wake up and lie in bed watching the light dance on my trophy shelves. I can taste it when I eat my corn flakes. It sits on my shoulders as I walk the halls of our school and kids stare at me and whisper, or look away because they're afraid to jinx me.

I can feel it when my mom kisses me on the forehead in the morning before heading off to work. I gave her such a hard time last year. Now I can make her proud.

And my dad, the last man I ever wanted to disappoint. There he is in his security guard's uniform, reading the sports section before going to work, studying a long article about me and our team, soaking up the moment with proud eyes.

I can tell that Coach Shea feels the moment, too. He seems to have shed five years. His eyes are brighter, his step lighter, his growls more menacing, and his pep talks more inspiring. "Two games," he told us before Saturday's practice. "Five hours of football, total. But make no mistake— five hours that will define you for years to come." His voice dropped lower. "I guarantee you'll remember those five hours when you're as old as I am. If you win the state championship, they'll be a source of pride for you. If you lose, you'll chew your hearts out about them, but you'll never be able to go back and change the result. So let's give everything we have, and maybe a little more."

We practiced brutally hard this week and closed the workouts off to writers and townspeople and even to our own student assistants. Partly Coach Shea did this to tighten our sense of team closeness, but I also think he wants to make sure the strategies we prepare stay secret. Coach seems inclined to rest Danny on Friday, just as he did when I got my bell rung against Midland and he had me sit out a game. But not having Danny will give our offense some real challenges.

It's not revealing any secrets to say that if we don't have a deep threat, Jamesville's defense will sit on our runs and stifle our short passing game. Luckily we've got Glenn Scott and Mike Magee, who both have the wheels to go long. I've been working with them on some funky deep routes, and if Jamesville tries to play us too tight, they'll regret it.

Danny didn't come to practice on Saturday or Sunday, and he skipped school on Monday to rest up and get checked out. But he showed up on Tuesday with the news that the docs have cleared him to play. Coach still didn't let him put pads on, but it was great to have Danny back with us, pacing the sideline. Lots of guys asked him how he was feeling, and Danny answered with a smile and a line like "How do I look? Ready to rumble."

He does look good—at least most of the time. I went over to his house on Tuesday after practice. We were hanging out, watching mixed martial arts, and Danny turned down the volume and glanced away from the screen.

"Chimes still ringing?" I asked.

He switched the set off, sat back, and covered his eyes with his hands. "The brightness of the screen bothers me a little," he admitted. "But it's getting better."

I ran into Carla at school a few times, and we nodded and exchanged hellos. As you've probably noticed, she's taking a little vacation from blogging, but I bet our number one sports reporter will do a great job of writing up our championship game. Since she's followed our story all season, I can't imagine winning the States and not having Carla describing exactly how it happened.

The local press, on the other hand, keeps cranking up the hype. Wednesday morning's newspaper had a giant side-by-side profile of Ricks and me, with the headline: "Ricks and Downing: The Two Best Schoolboy QBs in Jersey Go Head-to-Head." To illustrate the matchup, there were two big face shots of us positioned in such a way that we seemed to be glaring at each other.

I read it and then I put it aside and tried to forget it. I wasn't crazy about being called a schoolboy, and I have to admit that Ricks is better looking than I am. But that's not why I put it aside. It does something to you when your face is looking back at you from a giant picture in the newspaper. It's dangerous to see yourself blown up, out of proportion. That's the last thing I need this week. Remember that blue van, I keep telling myself. Think of that judge.

But it's hard to stay humble after an event like the pep rally we had after football practice this afternoon. A thousand kids packed the gym, and there were speeches and a cheerleading performance, and our marching band played their lungs out. We tromped in from the field in our muddy uniforms and were introduced one by one, with roars from the crowd. When I stood, there was such an explosion of cheering that it felt like a giant wave had picked me up and was carrying me along.

After the pep rally, I was hanging with some of the guys when I glimpsed Carla zipping up her coat and slipping out the door. I ran to catch her, which wasn't so easy because it was getting dark and for a girl who had had a recent knee operation she was moving pretty fast. "Hey, stranger," I said, "did that pep rally have pep or what?"

She glanced at me, and I couldn't tell if she was glad to see me or not. "Yeah, it was a real barn burner."

"Who's gonna write that rally up?" I asked.

"Chris McFee," she told me. "And Sophie took pictures." She lowered her head and tried to speed off into the shadows, but she was still limping a bit and I quickly caught up.

"Hey, could you slow down for a minute? I know my mom's rehab works wonders, but it's easier for me to keep up with Danny Rosewood."

She gave me a little smile and slowed down. Our footsteps thudded on the cold sidewalk almost in unison. "I hear he's been cleared to play," she finally said.

"Yeah, but Coach is probably gonna rest him. He hasn't let Danny put pads on or run drills all week."

"That's good," Carla noted, sounding glad.

"So what's going on with you?" I asked. "I miss your blogs."

"That's a little hard to believe," she muttered.

I didn't want to argue, but I had to say: "That's not fair."

"Why isn't it fair?" she asked, and if I were allowed to say that her eyes flashed, believe me they did then.

"It's not fair because I disagreed with you but I didn't call the thought police or even complain to the principal. I just told you what I thought you ought to do. So now you act like no one's allowed to disagree with you or else they're evil."

We had both stopped walking and we were facing each other. Carla said the last thing I would ever have expected her to say. "You know what, Jerry, you're right. You had a legitimate point to make and you made it, and I think you're wrong, but it was a fair argument. And I guess I'm just kind of sensitive because the other people on your side didn't fight fair. But I shouldn't take it out on you." She stuck out her right hand, and before I knew what I was doing, I took it and shook it.

"Okay," Carla said. "Good luck on Friday, Jerry. Kick some Jaguar butt. Bye."

"Bye," I repeated. "Hope to see you at the game. Ricks will be tough, but I'll give it my best shot." But she had turned her back and was already two steps away.

View 4 reader comments:

Posted by user **JaguarsSuck** *at 10:13 p.m.*
GOOOOO TIGERS

Posted by user **DanTheMANLookingFineAllTheTime** *at 10:13 p.m.*
Excuse me buddy, looks good MOST OF THE TIME? Don't know what you're talking about. Pretty sure that must have been a typo.

Posted by user **CrustyAlum** *at 10:19 p.m.*
This is a truly climactic moment for our community and
town. I would like for us all to take a moment to reflect on
this momentous occasion as well as the great football
history it brings to the fore for all of us. These days, with our
iPhoneVideoMobileBeeper contraptions, it seems everyone
is far too likely to walk right past crucial historical sites
like the Kendall football stadium where so many state
championship flags fly proudly without even noticing the
piece of our nation's history they are able to bear witness to.

Posted by user **@CrustyAlum** *at 10:22 p.m.*
~~Ah yes, the iPhoneVideoMobileBeeper generation. Give it~~
~~up, man. Go climb back into your coffin and take a nap for~~
~~the rest of eternity, dude.~~

Comment deleted by user Ms_Edison *at 10:25 p.m.*

From: Cjenson@kendallhs.edu
To: JerryQB@kendallhs.edu
Subject: Field trip

Hi Jerry,

Sorry I was sort of crabby after the pep rally. I hear you don't
have practice tomorrow, and I wondered whether you wanted
to go with me into Manhattan on a kind of field trip—for a story
I was writing, back when I was allowed to write stories. Might be
a change of pace.

Let me know,
Carla

From: JerryQB@kendallhs.edu
To: Cjenson@kendallhs.edu
Subject: Re: Field trip

_____

Hi Carla,

I admit I'm intrigued, and ordinarily I'd be up for it, but maybe not the day before a championship game. Please ask me again and I'll come.

Jerry

From: Cjenson@kendallhs.edu
To: JerryQB@kendallhs.edu
Subject: Re: Re: Field trip

Jerry,

Sure, I understand, it was probably a bad idea. I just thought maybe you'd be looking for distractions. But you should do whatever you think will set you up to grind Jamesville into the dirt!

All best,
Carla

From: JerryQB@kendallhs.edu
To: Cjenson@kendallhs.edu
Subject: Changed my mind

Hey, Carla, I thought about your offer and I guess I've changed my mind. The truth is, I won't be able to accomplish much tomorrow after the team meeting. I'll be too charged up. I'll probably just come home and bounce off the walls till my parents get home from work, and then I'll annoy the hell out of them till bedtime. So, if you still want me as company, I'll come. I have to admit, I'm a bit curious about your field trip.

I have two conditions. First, I need to be home by 9 p.m. so I can get a good night's sleep. Second, this trip stays just between the two of us. No one at our school can know about it. Coach might not love me going to New York the afternoon before the biggest game of the year. If you can agree to those two conditions, count me in. Oh, yeah, do I need to bring a notebook or dress up in any special way?

From: Cjenson@kendallhs.edu
To: JerryQB@kendallhs.edu
Subject: TBI: The blog entry no one else will ever see

Hey, Jerry, thanks for changing your mind and coming with me this afternoon. I told you we could make it back in time for you to get plenty of sleep for tomorrow's game.

I don't know what you made of the whole thing, but I thought it was fascinating and also pretty terrifying, and I wanted to write it all down while it was still fresh in my head. Here's the blog I'll never be able to post, for your eyes only:

Good morning, Kendall High. This is the silenced voice of your once and future sportswriter, temporarily on hiatus for bad behavior. (Boy, Jerry, it's hard to get used to this. It's really hard to get used to the idea that I'm not writing for anyone else to read. I guess I'm spoiled. I've been in the habit of thinking I could write down what I saw and what I heard and pass it by one teacher for editing and corrections, and then up it goes for the world to read. A small world, I admit, but still.)

(Last time I wrote, I let myself remember it was private, just one dedicated reader, and you saw what happened. By the end of the blog, I was feeling sorry for myself and sobbing onto my keyboard. Bad idea.

Instead, this is going to be written as if it could really be posted. Here's the blog that Carla would have written, if Carla still had a blog. Okay?)

I invited Jerry Downing to come with me on a visit I had arranged to a rehabilitation unit in Manhattan that specializes in traumatic brain injury, which everyone in the field calls TBI. I had arranged the visit through a doctor my orthopedic surgeon knows. I was planning to include it in the last installment of the story I was writing about sports injuries, which I thought would be about rehab in general. I was going to call it "The Long Road Back," or something like that, and talk about my knee and the way Jerry Downing's mother can always get me to do a little more than I think I can do. Then I was going to ask, "What if it isn't about muscles or tendons or ligaments? What if it's about brain cells? What does that mean?" and try to answer these questions from this visit.

So Dr. Abbot got in touch with someone named Dr. Klapper, and Dr. Klapper said I should contact someone named Pauline O'Donnell, who turned out to be the unit coordinator.

I called Pauline O'Donnell—she said to call her Pauline, but I didn't quite feel comfortable about that, but then I also didn't feel right calling her Ms. O'Donnell—that morning and asked if I could bring another journalist from my high school paper along. She said fine, so Jerry and I took the NJ Transit bus through the Lincoln Tunnel to the Port Authority Bus Terminal. I had been a little worried that things would be tense between us, because we've had some major arguments recently, but we actually managed to have a very civil conversation about what had been going on. We agreed that for the purposes of this trip, we wouldn't tell anyone about any of the controversy. We wouldn't talk about how the story might not get written, or about how I had gotten into trouble with the principal, or about Danny. In fact, we decided, we wouldn't even mention the name of our school or our school paper, unless we absolutely had to, just to keep things separate. No one needed to connect our visit to Kendall in any way. If we were asked where we came from, Jerry said, we could just say, oh, this little town in New Jersey, no one's ever heard of it. And we laughed.

I think we both felt good, maybe for different reasons, about getting out of Kendall—that little town in New Jersey—and leaving all our usual complications behind us. We talked very easily about trips to the city, trips with our parents, him getting taken to see the Christmas windows on Fifth Avenue every year when he was a little kid, me occasionally going with my mother to visit her office and eat a fancy business lunch. And then there's that moment when you see the Manhattan skyline out the bus window, and you know you're going under the river and into the big city, and we kind of grinned at one another, because neither one of us is really used to going into New York on our own, and it seemed kind of exciting. So into the tunnel and under the river we went, and then we took a taxi to the hospital, because it turns out that Jerry, just like me, is not supposed to take the subway in New York. I wonder whether all parents, in the end, read the same handbook.

Pauline O'Donnell turned out to be kind of grandmotherly, so then I really couldn't call her Pauline, even though every single other person we saw certainly did. We found her in a crowded office on the eighth floor of the hospital. There were three pairs of crutches leaning against the wall, and I almost tripped over a leg brace when I walked in. Pauline O'Donnell had short, curly white hair and bright red harlequin frame glasses, and she was sitting at what looked like a somewhat out-of-date computer, with one of those boxy screens, typing faster than the speed of light.

"Watch out for the prostheses!" she sang out as we walked in, without looking away from her screen, typed another thousand or so words, and then looked straight at me and smiled.

"You must be Carla!" she said enthusiastically, and stood up, dived forward over her desk, scooped up the leg brace, shifted it to her left hand, reached out with her right, grabbed mine and shook it, and then reached past me for Jerry's.

The thing about New York, I guess, is that there isn't that much space on the ground, so they build vertically. Everything seemed so crowded, compared to the hospital where my dad works. The offices were tiny and full of boxes and equipment and folders. The gym where she took us was cramped and dark compared to the gym where Jerry's mother puts me through my paces. To me, the hallways seemed kind of dim, and the rooms all had a slightly dingy quality. I'm sorry if that makes me sound like some kind of spoiled suburban princess, and I know it is supposed to be an absolutely first-class rehab facility, because Dr. Abbot told me so, but all I'm saying is, there didn't seem to be quite enough space, enough room to breathe.

Pauline O'Donnell went charging along the hallway, and we hurried behind her. I was carrying a brand-new reporter's notebook, and I had also turned on my tape recorder, because she said it was okay. I wasn't exactly sure where we were going. I could see we were passing patients' rooms, and I wondered where she was taking us. All three of us went bursting into the gym, where there were several therapists working with patients (all the therapists immediately said, "Hi, Pauline!").

"This whole unit is traumatic brain injury," she said proudly—and loudly. And for a minute I felt embarrassed, like she shouldn't have been saying in front of these patients that they had brain injuries. And I felt like we really didn't belong in there, like she was putting these people on display and that wasn't fair. I flipped open my notebook just so I could look at that instead of at the lady nearest me, who was taking very slow shuffling steps along the wall, holding on to a ballet barre.

But Pauline O'Donnell just kept talking in that same loud voice. "There are other kinds of brain injuries, of course. People can have injury after strokes, or after heart attacks, but our unit focuses on those with TBI, and because of that, we can offer medical support for the concomitant injuries sustained in the course of the specific traumas and rehabilitation services beyond those usually needed by stroke victims!"

I know that's what she said, since I have it on tape, and I got most of it down in my notebook as well, but she could obviously see that both Jerry and I looked a little blank, so she explained. "Our patients have had their heads hurt in a variety of different ways," she said. "Car crashes, motorcycle accidents, accidents on construction sites." She lowered her voice and said, so that only we could hear, "More than fifty percent of these injuries involve alcohol, you know. And that isn't just our statistic—that's nationwide." She shook her head. I looked up from my notebook and met Jerry's eyes; I knew he was thinking about his car accident, and I sort of hoped that this might show him that however bad that had been, it could have been worse—no one had been brain damaged.

Pauline O'Donnell had gone back to sounding like a kind of tour guide, talking loudly and clearly, like one of those people who take school groups around museums on class trips. "Because all of these injuries happened traumatically, we have to think about the whole patient here," she said. "It's more than just their heads—they often have injuries involving their arms and legs, their necks, even their kidneys or their stomachs. We're set up here to deal with all that and at the same time work on the brain injuries."

I could see that Jerry looked a little relieved.

"So these aren't people who got hurt playing sports?" he asked.

"No," said a man's voice, and we looked around. A young-ish man in a white coat with buzz-cut blond hair had joined us. He had a stethoscope looped around his neck and a bright pink tie that somehow reminded me of Pauline O'Donnell's eyeglass frames; I wondered whether there was some wear-bright-colors rule here on the eighth floor.

"This is Dr. Klapper," said Pauline O'Donnell.

"Hi, Pauline," he said.

"And this must be Jenny Abbot's patient," he said, "coming to check us out."

"That would be me," I said. "She operated on my knee."

"You're lucky," Dr. Klapper said. "Well, I mean, clearly the luckiest would be not to need surgery on your knee. But if you do need it, Jenny is the best of the best."

I introduced Jerry, and I could see Dr. Klapper look him over, kind of sizing him up. "Football?" he asked.

"Yes, sir," Jerry said. "Quarterback."

"*And* you're a journalist?"

"I don't know if I'd say that, sir," Jerry said. Then there was a pause, and he looked back at the doctor, then cleared his throat and said, "Um, wrestling?"

"Very good," Dr. Klapper said. "All-Ivy my junior year. But that's a while ago."

"Wow," Jerry said. "I'm really impressed."

"But I sure was no writer," Dr. Klapper said. "I think it's pretty impressive to be quarterbacking your team *and* covering the news."

"Carla here is the real journalist. But she's had me writing up our season for the school paper, and it's been quite an experience. And I do like to write."

"And he's good," I said, and then the two of them, Dr. Klapper and Pauline O'Donnell, looked from me to Jerry and back again, and I was suddenly kind of embarrassed. "So we've been working on this story," I said. Then I stopped myself. I had been about to say, "This story for the *Kendall Kourier*." Habit dies hard, I guess; that's just how I'm used to introducing myself. I would make a lousy secret agent. "Dr. Abbot probably told you," I went on, "I've been doing this series of stories about sports injuries. And I wanted to see what rehab really involves for people with traumatic brain injuries."

"That makes sense," Dr. Klapper said. "I heard this young man asking about people with sports-related TBI, and the truth is, from time to time we've had someone here on the unit who got hurt that way. Right now we have a college hockey player, really bad story. I'll tell you about that. And last year we had a college football player who had big-time neck injuries, head injuries, and a bunch of cracked ribs. But since this is inpatient, most of the people here sustained their injuries in other ways, as Pauline was telling you. But the important thing is that you'll be seeing relatively young healthy people who hurt their heads in a variety of different kinds of impacts—and the kinds of problems they have and the kinds of work we do to help them get back function. Those are very similar to the work that we do with anyone who has traumatic brain injury. People coming back after bad concussions, people who want to return to school or return to work—that's what we deal with here. Of course, first of all, they just want to return home."

He turned to Pauline O'Donnell. "I'll take them around," he said.

"Just bring them back to my office when you're through," she said, and hurried off.

Dr. Klapper gestured us toward a corner of the gym where a therapist was working with a patient. "Excuse me, sir," Jerry said, and the doctor turned to look at him.

"Is it okay for us to be here like this?" Jerry asked. "Should we ask if it's okay? Should we introduce ourselves? I mean, I know a lot of these people are kind of weak and all."

I was so glad he said that, because I knew exactly what he meant. I felt sort of bad, standing there in that gym, with someone giving me the guided tour. I remembered what Jerry had said about how I shouldn't have barged into Danny's hospital room, and it suddenly made more sense to me.

"It's fine," Dr. Klapper said. "You're with me. We have all kinds of students and visitors coming through. The patients understand that it's because we're a teaching facility and because we're a state-of-the-art therapeutic institution—people want to learn from us. Don't worry, I'll explain to the patients who you are."

He led us over to a corner of the gym where a tall, thin Asian woman was working with a bald-headed man who looked like he was maybe in his thirties. He was standing up, swaying just a little bit from side to side, dressed in scrub pants and a hospital johnny. There was a walker in front of him, like old people use, but he wasn't holding it. His arms looked very thick and muscular, like someone who worked out a lot, and I could see that there were tattoos on both forearms; the one nearer me looked like a snake, but I couldn't make out what the other was.

I am not supposed to use the names of the patients, so I'm just going to call them by letters.

"This is Mr. G," Dr. Klapper said, loudly and clearly. "Hello, Mr. G, how are you today?"

The bald man turned his head a little to look at the doctor. It was weird, but you could almost see how hard he was working, to turn his head, to answer.

"Good," he said, and his voice was a little bit thick. "I feel good."

"I'm glad to hear it," said Dr. Klapper. "Mr. G, I have two guests here with me today. Their names are Carla and Jerry, and they're students who are interested in learning about our unit."

Mr. G moved his head a little more, and I could see him focus on Jerry and me. I smiled at him, a little bit nervously, and he smiled back.

Dr. Klapper spoke again, same loud clear voice.

"Mr. G, do you remember where you are?"

"Hospital!"

"Excellent. And what day of the week is today?"

This took a few seconds, but he got the answer: "Friday!"

"Mr. G, do you remember who I am? Do you remember my name?"

Mr. G took his eyes away from me and concentrated on the doctor.

"I'm the guy with the loud ties who comes to see you every day," Dr. Klapper said. "So what's my name?"

"Doctor!" said Mr. G triumphantly.

"Doctor what?" There was a pause, and I felt really bad for Mr. G, since I could just tell, somehow, that he really wanted to get the answer right. Dr. Klapper didn't let him try for very long, he just gave his own name like it was no big deal. "I'm Dr. Klapper," he said, "and I'll ask you again tomorrow, and I bet you'll remember. Now, if you wouldn't mind, can you tell our guests why you're here?"

Again that pause, that kind of mechanical delay, while Mr. G turned to face us, met my eyes. I could see that his body was swaying a little more, and he reached out one arm and grabbed the walker to steady himself.

"Motorcycle!" he said.

"That's right," Dr. Klapper said. "You had a motorcycle accident. Very good job remembering! Okay, Mr. G, I will see you tomorrow. Look for the loud tie and remember, it's Dr. Klapper!"

He turned and started walking away, and Jerry followed him, and suddenly I could see that they both moved like athletes—their bodies looked confident in space and powerful. I watched Mr. G for another few seconds, and I saw the physical therapist start to work with him again, encouraging him to slide his foot forward and take a step, still holding the walker.

The doctor led us outside into the hallway, where he told us that Mr. G was thirty-four years old and had crashed his motorcycle into a van. He had been in a coma for almost a week, and after he woke up, he hadn't been able to walk or talk. "So he's made tremendous progress," the doctor said. "I don't know how much he'll get back in terms of memory, but he's very motivated. He has two-year-old twins, and you should see how he lights up when his wife brings them in to visit. And she's plenty motivated, too. She's been redoing the whole house so he can come home. Taken out all the area rugs, anything that might trip him, made all kinds of modifications, decluttered the place."

He took us into a hospital room, small and cramped, and introduced us to a lady who had been in a car crash. Then another room where there was a construction worker who had been hit on the head by a falling beam. With each of them, he asked if they knew where they were, if they knew what day it was, if they knew his name. The car-crash lady did know his name, and he congratulated her like she had just answered the hardest question anyone could ask. She had a huge flower arrangement sitting on her bedside table, and he asked her who had sent it. After concentrating really hard, she said, "Mom and Dad."

The construction worker couldn't talk very clearly, and there was some drool running down his face. On the whiteboard next to his bed, someone had taped up a big blowup of a wedding photo. I guess he was the groom, in a tuxedo, with his arm around his wife, in her wedding gown, about to cut the cake.

When we came out of that room and were standing in the hospital hallway, with nurses and physical therapists going by us, Jerry said, "Can I ask you a question?"

"Sure," said Dr. Klapper. I knew he was going to tell us again how the construction worker had made a lot of progress, and I could see that he was hoping that we understood how hard these people were working.

"Is this really related to what happens when people get injured in sports?" Jerry asked.

Dr. Klapper nodded. "Brain injury is brain injury," he said. "You're looking at more extreme cases here, of course, but concussions impair all the same brain functions that are hurt in our patients here." He smiled at us, maybe especially at Jerry. "I'm sure you're aware of all the recent interest in sports and head injury," he said. "All the controversy about concussion in the NFL, about professional hockey. Now they're even looking at what heading the ball does to soccer players."

I had read that, of course, but it kind of gave me a chill to hear it said by a brain injury doctor in this particular place, like he was reminding me that I had probably taken some hits to my own brain along the way. Still, I didn't see how heading the ball could be anything like what I had seen happen to Danny Rosewood.

"It's really shaking up professional football," Dr. Klapper

continued. "Back when I was training in medicine, we were never taught to expect the rates of chronic traumatic encephalopathy that we're seeing now. I might have expected to see it in boxing, where the whole point is to injure the head, but no one ever told us that so many football players are so at risk. Jerry, I bet your team trains and drills with a whole lot more emphasis on good form and protective equipment than anyone was even imagining a decade ago."

"It's pretty intense," Jerry said. "Put your head wrong when you tackle in a drill, and Coach makes you drop and give him thirty push-ups—and if there's any horsing around without protective equipment, forget it, you get benched."

"And they've outlawed spearing even in professional ball," Dr. Klapper said. "They've done a certain amount to make it safer. But it's still a violent game and people still get hit. Hockey, too. Same thing."

"There are former pro football players now who are suing the NFL," I said. "What kinds of effects do they have later in life?"

"Well, of course it's hard to tell, decades later, which injury caused which problem. Remember, guys who play pro football mostly played high school football and college football, too. They spent years taking those hits, and they may have been most vulnerable back at the beginning."

"Why is that?" Jerry asked.

"First of all, back when they were playing, like I said before, their coaches weren't taking these risks seriously the way yours does now. They weren't trained to save their heads, they weren't watched closely if they banged their heads. And second, well, what we didn't then understand is this: your brain isn't done developing when your body reaches its adult height. You take a top high school athlete, a top college athlete, they're as tall as they're going to get, maybe as strong or as fast as they'll ever be. You look at them and you think they're fully grown, top of their form. But it turns out the brain doesn't finish developing until your late twenties, so traumas and disruptions may injure it so that normal development doesn't happen."

Dr. Klapper gestured to a doorway a little further along the corridor.

"The last patient you're going to meet is the guy I told you about, the hockey player. And this isn't a typical injury—this is a worst-case scenario. That's what we deal with here: worst case after a car crash, worst case after a workplace accident. So worst case for an athlete, well, reinjury is bad, but worst case is what we call second impact syndrome, so you'll see the most extreme, but it's generally true that an injured brain is a vulnerable brain. That's why when I consult on athletes, I tell them they can't even consider returning to play until they're completely symptom free!"

"What kinds of symptoms?" Jerry asked. "I took a pretty major hit a couple of games ago, but I didn't have any symptoms."

The doctor looked at him, kind of close. "No headaches?" he asked. "No trouble when you study? Problems reading, memorizing, remembering?"

"Only trigonometry," Jerry said, "and I've been having those problems since second grade."

"I know what you mean," Dr. Klapper said. "Calculus almost did me in when I was premed."

You know, I get kind of irritated when smart people pretend to be dumb just because they're jocks. It's like girls pretending to be dumb because they're pretty. I mean, give me a break. I decided to ask a question and interrupt whatever game they were playing. "So what other kinds of symptoms do people have when they're just run-of-the-mill, not worst case, you know, when they aren't as extreme as the patients you have here?"

"Their eye movements, lots of blinking, their concentration, their memory, their timing—all those things that show up in everyday life but also show up in sports. You know, there are times when I've told someone that no, he can't go back and play, and I can just see he's relieved. Sometimes they'll admit that they know something's off. But you know how it is, Jerry, you're a quarterback. Sometimes they want to play so badly that they just go on kidding themselves that everything's fine."

He held up a finger in front of Jerry's face. "Keep your head still, follow my finger with your eyes," he said. He moved it all the way up, all the way down, all the way left, all the way right. "Good," he said. "Did any of those movements hurt your head?"

"Really," Jerry said, "really, I'm fine. I'm totally fine."

"Let's just go in this one last room and meet my hockey

player," Dr. Klapper said. It turned out to be the speech therapy room. The patient who was in there was the youngest guy we had seen. He looked like a college student, thin and kind of handsome, with very short thick brown hair and big brown eyes. But there was something off and just a little asymmetric about his forehead, like the right side was bulging out a tiny bit. He was in a wheelchair, with a neck rest propping up his head, facing a speech therapist, a woman wearing hospital scrubs and a jacket printed with letters of the alphabet, something you might imagine a kindergarten teacher wearing.

Once again, the doctor went through his routine of introducing us, telling us that this was Mr. L. The man in the wheelchair said nothing at all.

"Do you remember my name, Mr. L?" asked the doctor. The speech therapist held up a board covered with words and letters, and Mr. L moved a finger to point to the word *yes*.

"What letter does my name begin with?"

Again, the finger moved, and this time pointed out the letter K.

"Very good, Mr. L! Very well done!" Dr. Klapper sounded truly enthusiastic.

And then, right in front of the guy, he started to give us a little lecture on second impact syndrome. Mr. L, he said, was a varsity hockey player, very aggressive, very talented.

"As far as his coach knew, he'd taken a bunch of hits, but he'd never had a real concussion. But you know, hockey players can be even more extreme than football players. They think they're warriors, they think you play through the pain, right?"

Dr. Klapper put his hand on Mr. L's arm and squeezed it gently, through the hospital johnny. I was looking hard at the guy's eyes—like I said, they were big and brown—and I tried to see if he registered the touch or reacted to what the doctor had said, but I couldn't see any sign of it.

"In retrospect, we think he had probably had a string of minor concussions—maybe some he didn't even realize were concussions—and then he's in a close game, he gets checked into the boards, flips over, hits his head on the ice. I've actually seen the video, and it didn't look terrible. Or not terrible for a hockey player. It took him a minute to get up, but he signaled to the coach that he was fine, and then, all of a sudden, he went crashing down again. And when they got to him, one of his pupils was already big, which means that his brain was swelling."

It was a terrible, terrible story, and I couldn't believe he was telling it right there in front of the guy. They took him to the hospital, and the surgeons actually had to take out part of his skull—that's why his forehead still didn't look even. But in a way the worst thing was that this had all happened months ago. The guy had spent two months unconscious in the hospital after surgery, the doctor told us, and then two more months when they weren't sure he was going to be able to breathe for himself.

"He's been with us for a while now," Dr. Klapper said,

and I swear he sounded proud. "And he's come a long, long way. You can see how his hair is growing back where they had shaved it all off for the surgery. He can answer more questions week by week. We think there's a real chance, given how young he is and how motivated he is, that he may recover speech. He works so hard—he never gets tired, he always wants to push a little farther."

I couldn't tell what on earth he meant, though I smiled my best encouraging smile at the good-looking vacant-eyed guy in the special chair.

When we were out in the hallway, and he finally wasn't there in front of us, I had to ask, "Will he ever be normal? I mean, if he works hard, like you said, if he gives it more time, will he have a life?"

"He won't have the life that he would have had," said Dr. Klapper. "Like I told you, this is a worst-case scenario. You have to understand what happened in his brain, this second impact syndrome. Because there was already injury from all the previous hits, the brain doesn't regulate properly. So there's an additional blow, and it can even be a fairly minor one, but the brain just goes crazy, firing electrically, releasing neurotransmitters—those are the chemicals that carry signals in the brain—giving out alarm signals. It's all the biological processes, electrical, chemical, blood flow, all happening supercharged at once, and the autoregulation goes haywire. We think that the capillaries, the tiny blood vessels, just allow too much fluid up into the brain. It leaks out, and if the brain starts to swell . . ." He paused. "You just think about that gelatinous brain in there, inside your skull, being stretched and pulled and banged," he said. "And once you have an organ that's already been injured . . . well, then it's really vulnerable. And that poor guy got dealt a really bad hand. So you ask me, will he ever walk and talk, I'll tell you, he's young, he's motivated, his parents love him, they'll help out, but his memory, his cognitive skills, the speed of his processing—he's not going to be back to anything like he was. Best case, and this would be really good, he'll have speech that's kind of slow and kind of slurred and that will also be true of his thinking. There's been real injury done."

After Mr. L, I had had enough. There was something so terrible about all these interrupted lives, Mr. G's two-year-olds, Mr. L playing hockey in college, his parents, the construction worker's marriage, the car-crash lady's mom and dad. Dr. Klapper had called it second impact syndrome, what had happened to the hockey player, but it seemed to me that every one of these injuries had impact after impact after impact, infinite impacts on and on through the whole lives of the people who got hurt and their families. I couldn't stand it.

"I don't know if I could work here," I told Dr. Klapper. "Jerry's mom does physical therapy—she works on my knee, she's really good—but this is different."

"My mom works with lots of stroke patients," Jerry said, surprising me. "She works on their walking, but some of them can't talk, either. She says she first got into this from working with injured athletes, and she still does a lot of that, like with Carla—Carla's a soccer star, by the way—but my mom says now she likes the elderly patients, too. She says there are lots of different kinds of strength and lots of different kinds of bravery."

This is what I like about Jerry Downing, I have to say. Just when I think I have him figured out, he says something or writes something that I would never have expected.

I was still thinking about that story of the hockey player who didn't tell anyone that he had had concussions. So I asked Dr. Klapper another question. "People who have head trauma—traumatic brain injury—the important thing is, did they lose consciousness?"

"That's one important thing," the doctor said.

We were standing in a little corner of the corridor, the three of us grouped around a gray cart on wheels, with lots of drawers. I guess it was full of medicines. But I know enough to understand that there aren't any medicines that give people back their speech, or their memories, or their ability to answer questions.

"So do people always know if they've lost consciousness?" I asked.

"Sure," he said. "You ask someone, did it all go black, was there any time when you didn't hear the people around you or see anything—they know."

"Not always," Jerry said. "I don't mean like if a girder falls on your head, or something like that, but in some situations, like, say, a car crash that's not so serious, or a sports situation, couldn't you take a hit and have the wind knocked out of you and just not be sure if everything went dark for a few seconds?"

Dr. Klapper looked at Jerry hard again. They were almost the same height, and they both have this kind of square, open face. "Let's step in here for a minute," the doctor said, gesturing to the doorway in front of us.

We went in, and it was an empty patient room. There was a hospital bed, neatly made up, a bedside table, a blank whiteboard. All I could think was that one day soon, someone's family photos would go up on the whiteboard, someone would be lying in that bed maybe not recognizing the people in the photos. It seemed like the saddest place in the world, that empty room, waiting for someone whose brain had gotten hurt, and I stepped over to the window and found myself looking out on a street eight stories down and a matching big building across the street. I wondered if that was also a hospital, and if there were more hurt people behind those windows, and my knee was aching, and I wanted to go home.

"So, Jerry," Dr. Klapper said, "I'm wondering if maybe you did take a hit to your head and you actually are having some troubling aftereffects."

"No, sir, absolutely not!" Jerry sounded surprised. I turned back from the window and saw their two faces again, head to head, concentrating. "Like I told you, I got hit a couple of games ago, but it wasn't my head, and I didn't black out. I can just see that when you have all the wind knocked out of you like that, and everything hurts, it might be hard to answer detailed questions about exactly what happened."

"Jerry, I have to tell you, I have taken care of many athletes, and many guys your age. And this game of asking theoretical questions, does this sometimes happen, does that sometimes happen, is the second-oldest game in the book. The only older tactic is where a guy says, 'I have this friend, he's having headaches, he flunked his history test.' So skip the games and tell me, did you lose consciousness?"

"I didn't. I swear to you I didn't," Jerry said. "And I haven't had any symptoms at all since then like the ones you're describing. Matter of fact, I actually got my highest grade of the year in trigonometry the very next week. And I've been reading stuff and writing stuff no problem, and playing serious ball. I mean, believe me, I would know if my timing was off. Really, Dr. Klapper, I'm just trying to understand. Like you said, I'm trying to understand the way that guys talk sometimes when they've been hit really hard."

"People know when they've lost consciousness," Dr. Klapper said. He looked past Jerry to me, and I wrote it down on my reporter's pad, even though of course I knew the tape recorder would pick it up. "People know."

We all stood in the room in silence for a minute. I was willing Dr. Klapper to give it up, to stop. I'm not sure why, but I was. I didn't want him to ask any more questions, and I didn't want Jerry to have to answer.

I turned over a page in my reporter's notebook. I cleared my throat.

"Um," I said, kind of loud. "Um, Dr. Klapper?"

They both turned toward me, those square faces, those four clear eyes.

"I was kind of wondering," I said, "you've been so kind, you've given us so much time, and I'm sure you must be really, really busy. But could you tell me, what made you choose to go into this particular field?"

He looked at me, like he was trying to figure out whether I really wanted to know. I held my pen, poised over the lined page, ready to take down his words.

"It's just about the brain," he said, finally, and I thought I could feel all three of us relax. "The brain is so amazing—what gets stored there, how it reacts when there's injury, the way that things come back, even the way they don't. You can spend your whole life studying one tiny, tiny piece of the brain and never understand how it works completely. Or else you can accept that we don't fully understand it, but you can do this kind of medicine, work with people who are trying to repair their brains and repair their lives. And it's like Jerry's mother could probably tell you, there are a lot of small victories, and those small victories can give people back their lives."

I looked down at my notebook, writing as fast as I could.

As we were walking back to Pauline O'Donnell's office, Jerry asked another question. You know, in some ways he's a much better reporter than I am, I think. He doesn't ask predictable questions, he puts his whole self into everything he does. Maybe that's another thing about being a real athlete.

"Dr. Klapper, you're an athlete. You probably watch sports to relax. So doing the work you do, seeing what you see, what do you think about the lawsuits and the people who want to make changes—maybe even banning younger kids from contact sports—wouldn't that be going too far?"

"I love football," Dr. Klapper said, swinging us down the corridor at a fast pace that almost seemed like an insult to all those patients in their rooms. "Watch it every Sunday. Big Giants fan, ever since I was a kid. Besides, where do you start? Where do you stop? I showed you a worst-case motorcyle injury. Would I ban motorcycles? That'd be a great thing in the world of traumatic brain injury, I can tell you, but I wouldn't ban them. Then I showed you a worst-case hockey injury. Hell, I could show you a slew of car accident disasters, but the answer is, you make the cars as safe as you can, you don't ban them." He paused. "But sure, I'd rather see younger kids playing flag football, no question. No way that tackle is good for the brain. And I can tell you, Jerry, my body took plenty of punishment, but by the time I got to med school, I needed every last brain cell I had. Glad I didn't have a concussion or two along the way. Especially not two."

We stopped in front of the office where we had started. I put my notebook and pen in my left hand and stuck out my right. "Dr. Klapper, thank you so much."

"So if you had a son?" Jerry asked. "If he wanted to play football, you'd let him play, wouldn't you? I mean, follow all the safety rules, learn to tackle properly—but you'd let him play, right? You wouldn't stop him?"

"I do have a son," Dr. Klapper said. He reached around under his white coat, pulled a wallet out of his back pocket, and opened it to look for a photo, but before he could find it, Pauline O'Donnell popped out of her office, holding a framed photo of a very blond toddler clutching one of those Thomas the Tank Engine toys.

"Thanks, Pauline," Dr. Klapper said. We all looked at the photo.

"Jerry, I don't know how to answer you," he said. "I honestly don't know. I hope he will play sports. I think he'd miss out on half the fun in life if he didn't. But I'll tell you, if he comes to me in middle school and says he wants to play tackle, I don't know what I'll say. Because I'll think about . . . He's learning to talk right now, he knows new words pretty much every day. It's kind of amazing to see. So I think a lot about what's going on in his brain, about how everything is getting stored there, everything he'll use his whole life through. If he told me he wanted to do boxing, or tackle football, something like that which made it sure he would take hits to the head, I just don't know."

From: JerryQB@kendallhs.edu
To: Cjenson@kendallhs.edu
Subject: Strong stuff

Hey Carla,

I read your blog that will never be posted, and it's a real shame because I think it's some of your strongest writing. Thanks again for inviting me along. The trip took me out of all the madness and hoopla here—a break I kind of needed. Visiting the clinic didn't make me nervous about playing football tomorrow—I've always known the risks. But going to New York and seeing what we saw helped put everything in perspective. People have a lot more serious problems than high school football games. It's ten p.m. now on the eve of the battle and I'm about to turn in, and I have a feeling I'm going to sleep well.

I wanted to give you some good news. After we got home, I talked to Danny, who had just gotten off the phone with Coach Shea. Danny still insists that he's ready to play tomorrow, but Coach has decided to rest him no matter what happens. The docs have cleared him, and he wants to run, but Coach made it clear to him tonight that he won't be in for even one snap. I told you that we take care of our own.

So, anyway, it's nice to not have to worry about any of that and just look forward to a good, hard football game.

I'm sitting at my desk now, and I know that somewhere out there Joshua Ricks is getting ready for bed also. I wonder what he's doing and thinking and feeling. I've watched tapes on him all week, and I know the different weapons he has in his arsenal. I'm quick enough, but I've never been real fast. I wish I could do what he does, tuck the ball in and burst upfield like a running back, but the football gods didn't give me that. I'm a pocket passer. They gave me a strong right arm and the ability to see the field.

That's taken me a long way so far. Tomorrow we'll see if it's enough to take our team to the championship final.

Thanks again for taking me along today. I'm going to sleep now. See you at school tomorrow and then at the big game.

THE GRAND CRUSADE

Posted by user **JERRY** on November 30 at 11:07 p.m.

Nervous energy is a strange thing. I slept well on Thursday night—a deep, eight-hour dreamless sleep, but when I woke up, I immediately knew I was in trouble. I usually lie in bed for a while on game day, mulling things over, but this morning it felt like someone had plugged my central nervous system into the wall socket near my bed. I couldn't lie still. Almost the second my eyes opened, I popped out of bed and peered out the window into the first light. I knew the forecast—cold and clear—but I checked to see if there was any snow. Ricks is an elusive runner, and a slippery field would slow him down. But there was no snow, no hail, no sleet. Our defense would have to find a way to trip up the dual-threat-meister of Jamesville without help from the skies.

I tried to focus my mind, but my thoughts were whirling like a pinwheel in a winter wind gust, springing forward to the coming battle with Joshua Ricks, and hopscotching wildly back over the high and low points of my past year of shame and glory.

I started to panic a bit as I pounded through the cold and empty streets to Danny's house. You can't quarterback a quality football game if you're not locked in. I even found myself whispering a prayer. I'm not super religious, and I never pray for victory—I just don't see why it would be fair for a supreme being to favor one team over another. But as I jogged through our sleeping town, I thanked God for giving me the opportunity to play in a great game like this, and I also asked him to please help me stop feeling so wired. I'll win or lose it on my own, but I need to be able to think clearly. Just tell the bees to stop swarming and buzzing between my ears, and I'll do the rest.

I guess I was also concerned about all of you who are reading this now—my schoolmates, friends, and fans. You gave me a second chance to lead your team, and I'll never forget that. I wanted desperately to give Jamesville and Joshua Ricks my best Tiger bite, and I was afraid the pressure was getting to me.

Danny was waiting outside his house for me, all suited up in gloves and a red fleece cap that made him look like a tall and skinny Santa. "Hey, early riser, how do you feel?" I asked him.

"Ready to rumble," Danny said, even though we both knew that he wasn't going to be playing that day. He looked sad and a little angry, but I have to admit that on some level I was glad that Coach Shea was playing it very safe. "What about you?" Danny wanted to know. "How's the bazooka?"

"Loaded and ready to fire," I replied, and it must be Carla's influence but I couldn't help noticing all our references to war and military hardware. Let's face it: a football game is a battle, and preparing for one is like getting ready for combat.

"But I am a little more hepped up than usual," I confessed to Danny.

He studied my face for a moment and then grinned and swatted me on the shoulder. "I'd be worried if you weren't, amigo," he told me. "This is serious stuff, today. Let's go!"

Danny took off and ran like a demon. I tapped into my store of nervous energy to try to keep up and managed to stay with him through the fields and past the factory to the pine forest. We ran side by side through the stunted pitch pines, not saying a word. The movement and the cold air helped clear my head a bit, but not as much as I'd hoped.

I found myself wondering if Ricks could have stayed with us on our long run. I know he could have smoked me over a short distance. I remembered his face from the newspaper photos. It said in the article that he plays center field on the Jamesville baseball team and is one of the best high school prospects in Jersey. And in the winter, he runs indoor track and has set records as a sprinter and long jumper. If that isn't enough, Ricks has his own band in Jamesville— where the hell is that in New Jersey, anyway?—and apparently he is a hell of a lead singer. Now, I'm not usually intimidated by opponents. I've played against great runners and wonderful defensemen, but I'd never encountered a team with a star who might be far better than me at my own position.

Halfway home, Danny turned on his extra jets and started pulling away. I flew into full sprint and stayed on his heels for a hundred yards or so, and then I fell back, gasping: "Hey, Roadrunner, have some mercy. I need to save something in the gas tank for Jamesville." He didn't slow down, so I did—I wanted to make sure I didn't run myself out. By the time we reached his house, he'd opened up a two-block lead. Danny'd made a point—to me and to himself. He ran like his old self—the way nobody else ran—and by not using him against Jamesville, Coach was giving up an awful lot.

School was a blur today, even walking through the halls was surreal. Faces swung sideways to stare at me and quickly past me, eyes studied me and darted away. When a pitcher is throwing a no-hitter his teammates aren't supposed to talk to him for fear they may spook him. Well, at a school like Kendall, when there's a humongous football game looming, nobody wants to risk jinxing the quarterback. I walked in a strange bubble of silence as kids looked away and didn't smile back or speak; sometimes they even knocked into each other to clear a path for me, not wanting to jostle my right arm.

Someone should make a rule that if you're playing a post-season football game you don't have to sit through Spanish, chem, and trig. The bell finally rang, and I was first out the door.

A bus took us from Kendall High to Princeton University, where our semifinal game against Jamesville would be played. It was nearly an hour's drive, and our team was mostly silent, everybody getting pumped up in his own way. Hey, Carla, here's a good over-the-top war reference for you. We've been studying D-day in Ms. Fraser's history class, and I couldn't help wondering if this was a little bit like how it felt when American and British boats set off for Normandy in the darkness and suddenly, to all the soldiers on board the flotilla of boats, the life-or-death battle to come became shockingly real—the black waters of the Channel on an overcast night, a tight-faced commanding officer at the front of the boat, and your comrades and brothers-in-arms sitting around you, praying or waiting in silence as the French cliffs appear and the battle inches ever closer. What was the message that Eisenhower sent to his troops that fateful night? "You are about to embark on that grand crusade toward which we have striven these many months." We had started practicing for the football season in August, and now it was basically December and here we were, on this silent bus, rolling toward a fierce foe.

Coach sat at the front of our bus, alone, fingering his St. Christopher medal. He didn't say anything to us—he was saving his pep talk for the pregame meeting. I sat next to Danny and gazed out the window at the changing landscape. As we wended our way through forest, farmland, and small towns, I tried desperately to quiet my nerves.

There may be some positions on a football field where you don't need calmness and split-second decision making. I've never played linebacker or rushed a passer, so I don't know how much actual thinking goes on from play to play. Maybe they can get by on instinct and anger. But I can tell you that a quarterback has to be razor sharp from the coin flip to the final whistle. There are a million decisions to be made with every snap, and the tiniest error in time management or ball protection can be the difference in a game, and in this case an entire season.

Something told me Ricks didn't have trouble making decisions. He was a natural athlete—or maybe just a natural. Maybe he didn't have to work hard at being the star of a rock band, either. I realize now that I kept building him up in my mind as the day wore on and the game drew closer.

I was running out of time to get myself under control. After thirty minutes, I closed my eyes and tried to think of nothing at all—a zero inside a black egg, growing smaller till it was a silent dot in time and space. And then Danny said: "Hey, Jer, check it out, Princeton!" and I opened my eyes.

The Princeton campus was beautiful but a little unreal—Gothic buildings, perfectly kept. Okay, here's an admission: as I've been blogging about this season, I've followed Carla's lead and not written much about my own college application process and how many coaches and recruiters have called. I'd rather keep that private and use my blog to tell the story of our team. But I guess I should mention here that at the last possible moment, at Carla's suggestion, I'd dropped in an application to Princeton. I'll never get in—my grades won't be high enough—but when I'd found out the location of this game, I'd let their coaching staff know I'd be playing in their house. I hoped I wouldn't lay an egg in front of whoever they sent to scout me.

The Princeton football stadium holds nearly thirty

thousand people, and while I don't believe in luck, I did take it as a good sign that we saw a Tiger logo when we pulled into the parking lot. Princeton's mascot is the tiger—same as ours.

I was actually shaking during our pregame meeting. I held my hands together so no one would see. We went over a few key plays, and Coach Shea gave a great pep talk about how he had won the state high school championship forty-one years ago and what it meant to him. "Don't overplay it," he cautioned us. "Don't let the moment get to you and try to do too much. You each have a job to do on the field, and by now you know what that is. Just do your job to the very best of your ability—win the one-on-one battles and make a few brave choices when the spotlight sweeps your way—and no one can ask for more. I certainly can't. It's been an honor to coach you guys, and win or lose I'll never forget this season. But I think you have a destiny beyond this game. So let's show some pride and win this one for Kendall!"

From gloom to bright lights, and from the low voices of our tense locker room to thousands upon thousands of cheering fans. The powerful lights had been switched on above Princeton Stadium, and they flooded the field with a white, silvery radiance. The thirty thousand seats might not have been completely filled, but I sure didn't see too many empty rows. I stood there for a long second and drank in the moment—the marching bands playing fight songs, the bright lights shining down, the perfect turf field that seemed to glitter, and the fans who greeted our entrance with a roar.

He studied my face. "Go out with Rosewood right now," he commanded. "Look Ricks in the eye. Wish him good luck. And when you shake his hand, try to break it."

"Okay," I said. "Sounds like a plan."

Most teams have two captains, but our whole senior year, we've only had one—Danny. I was a little surprised, but on Coach's orders I jogged out with Danny to the fifty-yard line for the handshake and the coin flip. Joshua Ricks and Don Chambers—their defensive star—sauntered out to meet us. This was my first look at Ricks up close. He was three inches taller than me and more muscular. Quarterbacks aren't usually bodybuilders, but he looked like he had pumped an awful lot of iron. He was watching me closely but without expression, studying me with his gray eyes.

An official held a silver dollar in his palm and told Danny to call it in the air. Then he tossed it up, and it gleamed in the stadium lights as it flipped. "Heads," Danny called out in a strong voice. And sure enough, it landed heads. "We'll receive," Danny said.

The head ref nodded. "Okay, Jamesville kicks off. Guys, let's have a good, clean game. Wish each other good luck, and let's get it on."

Ricks stepped toward me, and we shook hands. I was vaguely aware that the press people had surged forward over the sideline and were snapping photos of us—Ricks and me—at close range. I saw the flashes, and I could hear the refs pleading with them, "Come on, guys, back up, give them some room."

Even the distant top bleachers were mostly filled
screaming Tiger and Jaguar fans, and there were a
TV cameras and photographers than I was used to.

I saw Sophie West standing next to the dozen o
fessional photographers, snapping away for the *Kour*
front bleacher near her, I spotted Carla in her gre
with a bright orange "Tiger Power" scarf looped aro
neck. Her dad stood next to her, and I wondered fo
ond if he was mad at me for writing about their fa
my blog. Very sorry about that, Mr. Jenson, if you're
this.

I saw my own parents standing together two rows
the Jensons, looking excited and a little nervous. They
and I waved back and then turned away from the ble
to face the field and my fate. My damn arms and
would not stop shaking. I wrapped myself up like a pa
legs together, arms crossed, and took a deep breath.
was I going to drop back and throw accurate passes wi
knees knocking and my right arm quivering?

A big hand came down on my shoulder. "It's no
cold," Coach Shea said knowingly.

I glanced around. No one was near us. "Butterflies,"
mitted softly.

"Those don't look like butterflies, I think they're p
dactyls," he said with a concerned smile, and leaned cl
"Is it Ricks? He's gotten to you? There's been a lot of stu
the press."

"Nah, it's not him," I answered. "I'll be fine."

I won't say I tried to break Ricks's right hand, but I didn't exactly stint on the grip. His own grip was strong and firm, and he smiled at me. "Good luck, Downing," he said.

"And to you," I said back.

He stepped forward a little more, his lips twisted up into a smile or a smirk, and I saw something in his eyes for just a moment. Was it the complete confidence of a natural athlete? I'd like to think so. But I read it as disdain. Even a kind of arrogance. "Thanks, bro," he told me in a low voice, "but I won't need it."

I looked back at him, and I thought: I know who you are. You're me, a year ago. You've never been taken down a notch. Well, go read the story of David and Goliath, because you may have the size and the attitude, but I have the sling. But I didn't say any of that. I just stared back at him, and all the jangling nerves and the butterflies I'd been feeling since the moment I'd woken up went away in a single stroke of football magic. Then I let go of his hand and broke the stare and trotted back to our sideline and said to Coach Shea: "Butterflies gone, Coach. Ready to go."

He must have seen something in my face that he liked because he slapped me on the back and said, "Downing, I got a feeling this is your day to shine."

Since a lot of you were at the game, I don't need to go over it play by play. And I don't want to seem like I'm bragging. But I kind of knew it the moment I set foot on the field. I was surer of it when I called a post to Glenn Scott on our second play and let it go thirty yards, and my tight spiral fell right into his fingertips. If you'd gone out there with a pencil and pointed the tip at the exact best spot for the ball to come down into his hands, that's where I put it. I wasn't aware that I completed my first seventeen passes, but I knew I was in a zone. Just before the half, running to my right, I tossed it all the way across the field to Magee streaking down the left sideline, and I knew it was a perfect throw as it left my fingers. Magee caught it at full sprint and took it seventy yards for our fourth touchdown, and that might have put the game out of reach.

All credit to Joshua Ricks—he tried to lead them back. He threw for one touchdown and ran for another and never gave up. I could see what skill he had, and what speed and what a powerful arm. I think he's going to be a pro athlete one day, and I'll be curious whether it's football or baseball.

But as dangerous as dual-threat quarterbacks are, don't discount the pocket passer. There are days when you drop back into the pocket and the action slows down to a crawl so that you can check off options, and it seems like you just can't make a bad throw. I've had games like that before, but never like this—never, ever like this.

Mike Magee caught three touchdowns, and did you see his last one? It was a fully extended dive to snare a pass I lofted into the right corner of the end zone. I had to angle it up over their biggest lineman, who had his arms raised and looked like he was eight feet tall. The ball spiraled up into the lights and then dropped back down into Mike's hands. He caught it as his body stretched out in a dive, and then he belly flopped hard onto the turf, and the Jamesville defender crashed down right on top of him. But that ball didn't pop out or even peek out. Mike cradled it like a newborn and put it to sleep. Way to go, Mike, not a bad catch for a soph!

Let me give a shout-out to our defense. Every time Jamesville tried to come back, we'd stuff one of their runners in the backfield, and when Ricks tried to match me bomb for bomb, our quiet but always tough three-year letterman Steve Henderson made that key interception that drove a stake through their hearts. You could see it in their eyes after that play—they were done.

I could never have had a game like this without great pass protection. Every time I dropped back, it felt like I was surrounded by the Great Wall of China, or at least the Great Wall of Kendall. Well done, guys!

And then there was Glenn Scott—our junior warrior and, at least in my book, a shoo-in for next year's cocaptain with Ryan Hurley. Glenn, you not only filled in for Danny but you did it with your own flair. My favorite play of the day wasn't one of the long bombs, but rather when you slanted up the middle for what was just supposed to be a first down, and the moment you caught it they hit you high and low, but you refused to go down and kept your legs moving and dragged four Jaguars seven extra yards.

And last but not least, there was that moment at the end of the fourth quarter when the clock was winding down and I glanced at the sideline and saw Coach Shea counting down silently with it. When it hit zero, he couldn't suppress a very small smile. Sorry, Coach, I know you pride yourself on never changing expression during a game, but that little smile meant so much to me. It wasn't a smile of gloating. It said, "Okay, we played with pride and passion and we're through to the final, and now we can find out just how good we are and what our destiny is."

Danny, my only regret today was that you weren't there for me to lay it in your hands a few times. Next week, pal. I saved some for you. Carla, I wish you could write this game up. I know you can't. But I'm really glad you were there to see it. Football Gods, thank you most humbly for giving me two hours like that. I ended up with thirty-one completions in thirty-five attempts for three hundred and forty yards in the air, with no interceptions. I threw six touchdown passes, and we buried the Jaguars 42–14.

After the game Ricks sought me out and shook my hand again. "Jesus, Downing," he said, "what the hell cereal have you been eating for breakfast?"

I thanked him and wished him well.

I really think that all I've been through this year: picking up garbage in public, and those sleepless nights when I was suspended, and wondering if my parents would ever trust me again, and looking in the mirror and hating myself and who I'd become . . . I really think that the weight of those experiences changed me and brought me to where I was on that field at Princeton. So let me take a very little bow—a cautious bow—and say, "Thanks to you all. Glad it worked out.

See ya next Friday when we play Albion High for the Championship of the State of New Jersey!"

View 4 reader comments:

Posted by user **TIGERSRULE** *at 11:56 a.m.*
Jerry, if I ever had any doubt we'd be seeing you in the NFL one of these days it's completely vanished. That was one hell of a game.

Posted by user **DanTheMAN** *at 1:13 p.m.*
No regrets, man. Next week we're gonna finish the deal. Would have been a waste of my talents today, anyway. Gotta save it up for the big show.

Posted by user **Photog_Sophie** *at 1:47 p.m.*
Click here to see the before-game shot of Jerry shaking hands with Ricks. We found out which one's a better QB, but you'll have to vote in this poll for us to find out which one's hotter. I'm also including a separate photo & poll for the back view . . . click here to vote on which one looks better in spandex!

Posted by user **Ms_Edison** *at 2:33 p.m.*
Given the importance of the victory, I'll leave this one up, Sophie. But I won't vote! Well, not on the second poll, at least.

From: Cjenson@kendallhs.edu
To: JerryQB@kendallhs.edu
Subject: Great game

Hey, Jerry, that was some football game. I screamed myself so hoarse I can barely croak tonight, and that's pretty unusual for me—I can usually talk no matter what. But there was so much to cheer—and an awful lot of it was you—that it was totally worth it. And I have to say, much as I wish I were writing this story, there is something kind of exciting about just letting go and watching the game, not worrying about taking notes, not rushing around to get every possible scrap of information—just watching the game. Especially a game like that.

Don't get me wrong, I haven't forgiven the principal. I think I should have been allowed to write up the game, and I'm looking forward to writing up the big one next week. I'm supposed to see Mr. Bamburger on Monday to apologize one more time and get reinstated, and I'm eager to be writing again. But I will say, I enjoyed being a simple spectator for once in my high school life. But come next week, when Growling Downing (Jungle Jerry?) leads the Tigers onto the field for the championship, I'm going to be telling the story, and it won't be a version that leaves out the hero, like some bloggers I could mention.

You were amazing, Jerry. Great game. Start to finish, I've never seen anything like it. Congratulations, good work, and please be proud of yourself. Take a real bow.

Carla

From: JerryQB@kendallhs.edu
To: Cjenson@kendallhs.edu
Subject: Re: Great game

Hi, Carla, thanks for your note. I wish you could have written up that game, but just say a few nice things to Bamburger on Monday and you'll be the one writing up the championship next Friday for sure.

It's turning out to be quite a strange weekend. Our phone never stops ringing. I'm taking some calls and doing a few interviews, and believe it or not there are even people waiting around outside our house. If I stick my nose out the door, in a few seconds I'm surrounded. I'm trying to ignore all the fuss and just keep a level head. I hang out with my parents and Danny, and when they're not around I talk to Smitty. Do you remember Smitty, our golden retriever? You insulted him, but he's a forgiving kind of dog, and he knows you weren't at your best that day.

At night when no one will recognize me, I go out walking through the streets of Kendall. Last evening I must have walked for two hours, from the railroad tracks to the golf course, from one side of town clear to the other. I passed near your house, but it was late and I didn't want to bother your parents again. As I walked, I kept thinking how this is my town, where I was born and grew up. This is also the place I disgraced. And now I'm so close to redemption, so close to giving everybody here what they want and deserve. One more game. Just finish it, Jerry. Well, I'm gonna give it my best shot.

I've been reading up on Albion; they're a dangerous kind of team. They don't have any superstars—no Sand River Monster or Joshua Ricks. They don't excel in any one thing, but they do everything pretty darn well. Unlike Kendall, they've never been in the state championships before—they've never even come close. But this year they've put together a scrappy bunch of guys who refuse to lose. Four times this season they were trailing in the last few minutes and each time they came back. In their semifinal game on Friday they trailed by fourteen points in the fourth quarter and somehow pulled it out. There's a lot of heart there, and we have our work cut out for us.

Well, good night. I'd better take one last swing at my trig. See you in school tomorrow.

Jerry

A BLOGGER'S FAREWELL

Posted by user **CARLA** on December 3 at 2:03 a.m.

Good morning, Kendall High. If any of you are online right now, you are about to see something just a little out of the ordinary. This is your sometimes sports reporter, Carla Jenson, doing the blog equivalent of setting herself on fire as a protest. No, don't worry, don't call in the counselors. I'm not threatening to kill myself. I'm going out in a blaze of something—call it glory or call it stupidity. And I would predict that everything you are reading right now will be gone, gone, gone in an hour or so, as soon as word gets back, so do me a favor: spread the word so at least a few people read it before it gets erased.

You're wondering what I'm gibbering about, aren't you? Last Friday, Jerry Downing threw the game of his quarterbacking life, and the Tigers soared with his every spiral. So why is Carla, the sportswriter, talking nonsense on her blog three days later when she ought to be covering every drumbeat of the approach to the final championship game?

Well, Carla the sportswriter is writing her last blog for the *Kendall Kourier*. So long, kids, it's been real. In case you didn't catch on yet, I am posting this without permission, without clearing it with Ms. Edison (let me make that clear, Mr. Bamburger—this is nobody's doing but mine. You can have my words removed [I'm sure you will] and prevent me from ever writing for the *Kourier* again [you've already told me that I can't] and punish me in all the ways you threatened, but it's only me, all alone out here, and for once, I'm going to use all the parentheses I want).

Maybe some of you have noticed that I didn't cover that glorious game on Friday, and that I haven't been posting on this blog for a week or so. To make a long story short, I was doing some stories on sports-related injuries, and I was building up to a final piece on head injuries, especially in football, but then Danny Rosewood got taken to the hospital after he got hit at the Midland game, and I posted a blog entry in which I made it clear that I thought he had been knocked unconscious but didn't want to admit it, and Mr. Bamburger called my house and made my parents make me take it down. (It gave me at least a tiny bit of satisfaction that he didn't have the technical savvy to take it down himself. We'll see if he's learned anything about the Internet over the past week.) And then he called me into his office and read me the riot act—no more stories about sports injuries, most especially not about head injuries, most especially not about Danny Rosewood's head injury. He told me I was silenced for the week. That's why I didn't cover the game on Friday; I was waiting out my sentence. And he hinted pretty strongly that if I gave him any trouble, I could kiss my college applications goodbye. So I did what any self-respecting high school senior with high SAT scores would have done. I swallowed and said yes sir, no sir, no excuse sir.

Okay, fast-forward to this morning. I swear to you, I

wasn't expecting trouble when I came to school. I was still a little giddy from the game Friday, from all the parties this weekend to celebrate. I didn't do much schoolwork this weekend, and I'm willing to bet neither did any of you. And I was thinking, too, that my punishment was about to be over. The cone of silence was about to be lifted, and I would spend the week posting football stories on this blog.

Instead, I get a message in homeroom: Mr. Bamburger wants to see me. I think he wants to tell me, "Welcome back, glad you'll be covering this championship week."

But the minute I walked into his office, I could tell it wasn't that. I could tell I was in really serious trouble, even though I didn't know why. He didn't get up. He sat behind his desk looking at me with a kind of, well, almost a kind of disgust. His desk was completely clean—standard executive intimidation strategy (I've heard my dad talk about it)— except for one little pink piece of paper, one of those forms that people use to take messages in offices that haven't gone completely digital yet.

He didn't get up, he didn't say hello. I walked in, sat down. He looked at me for another minute.

"I got a call this morning, Carla," he said, finally, pitching his voice a little lower than it usually goes. "I got a call from a certain Dr. Klapper."

Actually, I still didn't get it. Dr. Klapper is a doctor in New York who works with brain injury patients. Back when I was really working on that story, I had set up a visit to his clinic for last Thursday evening, and even though I was told not to write the story, I was still interested in the subject and I thought I would make the trip. Kind of on a whim, I invited Jerry Downing to come with me. We've been arguing about this head injury stuff, and I was curious to see what he would make of a traumatic brain injury clinic, and to be honest, I was a little anxious about going there alone. So the two of us went and visited the place for maybe an hour on Thursday. But I didn't write the story (well, actually, I did write something about the trip—as I'm sure Mr. Bamburger will be delighted to learn—but the only person I showed it to was Jerry).

"A certain Dr. Klapper," Mr. Bamburger said again.

"What was he calling for?" I asked.

Mr. Bamburger smiled, and it was a pretty awful, angry smile. "He was calling because he saw a TV story on Friday's game, and he wanted to congratulate me—to tell me that Jerry Downing is a remarkable young man. Just the kind of call I love to get—"

And then suddenly his voice changed and he was screaming at me, really screaming.

"*I told you to leave that stuff alone!* I told you no on the head injury story! No! I gave you another chance. I was going to let you write again this week, but you had to keep it going. You had to disobey me deliberately!"

I was scared. It was kind of like being slapped. It almost hurt to have him that mad, yelling at me like that. I was scared, and I started talking really fast.

"I wasn't going to write the story," I said. "Really, Mr.

Bamburger, it was just that I had the trip set up already and I sort of thought I should go—after my own doctor helped set it up, and Dr. Klapper was expecting me. I didn't think of it as disobeying you because I knew I wasn't going to publish anything." To me, my voice sounded weak and squeaky. I felt a little dizzy. I'm really not used to being in trouble, and here I was, in trouble up to my neck, and I hadn't even known it.

"So you thought it was okay to drag the quarterback into Manhattan the night before the semifinal game and have him walking around a hospital?" He was still yelling, maybe not quite as loud, but certainly way angrier than normal speech. "Did you ever see even an inch beyond your own self-serving agenda?"

I was frantic to make him understand. "It was totally safe, Mr. Bamburger," I said. "We were back in Kendall before nine, plenty of time to spare . . ."

He cut me off. "And I suppose you thought that was the right thing for the quarterback to be doing and looking at and thinking about the night before the biggest game of his career? Just tell me, what kind of a spoiled destructive drama queen are you? It's okay if the school is crushed and the town is disappointed, just as long as you can satisfy your need to be insubordinate."

"I wasn't trying to be insubordinate," I said, miserably. I knew I was about to break down. How could I have been so stupid? I was thinking. How could I not have thought of any of this, how could I have gotten myself into more trouble than I have ever been in, and how could I not have seen this coming?

But Mr. Bamburger wasn't really listening to me. He stood up behind his desk, and he towered over me. He was shaking his finger.

"You are *off* the *Kourier*," he said. "You will never publish another word in that paper or on the Web site. That self-indulgent blog of yours is done, and we aren't going to have any more like it. Over. Ended."

I was mad at myself because I could feel that I was on the edge of tears. I think it was partly rage, but it was certainly partly fear and sorrow. I had so many things I wanted to say: "But Jerry is eighteen years old and he can make his own decisions," "But nothing happened," "But Jerry threw a beautiful game the next day." But, but, but, but. I was trying to put the right sentence together, to say something without breaking down, but I had to gulp a mouthful of air instead. The principal stayed on his feet, thundering down at me.

"You are suspended for one week! And I want you to know that I will personally contact each college on your list and inform them that you have been suspended for bad behavior, insubordination, and attempting to undermine your school!"

"I wasn't trying to undermine my school!" I said, and I was shocked to hear that my voice was as loud as his. I wondered whether they could hear us in the outer office. I was thinking (how could I help thinking of this?) about the hours of filling in college applications, working on my essays,

assembling clips from the *Kourier*, about everything that he was trying to take away from me.

"I love this school," I said. "I love this school! And I think Jerry Downing is a great quarterback, and I would never do anything that would undermine him, either!"

Mr. Bamburger smiled another not-kind smile at me. He sat down at his desk, opened a drawer, and took out a manila file folder. I guess it was my file. He opened it, took a fat black pen out of his suit pocket, and made some notes. Then he looked up at me, like he could barely see me. "I don't like defiance," he said in a normal voice. "I don't like students who think they own my school, just because they have big-shot parents who can buy them whatever they want." He clicked the pen closed and put it back in his pocket, like I was all taken care of. "No further contact with the *Kourier*. No blog. One-week suspension for disciplinary reasons. Colleges to be informed by me, personally. I believe that takes care of it. You may go to your locker and collect your belongings. I want you off my school grounds in no more than ten minutes. And I want you out of my office right *now*. I have wasted enough time on this. I have a school to run and a championship to win." He picked up his phone and said into it, "Send the coach in, please. I want to speak with him here before we go meet with the mayor."

He was very deliberately not looking at me; he was trying to show me that I was already erased. He was back to thinking about important things and hanging out with the big guys. I was a bug and I had been squashed.

I stood up, then bent down to pick up my backpack. The outside pocket was partly unzipped and I could see, gleaming up at me, my tiny digital tape recorder.

I didn't stop to think. I turned my back slightly to the principal, slipped the recorder out, and pressed the little key to turn it on. Then I bent over the chair where I had been sitting, and as I slung the backpack over first one shoulder and then the other, I slipped the recorder back between the cushions, burying it as deep as I could. I did it, all alone. Me, myself, and I.

I'm not sure what I was thinking, exactly, because I was so scared and so angry. The truth is, right then, I hated him, and I knew that he hated me. The truth is, instead of crying, as I had thought I might, I wanted to scream at him and call him names and smash things. If I hadn't suddenly seen the tape recorder, I don't know what I would have done, stopped in the doorway, maybe, and made a speech, told him off. It was the way he was showing off his power and his control: I can erase you, I can ruin your life. It made me want to hit back and show him that I was even more trouble than he thought.

So I left my tape recorder tucked between the cushions of the chair. As I went out of the office, I passed Coach Shea standing right outside the door, bouncing a little on his feet. He looked at me as I went past, lugging my backpack; I must have been the only person he had passed that morning who hadn't said congratulations, but there was just too much going on in my head and I didn't think I could talk.

To make a long story short, I went to my locker, I put even more stuff in my backpack, took what I thought I might need. I was moving fast, even though I felt dazed. Everything around me seemed unreal—that locker with all the books and notebooks of Carla the good student, who does her homework and gets her A's and fills in her college applications. But no, I wasn't going to think about that. And I wasn't going to go find Sophie or stop in at the *Kourier* office. No time. Instead, within ten minutes, I was back outside the principal's office, lurking in the hallway.

And sure enough, the door opened and out came Mr. Bamburger and Coach Shea, walking fast, just as the bell rang and the hall started to fill with students. I turned away and started walking in the other direction, and I'm not sure they noticed me. So I went into the principal's outer office and told his secretary, in my best scared-little-girl voice, that I thought I had left my phone in Mr. Bamburger's office when I was talking to him just a few minutes ago. She let me go in and stood in the doorway watching me. (I don't know whether she knew I was a dangerous criminal or whether that's just how she treats everyone. As I keep saying, I'm just not used to being in trouble like this.) I went straight to the chair where I had been sitting and reached between the cushions.

"Here it is!" I said. I pulled out the tape recorder, holding it in my fist so she wouldn't be able to see exactly what kind of small rectangular electronic device I was clutching.

And then I went home, me and my backpack full of stuff from my locker, and my tape recorder. And I will admit to you that when I was finally sitting down in my own room, I did cry. I thought about my college applications, and about the championship game that would happen without my being in school for the days beforehand, without the buzzing talk in classes where we were supposed to be doing something else, or the silliness in the hallways, or the craziness at the pep rally.

And then I thought about the *Kendall Kourier*, and all the excitement of covering a championship countdown, and the way it would be happening without me. I sat there and I felt sorry for myself, and I cried. I thought about calling my mother at work, or my father, but to tell you the truth, I was scared. I didn't think I could handle one more person yelling at me right then.

So I washed my face and I sat down at my desk, and I listened to my tape recorder. So here's what was happening while I was cleaning out my locker. The little recorder picked up everything. It's a little muffled because it was recording through the cushions, with the coach sitting on top of them, but it's pretty clear.

The principal congratulates the coach, tells him great game, and the coach says thanks. Then the coach asks, "Wasn't that the kid who covers sports who was just in here?"

"That's over," Mr. Bamburger says. "She's done. She's off the paper. She's a spoiled rich kid who wants all the attention for herself. She makes things up, she twists the truth. She's done writing for our paper. She thinks she's better than the other kids, better than the doctors, better than the coach.

You know that little princess doesn't give a rat's ass about the school or the team or anything but herself!"

"She's a pretty good writer, actually," the coach says. "And she's got Downing writing, too. Some of it's kind of interesting. I wasn't sure it was such a good idea, but the guys on the team like reading him, and he's certainly having a hell of a season."

"She's got Downing doing all kinds of things," the principal answers. "I really wonder if that guy has any judgment at all! Smashing up that poor girl in his car. How come we have to win with a juvenile delinquent for a quarterback, answer me that?"

"He's having a great year," the coach says. "Honestly, Mark, I think he's put all that bad stuff behind him. I was worried that it was just weighing on him too heavily, but look at him now!"

"And he's going to finish the job, right? You're feeling okay for Friday?"

"To tell you the truth, the team we're playing on Friday is out of nowhere—it's a school that no one was expecting to see go this far. My guess is, they're playing on guts and glory right now. On paper, I think we're better, but when a team makes a run like that, you never know. I'm taking it very seriously, and I'll make sure my team does, too."

"But if Downing plays at the level he did on Friday—"

"If Downing plays at the level he did on Friday, there's no team anywhere going to beat us," the coach says, and you can hear how proud he is.

"And this week you're playing Rosewood, right?" Bamburger says.

"If we need him," the coach answers. "I've talked with his doctor, and he's fully cleared to play."

"We need him," the principal tells him. "We need everything. He's Downing's favorite receiver. We need our stars on the field for this one. I want him in that game."

There's a little pause, and you can hear fuzzy electronic noise on the recorder.

"Rosewood's father called me," Bamburger goes on. "Told me his son is crazy to play this week, that I can't let him miss the championship game."

"I know," the coach said. "He called me, too. He's good people."

"So that's decided," Bamburger says. "It won't be the first time we've pushed the envelope a little. No guts, no glory, right?"

Coach stays silent. Maybe he nodded, or maybe he didn't.

Then Bamburger changes the subject—or maybe not really. "We need to talk about your contract for next year, Tom," he says. "We have to go meet the mayor right now, but let's put it on the calendar for next Monday, first thing we deal with once we're state champions."

"Sure," the coach says. "I'd like that, Mark."

"Win the game," Mr. Bamburger tells him. "You think about winning this game."

"You think I'm not thinking about that every minute?"

"We're going to win, right, Coach?"

"We're going to give it everything we've got," the coach says.

Well, that's the story. I'm not even going to comment or analyze or editorialize, because I'm so wrought up and confused right now, and so angry and so scared, that I don't trust myself. I'll post a link to the recording <u>right here</u>, so you can listen for yourself and at least you'll know I'm not making things up. Or twisting the truth.

And that's it. They haven't changed the codes or the passwords, though I'm sure they will now. I'm sorry, Ms. Edison, I know you trusted me. But if I wait and think it over, I'll chicken out. So here goes. This is Carla's last blog post, and goodbye, everybody. Go Tigers!

View 3 reader comments:

Posted by user **ProudTigerMom** *at 2:27 a.m.*
You should be ashamed of yourself. You say "Go Tigers!" but you post statements that will hurt the school community just when we should be feeling proud. I hope this is indeed your last post. Goodbye and good riddance.

Posted by user **LateNightSteve** *at 2:45 a.m.*
This is an important story; I'm mirroring the link on my own page at <u>Steve's Weave</u>, though I hope it will not come to the administration unfairly silencing it here, on this blog. Just in case, though, I've copied it to my home servers so that the truth will be heard.

Posted by user **WolverinesSUCK** *at 3:01 a.m.*

The real scandal is that due to the fluoridation of the water
in American cities none of our young people have the necessary skull strength to withstand the impact of sports injuries
anymore. Read more about this important issue at my blog,
You Cannot Hide Fluoridation is EVERYWHERE and join the
movement to return our drinking water to its natural state.
This sort of chemical manipulation is exactly what brought
down the Roman Empire.

ERROR 404. Kendallkourier.com/Carlas_blog *cannot be found.*
This domain was permanently removed by user Ms_Edison *at*
6:00 a.m.

VENTING

Posted by user **JERRY** on December 4 at 2:17 p.m.

It was a regularly scheduled board meeting, but that was the only regular thing about it. I walked to school with Danny, and other players joined us along the way. Coach had told all the seniors to show up to support the team, even though we weren't exactly sure what that meant. As we got close, we saw cars zipping into parking spaces and townspeople hurrying along the sidewalk to get good seats, excitedly exchanging gossip.

Every year or two in Kendall, a board meeting becomes an event. There was the time a few seniors were busted for dealing drugs at school. There was the cyberbullying mess— I'm sure you all remember that fiasco. And of course there was the board meeting after my car accident when everyone wanted to vent about whether our school had a drunk driving problem.

This time it was Carla. The blog she had posted with her recording of Principal Bamburger had been taken down by the school authorities within two hours, but by then it had gone viral. It was copied and reposted and even picked up by some local news shows. Let's just say the coverage about our school and its football team—not to mention the principal— wasn't too flattering.

There was a rumor sweeping school that Carla was going to be expelled in the closed-door session after the public board meeting. No one had seen or heard from her all day—even Sophie West couldn't reach her. I didn't want to believe the rumor, but what she had done was pretty serious stuff. There was a lot of anger toward her in town for kicking up this stink just before our big game.

Board meetings are usually held in the high school dining hall, but this one was moved to the gym for the big crowd. I'm not sure exactly what people thought they were going to hear, but there was a buzz in the air. Everyone was excited—about our team, about Carla's post, and about some of the things that Bamburger had been caught saying on tape. Two local cable news crews were set up outside. They nearly mugged Danny and me for quotes. "Hey, Downing," a reporter called out, "how does it feel to be called a juvenile delinquent by your own principal?" Danny and I kept our heads down and plowed right on by them, with the other guys running interference.

We sat at the front of the gym, beneath the giant American flag that hangs from the rafters. We were all in our team shirts, and as the gym filled up, people came over to congratulate us. "Don't let this distract you," I heard again and again. "You guys just finish the job."

I saw Carla walk in with her parents and sit down near the front. Her mom carried a pad and looked serious and professional, as if she had come to argue a case. Her dad wore a suit, and I saw him shake hands with a few friends from the hospital. Carla looked tense and kept to herself. Except for a quick hello to Sophie, she didn't talk to anyone. She just sat down with her parents on either side of her and waited.

I had very mixed feelings. She shouldn't have taped Bamburger and created this mess and dumped on Kendall football the week before our biggest game. On the other hand, I've sat where she was sitting—in the eye of the storm of an angry Kendall board meeting—and I remember it well. You can sit there quietly and listen to people spew, or you can rise and try to defend yourself. Either way, it's rough sledding.

The president of the board, Mr. Carson, gaveled the meeting to order. He's a retired banker who never seems to be without a coat and tie. The superintendent of schools, Dr. Sparks, was sitting next to him. Dr. Sparks had just been hired in September, so this was his first community blowup and he looked a little nervous. I saw Principal Bamburger take a seat at the front table, and he also didn't look particularly happy.

The board conducted their regular business first. They approved the minutes of the last meeting and did minor budget stuff and agreed to hire a contractor to fix some problem with the heating system in the elementary school basement. Each time a board member would state a motion, there would be a little discussion, and then it would be called to a vote and passed, and they would move on. The truth was that no one in the cavernous gym could care less. That wasn't the show they had come to see.

After about thirty minutes they had finished their business

and Mr. Carson stood to address the crowd. "Good evening," he said. "We'll now move to the public forum part of
the meeting, where you get to speak up about what's happening in our schools. I know many of you have strong feelings, and you're welcome to present your opinions, but please
follow our ground rules. Let's be civil to each other and not
mention any student by name. Who'd like to speak first?"

Several hands shot up, and he called on a woman near the
front. She stood, and they brought her a portable microphone. I thought I recognized her, but I wasn't sure from
where. "My name is Mary Thomas, and I've lived in Kendall
all my life, and I confess I'm not a big football fan," she began.

"That's okay, Mary, we like you anyway," somebody called
out, and there was laughter.

"I work at the library," she went on, "and I love reading
and writing. There's a lovely young woman who comes to
the library often to study, and she's one of the best readers
and writers we've ever had. Maybe she overstepped and some
mistakes were made on both sides, but we don't want to lose
a student like that or tarnish her future. So I'd like to urge
that the board use restraint and remember that young people
make mistakes."

There was polite applause, but the librarian didn't sit
down. Instead, she pushed her glasses a little higher on her
nose and said: "I was also quite bothered by some comments
of the principal that I heard on the news. He appears to be
pressuring the football coach to win at all costs, and he also
says some pretty negative things about his students. And I

was wondering if he could explain what he meant by 'pushing the envelope' and 'no guts, no glory.'"

She sat down, and there was a silence. Bamburger made no move to answer her—he didn't flinch or even blink. He just sat there as if he hadn't even heard her.

"This is a public forum where you can express your opinions," Mr. Carson told us, "but it's not a time when we question our school officials. Yes, in the front."

A big man stood up. He was a former Kendall football player and a loyal Tiger booster, and he had a barrel chest and such a loud voice that he waved away the mic. "HEY THERE," he boomed. "First off, let me tip my hat to Coach Shea and the Tigers. We're so proud of you guys!"

There was scattered applause that knitted together second by second, till everybody in the gym seemed to be clapping. The ovation must have gone on for two minutes. All of us seniors stood shoulder to shoulder and let the applause cascade around us. "Hell," Danny whispered to me, "it's better than a pep rally."

"It *is* a pep rally," I told him.

When the ovation died down, the big man spoke again. "It's a damn shame that mud is being kicked on our program by one of our own students. Especially this week, when we should all be pulling together. But some people are so rich and selfish they feel they can do anything and get away with it. Now, I also heard what's on that tape, and the principal didn't say anything wrong. It wasn't about winning at all costs, it was just about winning. Maybe some of his words

weren't PC, but it was a private conversation. Taping somebody is against school rules, and taping your own principal is
just plain shameful. To hell with restraint. We don't need
that student at Kendall."

He sat amid loud clapping and shouts of "You say it,
Frank." I glanced at Carla. She squared her shoulders and
looked right back at the man who had just spoken.

"Let's keep things civil," Mr. Carson reminded us. Before
he could call on the next speaker, someone near the front
shouted out: *"So are you going to expel her or not?"*

"We're not going to get into specific disciplinary actions,"
Mr. Carson answered. "And please do not speak if you haven't
been recognized." He wiped his forehead with a white han-
kie. I had a sense that he didn't like where this meeting was
going. He was trying his best to keep a lid on it, but it was
like a flood tide, and any second it could bust through the
barricades. "Yes, Jim," he said.

Jim Porter, a lawyer and former mayor of Kendall, stood.
"Hey, all," he said with a smile. "I'd just like to clarify what
Frank brought up about taping a private conversation and
posting it. It's not only despicable but it's also illegal. It's akin
to trespassing."

"What about freedom of the press?" someone called out.

"Doesn't apply," Jim explained. "If she'd turned it over to
a newspaper or TV station, a case could be made. But since
she posted it herself on the Internet, there's no freedom of
the press issue here. You have a student who violated both a
school rule and a law of the land."

"Please don't call out questions, or discuss specific students, or I will end this meeting," Mr. Carson warned, and then he saw something and he kind of swallowed his words. Carla was standing. Her mother was trying to tug her back down, but she waved her hand, and someone passed her a mic. Mr. Carson told her, "You don't have to speak."

"I think I do," she replied, in a soft but clear voice. And then she spoke to us all: "Good evening, everybody. My name is Carla Jenson. I'm profoundly sorry to have caused so much trouble. Principal Bamburger, let me apologize for taping your words. I shouldn't have done that. I was scared and angry." Bamburger glared back at her from the front table but didn't say anything.

Carla went on in a louder voice. "Nobody wants our team to win this Friday more than I do. If you've read my articles, you know how much I care about our Tigers. But I felt there was another football story here that needed to be told. A story about a player who may not be ready to go back on the field, and a team that needs him to win, and a principal who is applying pressure. I understand what football means to all of us here in Kendall, but there are some things that are more important. That's why I did what I did, and if you want to kick me out of your school, in the end you'll be kicking me out for telling the truth. And we'll all have to live with that."

Carla sat down, and there was a moment of silence, as if the crowd was trying to figure out whether her brave words were admirable or haughty. A few people clapped for her, but there were louder jeers.

"This is the last time I'll remind you to remain civil," Mr. Carson sternly admonished the audience, but of course he couldn't control it. Carla had just put Kendall Football itself on trial. That's, I think, why so many people had come— they sensed that this might happen. And that's why Coach Shea had told us all to show up. For better or for worse, after she spoke the focus shifted from the rights and wrongs of taping the principal and the coach to our program at Kendall and the dangers of high school football.

An old lady asked whether the football player in question had been examined by a doctor.

Mr. Rosewood rose with dignity to explain that Danny had been cleared by his doctor to play before the Jamesville game, but they had rested him an extra week to be supersafe. "Now he's ready and raring to go," Mr. Rosewood said. "I love my son and I would never do anything to endanger him. And the last thing we need is to create a big issue and divide this town at just the wrong moment."

That drew sustained applause, and Danny, sitting next to me, nodded and shot his father a thumbs-up.

Several men in the audience who had played for Kendall related their colorful war stories of having been knocked out or injured on the field and returning to play with no bad effects. "It's part of football," they seemed to be repeating in different words. "You get your bell rung, you wait till the docs say go, and then you go back out and tear up the turf again. No guts, no glory is right. This has been going on for years and it's part of football."

A short young man with thick glasses stood up. "The

problem with that," he said, "is when a player's had a concussion, no one in the world can be sure exactly when it's safe—if ever—for him to return to the field."

"What are you, a doctor?" somebody heckled.

"As a matter of fact, yes," he said. "A neurologist at Kendall Hospital. I study brains. One of my jobs is to help decide when athletes who have suffered concussions should return to play. There are tests that we give, and there are prescribed formats that we follow, but the truth is that no MRI or CT scan, and no recovery-from-symptom checklist, can be perfectly accurate predictors of exactly when and how safe it is. We just don't know. We can't know. But what we do know . . ."

Someone called out, *"Sit down."*

"What we do know," the doctor continued, and he didn't seem intimidated, "is that there's groundbreaking work going on at the Boston University School of Medicine. They've taken the brains from dozens and dozens of professional athletes after death—and some amateurs—including one eighteen-year-old. They're not just testing football players' brains but hockey players', too. And what they're finding is incontrovertible evidence of extensive damage, throughout the brain, starting at a young age."

He sat down, and it was as if someone had cast a pall over the gym. Mr. Carson glanced at his watch. "We only have ten more minutes. Tom?"

Coach Shea stood up. "I've been the coach here for thirty years, and I'd like to thank you for your support. We run a clean program and we've worked hard this season and put ourselves in a place to win it all on Friday."

There was another ovation, as if by clapping for Coach people could wipe away what the neurologist had just said. "I may be a football coach, but I'm not a dummy," Coach went on. "I know that what they're finding out medically is very important. I care about my players like they were my own sons. That's why I rested Jerry earlier in this season, and that's why I rested Danny last week."

Coach Shea stood tall and looked proud, facing the community that had trusted him with their sons for decades. "But I know of no better vehicle for teaching life lessons and building character than high school football. When we win the championship on Friday, we're going to win something much more valuable for our town than just a trophy for the case. We're going to show eight hundred kids that they can be the best, that hard work can pay off, and that even a town like Kendall, with all its problems, can rise to the top. And that's important, too."

There was the loudest ovation of the night. All of us seniors were standing up side by side and clapping and hooting and hollering.

"Of course football is dangerous," Coach Shea admitted when the clapping finally died down, looking right at the young neurologist. "Always has been, always will be. We're doing everything we can to make it less so. Better helmets. Different rules. And we're trying to listen to you docs. In soccer, heavy balls hit heads. Are we gonna outlaw soccer?

In wrestling, people get tossed to the mat. In diving, you slam down into the water. All of these sports have risks, but they offer great rewards. Are we gonna tell our kids to sit home and study all the time and when they want to blow off steam to play tiddledywinks?"

People laughed. The neurologist didn't answer, but it was kind of easy to imagine him playing tiddledywinks.

Principal Bamburger walked out next to Coach Shea, put his arm around the old coach, and finished for him. "No, Tom," the principal said, "we're not going to settle for tiddledywinks. We're going to go on doing what we love to do at my school. At our school. Carefully. Safely. Never pressuring a student or a coach and following the advice of doctors, but also listening to our student athletes and their families. We're a proud football town, and we don't need to be told what to do or to have people break laws and accuse us of all kinds of bad things for publicity at just the wrong time." He glanced up at Carla. "Rules have been broken and examples must be set, so that I can run my school."

Carla's mother popped up to her feet. "I'd like to respond to that," she said. She was a small woman, but somehow her voice seemed as loud as the barrel-chested guy's.

"I won't allow a give-and-take," Mr. Carson said.

"My family's been taking, and I have a right to respond," Mrs. Jenson asserted. Then she did a very smart and brave thing. She walked down the bleachers to the front, so that she was standing next to Mr. Carson and sharing his mic, looking right at Principal Bamburger.

"My name is Victoria Jenson, and I'm the mother of the student who's been pilloried tonight," she said. "As you have already heard, she's fully capable of speaking for herself. But I'm also a lawyer. As a mother, I'd like to apologize if my daughter—in her youthful enthusiasm—went too far. She's very passionate about journalism. But she shouldn't have taped a conversation and she's sincerely sorry."

I glanced at Carla. Her eyes were riveted to her mom, and she gave her a slight nod.

"I think many of us want the same thing here: to put this behind us and move forward in a positive way," Mrs. Jenson continued. "On the other hand"—she looked at the superintendent of schools—"I am a lawyer, and since we're publicly discussing legalities now, I want to state publicly that if a decision is made to expel my daughter, the response will be swift."

Mrs. Jenson's gaze swung to Bamburger. I know I'm not allowed to say that her eyes flashed, but there were hidden flames that I think might have scorched the principal's striped tie. "Bullying and threats precipitated my daughter's error in judgment, her rights were violated, unsubstantiated and possibly slanderous comments about her may have been communicated to colleges, and the specifics of her case and her disciplinary status have now been discussed at a public board meeting. In my opinion, those matters are actionable and could have serious repercussions for those responsible."

Principal Bamburger stood up to face her, and his face was red. "Are you threatening me?"

She looked back at him and seemed to take his measure. "Unlike you, sir, I don't make threats, I don't yell, and I don't try to intimidate. But my respectful advice to the board, both as a mother and a lawyer, is to take a step back, and let's see if we can't find another road to walk down. Thank you." She walked back up the bleachers and sat down next to her husband and Carla. Mr. Jenson took his wife's hand, and then Carla took her other hand, and they sat together as a family, linked by tight grips.

Mr. Carson seemed inclined to say a few closing words and end the public forum, but at that moment a stranger, who had gotten hold of one of the portable microphones, unexpectedly took over. He looked to be in his forties, a tall man with an easygoing manner, wearing boots and jeans and a flannel shirt. Even though none of us had ever seen him before, he fit in well in the gym; he looked like another one of the concerned parents who worked hard and cared about their kids.

He walked to the front of the gym, where Mrs. Jenson had just stood, waved a friendly hand in a sweeping gesture, and said in a soft, polite voice: "Good evening to you all. My name is Gene Edmonds, and I'm not from around here. I drove here from Connecticut . . ."

"Then I'm afraid you can't speak at our town forum . . ." Mr. Carson said, but the man wasn't giving up his mic.

"Oh, I'll be brief," he promised. "But I do have something important to contribute. You see, I'm the president of a group called Dads Against Tackle Football. We now have more than three hundred members nationwide, and we're growing quickly."

"Turn his mic off," someone called out.

"Why?" he asked. "Are you afraid of what I might say? You don't have to be afraid. I'm not a doctor. I own a store in a small town, and I teach Sunday school, and I'm also a parent. My son Tad was paralyzed in a high school game and will never walk again. We do have many scientists in our group who could echo what the doctor in your audience was trying to tell you. Those doctors in Boston he was talking about—they have actual brain samples. They've done the hard science, right down to the cellular level. It's not just a theory. It's been proven."

Again people tried to heckle him, and again he pressed on. "Many years ago, it wasn't known for certain that smoking cigarettes was bad for your health, and it was kind of cool to do," he said. "But then evidence started to come in that smoking caused lung cancer. And schools did their part and educated young people not to smoke."

His eyes swept the big gym from floor to rafter. "I know this town," he said. "I've never been here before, but I've been to towns just like it in Ohio and Pennsylvania and Texas. I do a lot of driving. I know how seriously you take your football here. It's the quintessential American sport. Well, I have bad news for you. Football is dead. Especially for kids. No more Pop Warner. No more high school football."

He leaned slightly forward and continued with absolute conviction. "It just doesn't know it's dead yet. It may take a decade or two, but it will go the way of gladiatorial combat. The evidence that's mounting will be impossible for parents and educators to ignore. The private high schools will ban it first, and then the public ones, and then the colleges, and finally the professional leagues will disappear. There's no way to save it, either. People talk about redesigning equipment or changing the rules about tackling, but that's bull. The goal of tackle football is to hit people head-on and often head-first. The game is built around that, and there's no way to change it."

Then his voice got softer and a little thick, and suddenly our old gym went silent as people stopped shifting around or whispering and just listened to him. "I got a boy at home—a good boy, a nice kid—who used to run down the field and jump in the air when a pass came his way," the man told us. "Now he's in a motorized wheelchair and he's learning to work a computer by holding a pointer in his teeth, because he can't move from the neck down. It wasn't worth it. It's *never* worth it. This game isn't worth my son's spinal cord or your son's brain." And he looked directly at Mr. Rosewood. "Let's save our children."

He dropped his microphone on the floor, shot Coach Shea a look, and then walked up the stairs and left the gym. Nobody said a word to him. After he was gone, there was a very deep and heavy lingering silence.

"I guess that concludes our public forum," Mr. Carson said. And then he paused. Something told me he didn't want to end on such a sour note. Superintendent Sparks whispered something to him, and Mr. Carson nodded. "Unless one of our football team members would like to make a closing comment?"

We all looked at each other. "You're the captain," I told Danny. "Go for it."

"No," Danny said, "it's gotta be you."

"Why?"

"You're the quarterback. You killed Jamesville."

"Who cares?" I said.

"They all do," he told me. And then he put his hand on my shoulder and whispered, "Please, Jerry. As a favor to me."

Now, the last thing I ever wanted to do in my life was to speak at a big public Kendall Board meeting. But the other seniors were kind of pushing me up and people started clapping and the next thing I knew there was a microphone in my hand. I wanted to toss it back and jump off the bleachers and run home and think about the Albion game. Instead, I heard myself say: "Good evening, everyone. My name is Jerry Downing, and I have the great honor to be the quarterback of the Tigers this season."

I saw my parents in the audience. I also glanced at Carla, who was watching me with interest, waiting to hear what I had to say. The truth is, I didn't know what I was going to say, either.

"Listen," I continued, "I think it's time we all went home. I need good sleep this week so that we can beat Albion. I'm no expert on the science of head injuries, and I'm very comfortable leaving all that to the coaches and the doctors, who want the best for us." I didn't add, *And our principal, even if he thinks I'm a juvenile delinquent.* "I just want to play football," I said.

Again, I waited for silence and said: "On a personal level, nobody knows better than I do how you can screw up and get into all kinds of trouble. I'd like to thank this town for giving me a second chance. And I'd like to urge you to find that same generosity, kindness, and mercy and show it to my friend Carla, who did something she shouldn't have done. You heard her apologize tonight. She's part of our school family, and families don't kick out brothers or sisters—they find ways to forgive."

This time there was no clapping. I felt Coach Shea watching me, and Danny was right there, too. "What happened to me a year ago happened because I got too big for my boots," I admitted. "I thought I could do anything. I forgot I was just a seventeen-year-old and there were rules I had to follow. And that those rules and laws protect other people, too. I think Carla needs to remember that. There's no story here, even though she's trying to create one. Everyone's done the right thing. She didn't need to blow this thing up and put football on trial. Not this week. That man was wrong. Football's not dead, at least here in Kendall. It's alive and well and we're going to find a way to beat Albion."

Then I was done and I handed the mic back to Mr. Carson as the other football seniors came up and slapped five with me. Danny was right next to me, my right arm around his back. People were cheering and stamping on the bleachers.

I spotted Carla walking out of the gym with her parents. She turned once to look at me, and then her mom put her arm on Carla's elbow and tugged her away. I thought of going after her, but I never would have reached her through the crush. And what else was there to say? We had both told the truth as we saw it.

"Tigers, Tigers, Tigers," people shouted, and stomped and slapped me on the back.

"Okay, we're ready to begin the closed-door part of the meeting," Mr. Carson said into a microphone near me. "I'd like to ask you to all quiet down and leave the gym." But nobody was listening to him.

Nor, I think, did too many people pay attention when the news broke online a few hours later that the Board had voted for expulsion and Carla was no longer a student at Kendall High.

View 6 reader comments:

Posted by user **ExpulsionWasTooGoodForHer** *at 3:14 p.m.*
Carla has forever damaged our school's and town's reputation. To my mind she got off easy given how much trouble she has caused for everyone here in Kendall. She doesn't deserve to graduate with her class; we're better off without her.

Posted by user **CarlaFan** *at 3:25 p.m.*
I had been reading Carla's sports blog religiously for the past year, and she's the best sportswriter our school has

ever had. I'm betting she goes pro one day and I, for one, will look forward to being able to follow her coverage again.

Posted by user **TIGERFAN** *at 4:10 p.m.*
The hell with the principal, the hell with the school board and the blog girl, can we just focus on what really matters here and win the damn championship?

Posted by user **@TIGERFAN** *at 5:11 p.m.*
Amen. I'm not worried about one troublesome student in the halls at Kendall. What really worries me is that the aerial attack against Jamesville was great but football games are won on the ground, grinding out the tough yards, and I just haven't seen the evidence that we can do that. Where is the blocking up front? Where is the runner who can steamroll in from five yards out?

Posted by user **@@TIGERFAN** *at 6:44 p.m.*
You're out of your mind; we've never looked better. How can you doubt the up-front blocking capabilities after that play by #19 in the third quarter?

Posted by user **Photog_Sophie** *at 7 p.m.*
Click here for a photo of my friend Carla speaking up for herself at last night's town meeting. Carla, I'm so proud of you and we all miss you here at Kendall.

From: Cjenson@kendallhs.edu
To: JerryQB@kendallhs.edu
Subject: Speaking for myself

Hey Jerry,

Well, that was quite a meeting last night. Turns out you have hidden talents. Who knew you were such an effective public speaker? And then to write it up so quickly. You must really have the blogging habit by now, just one more little piece of my legacy at Kendall High.

Thank you for trying to defend me. I think. I mean, I think you meant well. You were trying to say, Carla did a crazy stupid bad thing, but the saintly townspeople of good old Kendall should find it in their hearts to forgive her, just the way they forgave you for getting drunk and smashing up a car and a girl's face. Well, thank you very much, Jerry, I suppose. I know you've struggled with the guilt you feel over what happened and what might have happened, and I really do respect that.

But I didn't get drunk, I didn't hurt anyone who trusted me, and I haven't smashed anything, except my own high school career. So even though I really do appreciate that you meant well, no thanks. I did something that was probably stupid, but the one who was at risk of getting smashed up was me. I took on someone much more powerful. I did something that was ethically dubious—and I won't ever do it again, so I have learned a valuable lesson as a journalist, I guess—but in the end, what you mean by dumb catchphrases like "putting football on trial" is really that I told the truth and I told it too loud.

Our principal is a bully and a jerk. He doesn't like me because he thinks I'm a rich princess, and he doesn't like you, either. I happen to think that he's wrong about us both and that he shouldn't be running the school. (And from what my mother says, he probably won't be running it too much longer. She says that by the time this all plays out, the school board will be happy to cut him loose for all the ways he mishandled this—and for the way he sounded on the tape. It'll be too late for me to come back to school, but my mom's pretty good at handicapping these things, and she says he'll be gone by next September. So there's another little Carla legacy, if it happens.)

So that's one truth: Bamburger is a bully and a jerk, and he's not very smart, either. But there's another truth here, too, and you know it, I think, Jerry Downing. Your friend Danny is at risk. And no matter how much the town cheers you when you do your shucks-folks-I-just-want-to-play-football act, you're no fool. You know this game is dangerous. I don't know how I feel about that guy who said high school football is dead, but I bet he's at least right that we're going to be hearing more speeches like that in the next few years. And you know that Danny isn't telling the truth, whether he knows it or not, about what happened to him, and you know that the coach is worried, and you know that the principal doesn't care, and you know that he's pressuring the coach to play him. And the funny thing is that I think you knew all that even before Carla the Criminal taped that conversation and posted it.

So, sure, football is on trial, but that's not my doing. That's something that everyone who cares about the game is going to have to face and think about. And who knows how it will come out? But I will tell you this, Jerry, even though I'm pretty pissed off at you right now, I cannot stand to think that if you took a few unlucky hits in these games that I love to watch and love to write about, something might happen to you. I could joke and say, "Maybe you'd get that nonsense about eyes flashing knocked out of you," but that's not what I mean, and you know it. You have a way of thinking and writing that's yours and nobody else's. I make fun of you sometimes and I think you have a lot of growing up to do, and it makes me really mad when I think about you standing up in front of that meeting and saying I created this issue for no reason, but when I think of the possibility that you could get your brain banged up, again and again, till your thinking was dulled and you couldn't form the same kinds of sentences, and you just weren't the same you . . . Well, I have to tell you, Jerry, like the guy from Connecticut said, it's just not worth it.

Which doesn't mean I won't be out there cheering for you against Albion. I hope you have a great game and nobody gets hurt and Kendall wins the championship. Really I do. And I'm no coward—I'll be at the game, even though I don't go to the school anymore. And I'll shout your name and cheer, really I will, and I'll even mean it.

Go Tigers,
Carla

P.S. I guess I'd better say, don't worry about me too much. It looks like I'll be all set to finish out the year in private school. I suppose that would prove Bamburger's point about the spoiled princess, or your silly view of my McMansion and all the money we have to waste, but what the hell are you supposed to do when your principal gets you expelled in the fall of your senior year? My mom says we won't fight the expulsion directly—it would take too much of my school year (though I know she's already gotten an injunction and filed three lawsuits, and I gather it's going to cost Kendall quite a bundle, speaking of wasting money)—and instead we just use it to take Bamburger down. And sure, I hope this doesn't do me too much damage with my college applications (I've already started writing the new essay, and believe me, it's a doozy. And I got to use some of that great stuff on head trauma, too). But I think I'll be okay, just kind of sad about the way this all played out. But I'm still hoping to see you beat Albion.

ALBION

Posted by user **JERRY** on December 20 at 8:09 p.m.

It's taken me a few weeks to write this up, and I think it's the longest thing I've ever written. But, hey, it was the biggest game of my life, and they've expelled the best sportswriter we had at Kendall, so I guess it's up to me to finish this story, just like it was up to me to finish the season. So here is the story of my championship game.

All week long, it was stormy. Not just the weather, though we had strong wind gusts and freezing temperatures and more than six inches of snow. Starting with the board meeting on Tuesday night, bad news seemed to whistle down on us from the gray skies. Carla was expelled. Coach Shea's brother—who lives in Boston—had heart trouble, and Coach Shea had to rush to a hospital there and miss practice on Wednesday. Coach Horton ran the show while he was gone, and he took us outside to get us used to the subzero temperatures. Granger busted a finger sliding on an ice patch, and on Wednesday night I came down with the flu.

Thursday I was flat on my back, popping Advil, drinking hot liquids, and feeling lousy. I had all the symptoms: weakness, aches, fever, a sore throat, a bad cough, and nausea. Mom stayed home from the clinic to take care of me, and our doctor made two house visits.

I spent most of the day in bed wondering how I could play in such condition or if I would have to let Ryan Hurley take over. I had put so much work into the season that I couldn't imagine not leading our team. But it's also hard to imagine quarterbacking a championship football game when you're on your knees puking into the toilet.

By Thursday night I was a little better—I could at least stand up without feeling dizzy. Coach Shea came to visit, and we sat at the kitchen table sipping lemon tea and going over some new plays they had put in. "I gotta tell you, Jerry, you don't look good," he said when we'd finished.

"I'm on the mend," I told him. "It's just one game. Two hours of football. When the whistle blows, I'll be ready."

"I hope so," he said, and I knew he was in a bind. Sick or not, I had thrown for three hundred and forty yards the previous Friday, and newspapers now were calling me the best high school quarterback in the state. We were favored to beat Albion, but a lot of that was due to my passing performance against Jamesville. All the reporters agreed that Albion was a superhot team and they stacked up very well against us in the other phases of the game.

Danny Rosewood called up after Coach had left. "How are you doing, amigo?"

"On the mend," I told him. "I'll be okay for tomorrow. What about you?"

"I've been practicing with pads," he said. "They're still taking it a little easy on me, but I'm good to go. What about our run?"

I had been thinking the same thing. As you know from reading my blogs, Danny and I had had a little ritual since Pee Wee football. We'd never missed a morning run together on a game day. "Danny, I gotta level with you. I'm gonna need every last bit of energy for Albion."

"I figured that," he said. "No problem. Anyway, it's supposed to be a real icebox tomorrow. I'd rather be home in my nice warm bed."

I spent a little time on the computer Thursday night before turning in. I had a million e-mails from people concerned about my health or wishing me good luck. None of them was from Carla. I hadn't heard from her since the e-mail she had sent me on Wednesday, the day after the town meeting. I figured she was pissed off, like she said, and was probably busy getting set up in a new school. But I did read over that paragraph where she wished me luck a couple of times, and I hoped she really was telling the truth about coming to the game.

It's not good to read press the night before a game, but I couldn't help myself. There were several breakdowns of Kendall versus Albion, position by position. Their swarming defense had given up fewer yards on the ground per game than we had, and they were great at sacking quarterbacks. Their running game consistently generated more yards than ours. Their quarterback, Martinez, had only thrown one interception and given up two fumbles all year. He didn't light it up with long passes, but he was a smart field general and by all accounts a tough cookie.

I had read somewhere that warriors sleep well before battles, and I always took it as a point of pride that I conked out as soon as my head hit the pillow. Not this time. I lay there, feeling weak and a little feverish, and I kept waiting for the lights to magically switch off. Minutes passed, and then hours started to drag by. I didn't count sheep, but I did say a prayer asking God to please give me some rest and let me wake up feeling like my old self. I remembered the story of Moses leading the Israelites through the desert to the promised land but not being allowed to set foot there himself. Had I led Kendall this far, only to be felled by a stupid flu bug?

Finally I drifted off. I dreamed of a car crash. I was at the wheel and the road was icy and I knew we were going to crash but I couldn't stop. Some teammates were in the car, and we were approaching train tracks. I could see a train coming. I tried to jam the brakes, but it was like we were locked on the road, and then I woke up screaming and drenched in my own sweat.

Mom was in the room in a few seconds, and I told her it was just a nightmare. She gave me a long look, then took my temperature and said that I was still feverish. "Let's keep you home from school, at least in the morning."

"Mom, if I don't go to school, I can't play," I told her. "School rules."

The nightmare stayed with me as I took a shower, dosed myself with maximum Advil, and got dressed. I remembered my real car crash and being helped from the wreckage, feeling my arms and my legs and being surprised that each of them was okay and I was functioning fine. Then I had realized that the ambulance crew was focusing on the accordion of a car and someone still inside it was moaning. That had been the beginning of my very real-life nightmare, and this bitter cold day was supposed to be the end of it. This was the day I had been looking forward to for months, redeeming myself by working hard and keeping my nose clean and bringing a state championship home to Kendall. Unfortunately, I felt like total crap.

I dragged myself around from class to class and period to period, and I kept drinking hot liquids every chance I got. Coach Shea had the school nurse check me out during my lunch period, and she announced that my temperature was two degrees above normal. "He's not perfect, but he can play," she told the coach.

"He looks like death warmed over," Coach grunted.

"Thanks," I said. "Real flattering description. But I'm really feeling much better."

He stared back and growled: "Don't blow smoke at me, Downing. You think I haven't seen my share of flu over the years?"

Then we were on the bus, zipping down the highway, and I was sitting next to Danny. He had his headphones on and was listening to something, but I was watching cars roll through the ice and slush around our bus and trying not to think about how I should be feeling. I should have been feeling excited and primed, with that tension that builds all day in your gut on game day till an hour before start time you can barely sit still. But my stomach felt empty, as if someone had drained it with a hose, and instead of electric excitement there was still more than a tinge of nausea.

"Let me see what you're listening to," I said, and pulled Danny's headphones off and tried them on for size. The volume was real low. "What the hell?" I asked. "I can barely hear the words."

"The words don't matter, it's the beat," Danny said, pulling his headphones back.

For some reason I remembered when we were at his house, watching mixed martial arts, and he had kept turning the sound lower and then switched the set off. "Loud volume still bothers you?" I asked.

He gave me a look, as if to say that was ridiculous. "I'm just in a mellow mood. Never been in a state championship before. Hey, check that out!"

And there it was. MetLife Stadium, home of two professional football teams and the venue of our state championship football game. Even from miles away it looked enormous.

"Ever been to a game there?" Danny asked me.

"A couple of times. You?"

"Never," Danny shook his head. "It's huge," he whispered, a little awed.

"I never thought I'd be playing inside it," I whispered back.

By then other guys on the bus had spotted it, and you could feel the excitement kick in.

You work for months, three or four hours a day, in the pouring rain and the freezing cold. You start out in August, on a patch of grass in a hick town in a corner of New Jersey, a bunch of guys doing push-ups and squat-thrusts and running the plays from last year. And you tell yourselves that if you do everything right, you will one day find yourselves on a grand stage, playing for the bragging rights of the whole Garden State, but all along it still feels like a crazy dream.

And then, *bam*, it happens—we were inside MetLife Stadium, which holds more than eighty thousand fans. We were down on the emerald turf field in the bright lights, gathered around Coach Shea. It occurred to me that this was the last time I'd hear him give his pregame talk—everything that happened now would be for the last time.

"Downing's gonna start," he said, "and we'll see how long he can go. If Hurley goes in, that's great, too. We have two fine quarterbacks on this team, and either one can beat Albion. Right?"

"Right!" we roared back at him.

"You guys want it, don't you?" he asked.

"Yeah!" we thundered.

"You deserve it for all the hard work and pain and blood and guts you've put into this year, don't you?" His voice seemed louder than all of ours combined.

"YEAH!" We matched him decibel for decibel.

Then his voice dropped low, to almost a whisper. "Then go out there and take it. Go out there and play like the proud men of Kendall that you are, and *take it from them!*"

And we were roaring, and jumping, and slamming each other on the pads, but even at that moment when I was carried away by emotion, I felt the flu bug stirring.

They kicked off, and we started on our own twenty. I looked around the huddle and saw my old friends and comrades, and I tried to squash that flu bug and rise to the occasion. "Guys, we're gonna do it just the same way that got us here. Let's start with a short hook to Rosewood and move the chains."

I dropped back into my pocket, and he streaked off the line and then buttonhooked back, but my pass was three feet short. I could blame it on the strong wind or the numbing cold or the flu, but it was an ugly pass. We tried a run up the middle, but Magee got tripped up by two guys behind the line. You could see that this team, Albion, was for real. They were talking to each other, psyching each other up, not the biggest guys in the world, but they believed.

Third and eleven. I called a long slant to Glenn Scott, but he was blanketed by the coverage. I checked off to Danny, but he had two guys on him. I looked for a screen to Magee, but there was no time. Albion's pesky rushers had broken through my wall, and I felt their hands grabbing me. I took a step and wrapped up the football and someone spun me around. I tried to break away, but three of them had me now and they knocked me to the turf and piled on top. It wasn't a hard tackle, and when they got off I rose to my knees. Then I threw up in front of thousands of people, not to mention the cable TV audience.

We punted, and I stood on the sideline wrapped up in a coat and a blanket, sipping something hot. Coach Shea walked over and took one look at me, and said: "Sorry, Jerry, but you're done for the day." He always called me Downing, so I knew he really felt bad about it.

I didn't even fight him. I just nodded and lowered my head.

Ryan Hurley went in the next time we got the ball, which was six minutes later because Albion marched it down with short runs and tic-tac passes and scored a touchdown.

And Ryan tried. They all tried. Magee tried to bull it up the middle, and Glenn Scott got us two first downs, and near the end of the second quarter Danny made a one-handed catch and ran it all the way in for a touchdown to put us on the scoreboard. But by then we were trailing 21–7.

Danny came right over and sat next to me, still breathing hard from his long sprint down the sideline. "How ya doing, Jer?"

"I've been better," I told him. "Nice grab."

"When I caught it, I knew I was gone," he said. "It felt like I was flying."

"You *were* flying," I told him. "You ran away from their whole team."

"To tell the truth, they're not that fast," he said, sounding a little perplexed. "And they're not that big, either. They really don't seem like they should be as good as they are."

"The only problem is, nobody told them that," I replied softly.

We headed into the locker room at halftime down 31–7. The Kendall fans were quiet. Even our marching band had fallen silent. I saw my parents, and my mom looked concerned. Dad gave me a "fight on" fist pump, and I shook my fist back, but it felt like we were just going through the motions. I spotted Carla sitting with her parents on a bleacher right smack in the middle of the Kendall section. Good for them for showing up. Our eyes met, and she mouthed something. I think it was "Good luck" or "Fight hard" but it might have been "You suck."

And there was no doubt that we had stunk it up. After the first half against Sand River, we had trailed 14–3, and that had seemed like a big mountain to climb. But an eleven-point comeback was doable, and we had never stopped believing in ourselves. Now we were down twenty-four points to a really good team, a team that was supersolid in every phase of the game. I saw a lot of heads hanging as we trudged off the field for halftime.

Cold never bothers me during a game, but this time it felt good to be indoors. Coach gathered us around, but he didn't give us his usual fiery pep talk. "I want you to know that I've decided to retire," he said. "This will be my last game coaching Kendall. These guys are tough, and we didn't have a great week to prepare, and we've lost our starting quarterback, so if we want to make excuses we've got a boatload of them."

He broke off and let out a long breath. He looked a little old and tired. He said softly: "But that's not how I want to go out. And I don't think that's how you guys want to go out. We can do anything in one half of football, if we set our minds to it. Right, Leo?"

Out came his surprise guest, Leo Keller, the only guy from Kendall to ever make it to the NFL. He must have been fifty, with some white hair, and he had a slight limp. But he still had the rugged frame of an outside linebacker who had played ten seasons in the NFL. He looked around at us, and then he chuckled. "No, I'm not sure that is right, Coach. You fellows look whipped," he told us. "Don't pretend it's the cold weather. It's not your preparation, either. Those boys from Albion just want it more. They stuck it to you in the first half, and if they go out and score one more time it's over. Simple as that."

He pulled a chair into the center of our group and sat down. "So how do we change the momentum?" he asked. "Tell you what. I was part of one of the greatest comebacks in the history of the NFL. In Chicago, on a day a lot colder than this, we came back from thirty-five down. How does a thing like that happen? You can't explain it by more passing yards or better running plays or new tactics that the coach sends in. It was none of those things."

Again, he was silent, looking around at us. His brown eyes were intense, measuring us. "I can still remember that Sunday, crystal clear and cold. We were getting crushed, and then we turned it. Not all at once, but you could feel it happening. The other team could feel it, too, but they just couldn't stop it. And it wasn't one play, or a lucky break, or something that fate handed us. Nah."

He stood up and folded his hands over his big arms so that his two Pro Bowl rings flashed, and his voice got a bit louder. "Here's what it is," he told us. "Sometimes something a little freaky happens and a team decides not to lose a game like this. They make that decision in their hearts, as a group, that *they will not lose*. Then they go out and, play by play, they impose their will. They turn the momentum. They put their shoulders to it, and they slowly shift it. Somebody toss me a football."

Somebody threw him one, and he caught it and held it as if he were going to run with it. His hands were so big that the football almost disappeared inside. "Man, I love this game," he said. "I gotta tell you, I miss it terribly. I was there on Tuesday night when that sad man from Connecticut said that football is dead. He got that wrong, but he got most of it dead right."

Leo Keller looked down at the football. "You can't change this sport by making the helmets more cushioned or the tackling safer. Football is what it is, for better or worse. Somebody smacks you, and you smack 'em back. Somebody knocks you down, and you get up and hit them even harder. The beauty of the game is its ugliness. It's a fight in an alley. So if you guys want to win, you gotta decide, as a group, that you're gonna get up off the floor and start punching back."

He held the football up in his right hand and turned it so that the laces caught the light. "That's all I have to say to you. Fate has stamped you as the losers tonight. Everybody in this stadium feels it. Hell, your own parents feel it. And

I can tell you feel it yourselves. I see it in your eyes. If you want to be state champs, you're going to have to put your shoulders to this game and turn that fate play by play, till you remake your own destiny."

"Everybody kneel and link hands," Coach Shea said, and we did. Danny was on my right, and Leo Keller was on my left. My hand seemed to disappear into his huge paw. "Two minutes of silence," Coach said, and we were quiet. I could feel Leo's two Pro Bowl rings.

It was a strange thing, but those two minutes seemed to last a very long time. Instead of shouting at us, Coach had given us a chance to look inside ourselves, and I was surprised by what I saw.

Maybe it was the fever, but kneeling there, I had the craziest thoughts. I remembered the Pee Wee game when they first tried me out as quarterback and I threw four touchdowns. The way the parents had all gaped at me. I remembered my dad's tight face when he was laid off, and how he kept going out looking for jobs and coming home and not saying much. And for some reason I thought of my grandfather when he lay dying and I went into his hospital room to say goodbye. He smiled at me and said, "God bless you, Jerry," and reached out and touched me with his hand.

"Okay," Coach Shea finally said, and he sounded a little choked up. "This is going to be my last half as a coach, and whatever happens, I'm really proud of you guys. Now let's go play some football." We stood up, and the guys started to head out.

Ryan Hurley walked out the door first, and they all followed him. Nobody said anything.

I took a step toward the door, but Leo Keller grabbed my arm with his left hand. In his right, I noticed he still held the football. "C'mere a minute, Downing," he said softly, and drew me a few steps away. Then he let go of my arm, and we were facing each other, alone in the large locker room. "I got bad news," he said. "It has to be you. Know what I mean?"

I shook my head.

We were standing near a long polished wooden bench and a row of gray metal lockers. He smiled at me and said, "I see how it is. I know how sick you are. I've been there. But without you it doesn't work."

"Ryan can do the job," I told him.

He shook his head. "You're the man." He flipped me the football he'd been holding and shot me a wink. I'm pretty sure he was telling me: here, this belongs to you. Then he turned and walked out.

We kicked off to Albion to start the second half, and our defense held them three and out. I thought about what Leo had said and then I walked up to Coach Shea and told him quietly, "I want to try going back in for one set."

He didn't even hesitate. "Not gonna happen, Downing. You look like a corpse. This is Hurley's game now."

They punted and we took over the ball, and I was still standing on the sideline. Ryan Hurley stayed in at quarterback, and he tried to shift things in a hurry. He threw three long passes, but none of them connected, so we had to punt it back to Albion, and time kept ticking down.

Coach Shea was standing next to Coach Horton, going over defensive formations. "Hey, Coach," I said.

"Busy," he grunted.

"You gotta put me in," I told him.

"I'm gonna put you in a hospital, first chance I get," he said without looking up from his clipboard. "You're sick as a dog. Let it go, Downing."

I grabbed his arm so that the clipboard fell to the ground, and I turned him. Coach is not an easy man to turn. He glared at me. "What the hell?"

I met his eyes. "Put me in the game or . . ."

"Or what?"

"I'll kick your ass."

His sandblasted face twitched. "Yeah?" he asked.

"Yeah."

He looked back at me a second more, and then his lips twisted up in a tiny grin. "Okay, Downing. I don't want to get my ass kicked in my last game as coach. One piece of advice. If you puke again, try to puke on one of them."

Our defense held Albion, and this time Coach sent me out. There were ten minutes left in the third quarter. When I stepped onto the field, the Kendall fans let out a roar, and our band played our fight song.

We stood in the huddle, and I could see that the guys wanted to believe. They were waiting for me to start throwing bombs. And suddenly I understood that if they were waiting for it, Albion must also be. "They know I'm a passer," I said. "They'll think we're desperate. So let's cross them up and get our running game going first."

Sure enough, they were guessing pass, so when Brian Hart took it right up the middle, he gained fourteen before they brought him down. Next play I ran an option and they were all waiting for the sideline pass, so when I flipped it to Magee, he had plenty of daylight to run.

I only threw two short passes on that whole drive, and it wasn't exactly pretty, but we played smashmouth football, and our line outmuscled theirs in the trenches. All those hours in the weight room paid off, because foot by foot we shouldered and shoved them backwards. We scored on a draw, with Hart running seven yards straight up their gut, and it was 31–14. We were still down two touchdowns and a field goal, and our drive had eaten up seven precious minutes, but we had started to turn it.

Next time we got the ball, we stayed with the running attack and made two first downs. Now they were sitting on the run, loading up the line. In the huddle, I glanced at Danny. "I hear these guys aren't so fast," I said.

"Nope," he agreed.

"Then let's smoke 'em," I said. "I'm gonna fake it to Glenn short and hit Rosewood on a streak." A streak is a straight sprint toward their end zone, where our receiver challenges their coverage people to a fifty-yard dash and lets it all hang out. There's nothing fancy about a streak—it's pure speed. I looked at my pass protectors. "For this to work, you guys gotta buy me a few seconds." I could tell they were plenty determined. We broke the huddle, and Danny and I didn't so much as glance at each other. We'd been doing this too long to give the defense any clues.

I got the hike and stepped back into my pocket, and my wall held for a second, two seconds. My pump fake to Glenn froze their defense and bought me a third second. Then I looked long. They had their fastest cover guy on Danny, and their free safety was slanting over to help out.

Danny was thirty yards deep now, running with that peculiar gait of his that doesn't look like a full-on sprint but it gobbles up yards. Their cover guys were both still deeper than him, but I couldn't wait much longer.

I could feel my pocket starting to collapse behind me. I stepped up to buy myself one more precious heartbeat, and then a hand grabbed my shirt and I knew they had me. Danny and I had been doing this since Pee Wee, and I trusted him to get behind them and run under it. I threw it high and hard and got yanked to the turf. The crowd roared, and by the time I got to my knees Danny was five steps ahead of the guys chasing him, and then he was in the end zone.

And that was when the momentum shift became a momentum tidal wave. You could feel the weight of it swelling on our sideline. You could hear the roar of the wave in the bass drum of our marching band and in the chants of our faithful fans. "Kendall, Kendall!" This day belonged to us now, and our town would not be denied.

All credit to Albion High. Martinez kept running smart,

disciplined plays, but we were knocking down his passes and stuffing his runs. Their defense hunkered down and slowed our running game, so I went airborne more often. In the middle of the fourth quarter—with the score tied at thirty-one—I hit Danny on a sideline route, and they tackled him hard. He held on to the ball and got up fast, but Coach took him out of the game and sent him off the field to get checked out, so I finished the drive with Scott and Magee for targets.

I was passing well now, back in the rhythm that had destroyed Jamesville. I went short, short, and then long to Glenn Scott, who caught a slant-and-go and ran it all the way in for a touchdown. Finally—with five minutes left to play—we had our first lead of the game.

That should have been that. Albion had blown a twenty-seven-point lead. We had dominated them the whole second half. Now we had pulled ahead, and they should have wilted. We kicked off and tackled their return guy in the coffin corner, between their end line and the five-yard line. They had to go ninety-five long yards against our suffocating defense. No way that was gonna happen.

Then a strange thing happened. These kids who came from a football program nobody'd ever heard of and didn't have a single star player on their team did something I didn't expect. They got up off the turf and smacked us back. They had been down many times this season, but they had never been counted out, and they started playing mad.

Martinez put this crazy drive together that started as

slow as a tractor, and I kept waiting for us to stop him, but they made play after play and kept on rolling.

Danny walked up to me and we stood side by side, watching. "How are you doing?" I asked. "Looked like you got your bell rung again."

"No, Coach was just being careful." We watched as they made yet another first down. There were two minutes left and they had crossed midfield. "No way they'll march it all the way in," I said. "Our defense is too tough."

Danny glanced quickly at the scoreboard and shrugged. "Lucky we have an eight-point lead."

I looked at him. Danny's like a walking calculator. Straight A's in math all the way through school. "Danny, we have thirty-eight and they have thirty-one. It's a seven-point lead."

"Oh, yeah," he said, and blinked. "Seven. No problem. 'Cause they'll never get a touchdown." And just as he said it, there was a roar from the crowd because Martinez had threaded the ball through three of our defenders to his best receiver, who ran it in: 38–37. All Albion needed was to kick the extra point and hold us and they'd send the game into overtime.

But they didn't line up for the extra point. They went for the two points and the win. Martinez hiked the ball and pitched it to his running back, and they ran a sweep to the right side.

It looked like we had the sweep covered, but somehow their back kept angling toward the sideline and our goal line, and then he hurdled clear over our last tackler and extended the ball as he fell, and the ref raised both hands. Touchdown. He had broken the plane of the end zone. We were down by one point with less than two minutes left.

They kicked off, and Mike Magee ran it back to the thirty, and it was time for our last drive of the season, and of my high school career. Coach came over and put his hand on my back and said, "Get this one, Jer. You fought back from a real hard place, and you deserve it."

"We all do," I told him. "The whole town. We'll get it done."

We went out there and some of the guys looked a little nervous in the huddle. "Forget the crowd," I told them, and I had to speak loud because the crowd was roaring. "Forget the score. Let's just make one play at a time and we'll win this thing."

I've never run a better drive under time pressure. I picked up two first downs to take us to midfield, and then on a fourth and five I hit Danny on a long slant to get twenty more, down to their thirty. He got up a little slowly and ran to our huddle. "You okay?" I asked him.

"Fine," he said, blinking. "Let's take it in!"

Thirty-five seconds left. Our field goal kicker had hurt his leg before halftime and was limping around on the sidelines. Our backup kicker was not at all dependable. We had two time-outs, and we had to take it all the way into their end zone. Runs wouldn't do it. Short passes were risky, too. And our kicking game was done for the day. I had four shots at a game-winning touchdown pass.

I took my first one at Glenn Scott in the right corner, and he almost pulled it down, but their defender got a hand on it at the last second and knocked it away.

My second shot was a crossing pattern. Danny and Mike were supposed to cross up the middle and I would hit Danny as they came out of it. But Danny went the wrong way, so they never crossed, and Mike was double-covered. I waited and then I barely managed to throw the ball away before I got popped.

Third down. Eighteen seconds left. Coach called our second-to-last time-out. I hurried over to him, and he told me we were running a post to Danny. I looked back at him. "I'm not sure about Danny. When we ran the crossing play, he cut to the wrong side."

"He can run a post route," Coach said. "Straight to the goalpost, and you'll drop it in his hands. He's our go-to guy, Jerry. This is for all the marbles."

I ran back onto the field, and we huddled up and I called the post. "You good with that, Danny?"

"Yeah, sure." He blinked. "Let's do it."

I heard something in his voice. "What is it?" I asked. "What's wrong?"

"Nothing," he said. "It's just the crowd noise."

I studied his face.

"Jerry, we gotta break the huddle," Magee warned.

"A delay of game here would kill us," Glenn pointed out.

But I was looking at my oldest and best friend, and he was blinking and looking back at me. "Let's go," Danny urged softly. "We can do this."

I was remembering how he kept turning the volume down when we were watching mixed martial arts on TV, and how his hip-hop music was turned so low, and the fact that he got the score wrong on the sideline. And now I was watching him blink and look back at me and say, "Let's go."

Every bone in my body wanted to hike the ball, throw it to him, get the touchdown, and win it for Kendall.

"Okay," I said, "let's go." We walked toward the line of scrimmage, and I started the snap count, and then I broke it off and signaled for a time-out.

"Jerry," Brian Hart who was in the backfield said, "what are you doing?"

Coach Shea was shouting from the sideline: *"Hike the ball! Run the play!"*

But the ref had seen my signal and he gave us our last time-out.

I walked over to Danny. "Come," I said.

He looked back at me, and I saw how much he wanted to stay on. It was his dream and it had been since he was a little kid in Pee Wee. And it had been my dream, too, and the dream of all those people in the stands, shouting at me to run the play. Our marching band was halfway through our fight song. Principal Bamburger was up there, and Superintendent Sparks, and the mayor of our town.

"Come on," I said, and I took Danny's arm. I led him off the field, and he seemed like he might protest, but he never did. He stumbled once as we walked, but I caught him.

Coach Shea was hurrying toward us, but someone beat

him to it. Danny's father had been watching the whole thing from a front bleacher, and I guess he had jumped to the field, and he met me first on the sideline. I looked at him and I didn't have to say a single word. He read my eyes through the two bars of my face mask, and he nodded to me very slightly. He put his arms around Danny and said softly, "Come on, son," and led him away.

I sprinted back on the field, and we huddled up, and I called the same post play, but for Glenn Scott. He streaked out toward the goalpost, and I led him perfectly, but he was a half step too slow, and the ball grazed off his fingertips. There's a good chance Danny would have caught it.

We had no time-outs, so I called our last play myself— a crossing route where Glenn and Mike would end up in opposite sides of the end zone. The ball was hiked, and I faded back and watched them cross. Glenn was my first choice, but he stumbled. I felt the pressure and looked to Mike Magee, but he was covered step for step. Hands were grabbing at me, so I lofted it up into a corner of the right end zone where only Mike could possibly catch it, and I said a little prayer as I was clobbered.

The ball came down a few inches beyond Mike's desperate dive. Danny is four inches taller than Mike. Maybe he would have stretched for it and caught it.

We lost the game and the state championship, and that's something I'll have to live with for the rest of my life. My flu is gone now, and I'm clearheaded, and I still can't quite believe our big chance is gone. I wake up every morning and watch the first light on my trophies, and I think how close we came to winning it all.

I walk through the halls of school and there are some really awkward looks. Even though nobody's said it, I know what they're thinking: "You cost us the championship."

People in Kendall do say it. They say it in a million ways. Straight out in anger: "What the hell were you thinking?" And from the side: "Why couldn't he have played one more play?" And sometimes they pretend to understand: "I know he was your friend, but . . ."

That *but* comes back to me at night, when I lie in bed torturing myself about the championship I'll never bring to our school. We were so very close, and now it's gone forever.

I never talked to Coach Shea directly about what happened in the last minute of the game and why I walked Danny to the sideline. But I think he understands. Since he's retiring as football coach, he was cleaning stuff out of the coaches' office the other day, and he saw me passing by in the hall and waved me over. There were piles of old football equipment and signed team balls and diagrammed plays from seasons gone by. "Look at all this junk," he said. "Twenty-five years of it. Some of it's going home. Most of it's going in the Dumpster."

He bent and picked up a hat. "Hey," he said, "here's the hat I got when we won the state championship way back in the Dark Ages." It was an orange cap, old and faded, with a *K* above the bill for Kendall and two gold stars on either side of it. He handed it to me. "You take it."

"I can't take that," I told him. "It's yours."

"It doesn't fit my fat old head anyway," he said, and then he put it on me. "Life isn't always easy," he noted in a low, gruff voice. "You take your best shot." He was looking me in the eye, and I nodded back at him.

"Yeah," I said. "I know. Listen, I'm sorry . . ." I began to explain and apologize.

He thumped me lightly on the shoulder, cutting me off. "Hat fits you pretty good," he told me. "Wear it with pride." Then he shrugged and stepped away and picked up a garbage bag filled with what looked like a half century of shoulder pads and jockstraps. "Look at this mess. I better call in a dump truck."

Anyway, that's the story of Kendall's football season. Carla got me started writing this blog, and I wish she were still in our writing class to critique my final effort.

I'm gonna stop writing and go to sleep now, because tomorrow Danny and I agreed to meet for an early-morning run. He hasn't said much to me since the Albion game. But he's still my best friend in the world and a hell of a runner, and maybe, just maybe, if I get a good night's sleep I can stay with him.

From: Carla.Jenson@Farragutacademy.edu
To: JerryQB@kendallhs.edu
Subject: New school, old friend

Hi Jerry,

I should have written you sooner. Sorry. I was kind of emotional that weekend after the game. Well, I guess I wasn't the only one. And then there was the new school, and some trouble transferring my old e-mail into their system—note my swanky new e-mail address.

I'm not writing to talk about the game. I hope you could hear me cheering, although I guess it's not very likely in a place that big. But I want you to know that I was screaming "Go Jerry!" from the moment they put you back in the game up till the very last second, and I do mean that. You are an amazing player and, God help me, I do love watching football, I really do. And I'm really glad to know about what happened in the locker room at halftime that sent you guys back out there to accomplish that miracle. Because it was a miracle, no question. I know I said I wouldn't talk about the game, and I know you didn't quite get it done, and I know why. But just remember, you gave us a miracle, we cheered and shouted, and we watched. You made it a great game. But the other team made their miracle, too, just like you said on your blog, and even great games end, one way or the other.

I just have to say one more thing about the game, Jerry. You can't beat yourself up about the *what-if*s, especially not in sports. Danny might have stayed in and caught a pass. Danny might have stayed in and dropped a pass, or gone the wrong way again, and then everyone could be dumping on him, instead of on you, and you could be beating yourself up about how you knew he wasn't okay and why hadn't you thrown to Mike Magee and maybe Mike Magee would have caught it. I know you like battle metaphors, Jerry, but you can't unstir something once it's stirred, and you can only take a drive forward. You gave us some great moments, and I cheered and cheered and cheered.

And I don't know whether it's any comfort or not to know that a few dozen miles away on the carefully manicured lawns of Farragut Academy (I know, if you were writing this, it would probably be a palace, a small university, peopled by students in designer clothes that cost more than the average Kendall citizen earns in a year, but actually it's just a pretty good New Jersey prep school with some aspirations and some affectations. They think I'm going to help their Ivy admission numbers, and mostly everyone just talks about college admissions, just like back in Kendall), nobody even knows there was a game. We all live in our own little worlds is I guess what I'm saying, and all you can do is play by the rules of your own particular little world and try to do the right thing. And I think you tried.

There are some things I would like to say to you, and some things I probably don't really want to say, but maybe in a month or so, we should take that bus into Manhattan again and do something. And I don't mean visit a traumatic brain injury unit, though I know you think that's a pretty fun afternoon in the big city. Go to a museum, or a weird old movie, or just walk around a little. We don't have to talk about the game (we can see if I do as good a job at not talking about it as I did at not writing about it), or about the season, or about my crimes and misdemeanors, or about what you said at the town meeting. We could talk about writing and the experience of putting your life up on a blog, or about college. I'd like that.

One thing I'm afraid we might have to talk about. I feel bad about this, but I know there's been some stuff in the papers. I don't think that it's for sure yet that the hospital will close, but I do think it's true that my dad is seriously considering another job this time, and I don't know whether he would be doing that if he believed that they were going to keep the hospital open. And sometimes I have this bad feeling that maybe he got angry at the town, or he stopped believing in the town after what happened to me, and he just stopped fighting. But that isn't true. He hasn't stopped fighting. He still wants to keep it open. And he's been worried about this for a long time. And it would be total arrogance for me to think that my stupid little issues could end up affecting a whole town. But we'll see what happens, and I hope people won't blame my dad if it's not good news.

You're a good writer, Jerry. I really like your description of the game. It's much, much better than anything I could have written. I won't tell you now what I think are the good phrases and the bad phrases, because, overall, I think it's a strong piece of writing. It sounds like you, and it sounds like football. I printed it out, along with all your blogs from this season, and I'm going to save them with my own writing. I know I'll read them over, and I know I'll read more because I know you'll write more. And I'll always be proud that in my admittedly somewhat checkered career on our school paper, I was the one who signed up Jerry Downing and got him writing. And he told the story of a pretty interesting football season, as only he could tell it. Good going, Jerry. I don't know if anyone has said congratulations to you lately, but I'd like to say it now.

Congratulations on your season,
Carla

SQUARE FISH

DISCUSSION GUIDE

SECOND IMPACT
by Perri Klass and David Klass

Discussion Questions

1. Most of us participate in sports with the intent to win. Football is a team sport, and the entire team is going for the championship. Should one team member's well-being be placed above the group's?

2. Does a school principal have a legitimate authority to limit free speech in the interest of the school? Can you think of other ways Carla could have gotten around the principal's order to postpone making her report on concussions public? Could she have enlisted Ms. Edison's help? What would you have done?

3. Do you think gender played a part in the principal's treatment of Carla? Would he have been more tolerant if she were a boy?

4. Jerry was shunned for taking Danny out of the game and blamed for losing the title for Kendall High. Would it have made a more satisfying end to the book if someone in authority, like the coach, had publicly praised him for his action? Would it be credible?

5. Winning a game is celebrated, losing is no fun. What do you think it will take to change the culture and make contact sports safer? Do you think contact sports should be banned?

6. What role does Jerry's past mistake—the accident caused by drinking and driving that got him suspended from the team and in trouble with the law—play in the unfolding story of the current season?

7. Can football be made safe, or is the game doomed—especially on the high school level—because it exposes young brains to repeated trauma with the risk of irreparable damage?

8. How does a town come to care so much about a high school sport?

9. If a seventeen-year-old wants to play on his high school football team, but his parents think it's too risky, who should have the right to decide?

10. If a high school football player gets badly hurt, should his parents be able to sue the school, the way that former professional players are now suing the NFL?

11. Are Carla and Jerry going to regret any of the things they've posted on the Internet? What could come back to haunt them, and how?

12. How do you think your school would treat a star athlete who got into the kind of accident that Jerry got into? How do you think your school would treat a student who wrote the kind of story that Carla writes, criticizing a winning sports team?

13. Does the information that we're all learning about head trauma in football change the feeling we get as spectators watching a hard-fought game?

GOFISH

DAVID KLASS & PERRI KLASS

What did you want to be when you grew up?
David: A baseball player.
Perri: A naturalist.

When did you realize you wanted to be a writer?
D: Growing up in our family, it was sort of expected that you would become some sort of writer. But I don't think I considered the possibility of even partially supporting myself through writing till my first novel was published when I was twenty-three.
P: I always wrote for pleasure, and I published my first short story as I was starting medical school.

What's your most embarrassing childhood memory?
D: I once tried to punt a football, and somehow kicked myself in the mouth. The dentist asked me what happened and when I told him, he fell off his stool laughing.

What's your favorite childhood memory?

D: Eating dinner at the kitchen table in our old house in Leonia, New Jersey. My mother wasn't a great cook, but she had a few dishes that she made very well. It was a nice family, and we all loved food.

P: Our father used to read aloud to us in the evenings. The stories of P. G. Wodehouse gave him a lot of opportunities to talk in different accents.

As a young person, who did you look up to most?

D: My parents. They were as happy and lovely a couple as I've ever met.

What was your favorite thing about school?

D: My answer here will be very different from Perri's answer, but I loved sports and always looked forward to phys ed, and to a team practice after school.

P: Well, as David suggests, I hated gym passionately. And I think I was generally not a very happy camper—as you can probably tell, I'm the crankier sibling. But I did have some great teachers, especially literature teachers, in my last years of high school. I was part of an alternative high school and a lot of community members, including college teachers, taught classes.

What were your hobbies as a kid? What are your hobbies now?

D: I played chess, and several different sports. I still play competitive soccer at fifty-three, but my game has gotten slower and dirtier.

P: My major hobby is knitting. I'm also very interested in food and travel.

Did you play sports as a kid?

D: Yes, I played baseball and soccer seriously, and a number of other sports like tennis and basketball for fun. I've used those sports in my YA writing, and written novels about baseball, soccer, track, basketball, and wrestling.

P: I played no sports and I still don't. I'm a big Red Sox fan, though, so I had a pretty good time as a spectator in October, 2013. Go Sox!

What was your first job, and what was your "worst" job?

D: My first job was delivering papers. My worst job was working as a file clerk in a law firm.

P: My first job was working on the Floating Hospital, a ship which takes kids out on the water around New York City and provides medical services and activities. I worked on the "playdeck" when I was a high school student. I guess I've been lucky—I can't think of a "worst" job.

What book is on your nightstand now?

D: *The Patriarch*, a biography of Joseph Kennedy. I read far more nonfiction than I did when I was younger.

P: A novel, *The Good Lord Bird*.

How did you celebrate publishing your first book?

D: I was living in a small town in Japan, and when the letter came from Scribner's that they would publish the book, I had no one to tell and celebrate with. I called my parents back in America, and then went out onto the terrace and drank a beer.

P: I was a medical student and kind of stressed out most of the time. I probably went out to dinner to celebrate, but I have to admit I don't remember it.

Where do you write your books?

D: I have a library in my apartment in New York, and I write there. I also belong to several gyms, and during the day they have tables and wireless Internet, so I combine writing with a workout.

P: I work at home or in my NYU office.

What sparked your imagination for *Second Impact*?

D: I had read newspaper articles about the dangers of head trauma and tackle football. Perri and I enjoy writing together, and this seemed like a natural topic for us, and one that we were both interested in.

What challenges did you face writing this book together? What was that process like?

D: We had collaborated on screenplays before, but never novels. I found this much more difficult. Perri cares a great deal about prose, and we were pretty tough on each other. We kicked chapters back and forth, making lots of suggestions, and were both helped tremendously by our wonderful editor, Frances Foster.

P: We talked through the plot together, but as you can see from reading the book, it's a kind of dialogue between two characters with very different personalities and very different narrative "voices," so we each got to write one of them. I don't think we could have managed a page if we were both trying to write every sentence.

Have you ever played football or other contact sports?

D: I played intramural tackle football in college, with full pads.

P: Nope.

Have you ever had a concussion?
D: I've never had a concussion, but I have taken some hard hits.
P: Nope.

Did you grow up in a football town?
D: Leonia, New Jersey, was not a crazy football town, but the varsity football team was a pretty big deal.
P: My recollection is that the Leonia Lions were not having winning seasons during our high school years, but there were certainly people who cared about the team a lot, and there were pep rallies and a pep club.

What do you think are the biggest pressures high school athletes face?
D: I think this depends on the athlete and the sport. With team sports like football, I found the greatest pressure to be not letting my teammates down. My family was not athletic, but I have friends whose parents put a great deal of pressure on them. And then there's the pressure for elite athletes to perform well enough to get a college scholarship.
P: Nowadays, you hear a lot about parents who hope that a high school student's athletic prowess will lead to the kid being recruited by an elite college or getting a college scholarship, and sometimes those kids get worked so hard in high school that it really takes a toll. There's a lot of concern in pediatrics about the increase in injuries among high school athletes—the younger pitchers needing Tommy John surgery, the ACL tears, and whether some of that goes back to that kind of pressure.

What do you hope readers take away from this book?
D: I'd like readers to enjoy the story of the book, but to also gain an understanding of the complexity of this issue. I love

watching football as much as anyone, but after researching and writing this book, I would not allow my own kids to play tackle football.

P: I hope readers come away with the sense that this is not necessarily a story with good guys and bad guys, that well-meaning people who care about athletes and care about athletics can find themselves faced with ambiguities and difficult decisions.

Who is your favorite fictional character?

D: Two spies who couldn't be more different—Ian Fleming's James Bond and George Smiley in the John le Carré novels.

P: Okay, I'll go with a spy as well—Harriet in *Harriet the Spy*.

What was your favorite book when you were a kid? Do you have a favorite book now?

D: I loved Jack London's short stories and his novels, particularly *White Fang* and *Martin Eden*. I don't have one favorite book now, but I just finished a collection of Byron's letters and I think he was a magnificent writer.

P: I might stay with Harriet, though I was generally a big fan of some of the older girls' books as well, from *Little Women* to *Anne of Green Gables*.

If you could travel anywhere in the world, where would you go and what would you do?

D: I loved Asia as a young man, and would love go to back with my family. I'd like to show them some of my old haunts in Japan, and also explore Thailand and Vietnam.

P: I'd probably go to Asia as well.

If you could travel in time, where would you go and what would you do?

D: I'd like to go with Hannibal over the Alps and attack Rome. He really deserved to win that war.

P: I might travel with Darwin on the *Beagle*.

What's the best advice you have ever received about writing?

D: I once met John le Carré and he told me to get out of Hollywood before it destroyed me.

What advice do you wish someone had given you when you were younger?

D: Chose one or two foreign languages, start them when you're young, and stick with them till you're completely fluent.

Do you ever get writer's block? What do you do to get back on track?

D: I've never gotten writer's block.

P: I sometimes bog down on a particular project, so it helps to have more than one thing going at a time.

What would you do if you ever stopped writing?

D: I think I will always be writing something. I may stop writing screenplays soon.

What do you consider to be your greatest accomplishment?

D: Raising two nice kids.

What do you wish you could do better?

D: I wish I could sing on key. My entire family makes fun of my singing ability, and they're probably right.

What would your readers be most surprised to learn about you?

D: I write two very different kinds of things—YA novels that are mostly coming-of-age stories, and action screenplays for Hollywood.

Daniel was looking for acceptance—but the secrets
he uncovers about his father will force him to
make some surprising moves himself.

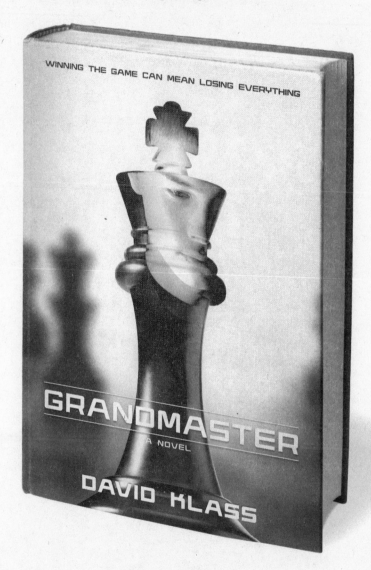

Keep reading for an excerpt of

GRANDMASTER

1

Chess club was done for the day, and so was I. I had played three games that afternoon, two of which I'd managed to lose in the first fifteen moves. I tried to remind myself that I had just taken up the game six months ago and was still learning the basics, but there were times when I wanted to heave the nearest chess set out the window and never touch another rook or pawn again.

I pulled on my coat and headed out the door. Suddenly a hand yanked me back into the empty room and I found myself alone with the two senior co-captains of the chess team, Eric Chisolm and Brad Kinney. "We need to talk to you, Patzerface," Eric said as Brad locked the door.

A "patzer" in chess speak is a beginner who barely knows the moves and is a pushover to beat. It's like being called a combination of chump, rookie, and dufus. Given the unfortunate similarity of my name to "patzer," I had been called it many times since I first walked in the door of the chess club. But "Patzer-face" was a new twist by the co-captains that I didn't particularly like. "Actually my name's Pratzer," I stammered, glancing from one to the other to try to figure out what was going on.

Eric Chisolm was senior class president, a turbo-charged student and a superachiever with intense black eyes who had never gotten less than an A in his life. He was a grind—maybe not brilliant but he outworked everyone else. He literally could never sit still—even when Eric played chess he was always fidgeting, getting up for water, and pacing behind his chair, probably doing his calculus homework in his head while figuring out a next move that would destroy his opponent. He was the son of a heart surgeon, and everyone knew he was going to be the valedictorian, go to Harvard, and discover the cure for cancer.

Brad Kinney was less intense but more naturally talented. He was tall and rugged, with a grade point average that glittered as brightly as the huge trophies he won as captain of the swimming team and contributed to our school's trophy case. For fun, and maybe to make us all even a little more jealous, he dated the prettiest girl in the freshman class. He was the best chess player in our club—a master at eighteen who regularly won local and regional tournaments.

At another school the two of them probably wouldn't have been caught dead on the chess club, but Loon Lake Academy had the oldest and strongest chess team in New Jersey—the

Looney Knights—and it was cool to be on it, especially if you were Eric Chisolm or Brad Kinney.

I was not Eric or Brad—I was Daniel Pratzer, apparently also known in certain circles as Patzer-face. I was not tall or brilliant or rich. The admissions office must have accepted me because it was a weak year and my combination of mediocre scholarship and undistinguished extracurriculars was just enough to pass muster.

My grade average hovered above C+, resisting all my attempts to lift it into the B range like an airplane that has reached its operational ceiling and can't gain a few more feet of desperately needed altitude. I could play a bunch of sports reasonably well, but the electrifying soccer run and the diving baseball catch forever eluded me. I had decided to join the chess club on a whim. The school sports teams practiced for more than two hours every day, and since I was still struggling with the homework load I didn't have enough free time or ability for them. Chess met every Tuesday, and I thought the club might be a good way to make some new friends.

"We know what your name is, Patzer-face," Eric said. "That's why we need to talk to you."

"What about my name?" I began to ask.

"Sit down and shut your trap," Brad advised with his usual charm.

I sat at a desk and waited nervously. Was this some kind of freshman chess club initiation? Would they do something awful to me with rooks and bishops, leaving scars that would last for the rest of my life? I had only been at Loon Lake Academy for seven months, and had so far managed to fly under the radar of the cool-and-cruel crowd.

I glanced from one senior co-captain to the other and tried to figure out what these two towering school icons could possibly want from me.

"What are you doing this weekend?" Eric asked.

"Nothing special," I told him. "Staying home. Watching some junk on TV. Rethreading my sheets."

"Rethreading your what?"

"It was a joke," I explained.

"His sense of humor's worse than his chess playing," Eric grunted to Brad.

"You're not going to be rethreading anything this weekend," Brad told me. "Don't make any plans."

"What's this about?"

Brad plunked his big frame down on the desk next to my chair and folded his arms, staring at me with his bright blue eyes. It didn't seem fair that a guy who could swim fifty meters in thirty seconds and had the physique of a Viking raiding-party chieftain was also a chess master, with a rating well above the 2200 norm. "We know about your father," Brad announced.

"Huh?" I gulped. What was there to know about Morris Pratzer except that he was the shortest, baldest, and no doubt poorest father to ever send a child to Loon Lake Academy? He was practically mortgaging our house so that his only son could go to this fancy private school.

I don't mean to be critical—my dad's a good guy who works

long hours at his accounting firm and sacrifices everything for his family. He also has a lighter side and some notable hidden talents that he sometimes reveals at parties: he can wiggle his ears, arch his eyebrows in opposite directions, and do a half-decent Elvis impersonation, but he's not the sort of "A-Lister" that people suddenly dig up revelations about.

"There's a chess tournament this weekend in New York," Eric said, as if that explained everything.

"Didn't see it on our schedule . . ." I replied cautiously. The truth is I rarely looked at the tournament schedule because I wasn't on the five-member travel team. Nor was I on the seven-member backup team. I was on the euphemistically titled Regular Reserve Roster, which meant they would use me when necessary—which was no doubt never unless a comet struck Loon Lake and killed the dozen players ahead of me.

"That's 'cause it's not a regular school tournament," Brad cut me off. "It's a new kind of tournament. A father-son tournament. Each team needs six players to enter—three fathers and three sons. It's at the Palace Royale Hotel in New York City. There's twenty thousand dollars in prize money. Ten grand for first place. Do you understand now?"

No, I didn't understand. Eric and Brad were strong players and I knew their fathers were both experts, but I was a patzer and my dad had never played a game of chess in his life. When I joined the club and brought some pieces home, I offered to teach him how they moved. "No thanks, Daniel," he said, laughing. "I don't have the mind for it."

I looked back at Eric and Brad and shook my head. "I don't get it. I won't help you much and my dad doesn't play."

Eric dug out a piece of paper. I saw that it was some kind of computer printout. "Your father is Morris W. Pratzer?" he asked, like a prosecuting attorney nailing an evasive witness.

"Yeah."

"We needed one more father-son to join us so we ran the dads of all club members through the Chess Federation ratings database, going back three decades."

He showed me the paper. My father's name and rating were there with an asterisk because his rating hadn't changed in almost thirty years. I stared at it. According to the printout, Morris W. Pratzer had been a grandmaster, rated well over 2500. "This is a mistake," I said. "Don't you think I'd know it if my father was a grandmaster?"

"Apparently not, Patzer-face," Eric said.

"Go home and have a father-son chat," Brad urged, handing me a sheet with info about the tournament. "Find out the source of this little misunderstanding. Tell your dad we humbly invite him to join us this weekend in Manhattan, and if Grandmaster Pratzer doesn't show up we'll wring his son's neck."